The Trump Legacy

What might have happened

A Grady Franklin Novel

By W. Gary Claytor

The Trump Legacy is a work of fiction. The characters are not real. The events are not real. The book offers an alternative reality of what might have happened. The programs, operations and organizations simply don't exist. It is the intention of the novel to entertain not to advocate for an action or undertaking.

Table of Contents

1. Grady

2. Matt

3. The Group

4. Plumbers

5. The Staff Meeting

6. Targets

7. Security

8. Summer

9. Development

10. Rowdy

11. Ellie

12. Rex

13. Debbie

14. Southern Baptist

15. Wildfire

16. The Meeting

17. End Game

Grady

Grady got up from the kitchen table to answer the phone. He checked the caller id and said,

"It says the White House."

"Well, answer it."

"Hello."

"Mr. Franklin?"

"Yes."

"Please hold for the Attorney General." Grady looked his wife and said, "I'm on hold for the Attorney General!"

"What's the Attorney General doing calling from the White House? Doesn't he have his own office at the Justice Department of something?"

"Apparently, he is getting ready to talk to me on the telephone. Maybe he is trying to impress me or something."

"Yeah, well it's working."

"I'm listening to muzak. I don't know the song but it sounds familiar." Several seconds passed and then,

"Mr. Franklin?"

"Yes."

"This is Robert Barnes, How are you?"

"I am fine."

"How are you enjoying retirement?"

"It's great! I highly recommend it."

"Well it's not on my bucket list right now, but someday, who knows. Listen, the reason that I'm calling is we have a little problem and we'd like you to come take a look at it. You may have heard something about the 2016 election and some of the things people inside the government did to use their positions of power to further their own political agendas."

"Yes, I've heard something about that. It's kind of been on the news a little."

"Well, unfortunately, it's been kind of a one way street around here. We would like to set up a task force to look at some of these issues. I would like you to come to Washington where we could talk face to face. Are you available tomorrow?"

"Sir, I think there has been some sort of misunderstanding. I'm not really in the market for a job. I'm happy in my retirement. My wife and I are settled into a quiet lifestyle. The hustle and bustle of Washington, DC is the furthest thing from my mind." There was a pause on the line and then,

"Mr. Franklin, I don't think you understand. I have spent a considerable amount of time with your file."

"I have a file?"

"Twenty five years as a Postal Inspector, three years as an Inspector-Attorney, and one year as a Special Assistant US Attorney. Dedicated, hard working, loyal but most importantly, values integrity above all else. Gets the most out of the people who work for him and not afraid to speak truth to power."

"That last one didn't always work out well for me."

"Don't worry about that. You are not going to be speaking to the President. But let me make myself clear, the President of the United States has asked you to serve your country and based on my reading of your file, you are not the type of person who says no to such a request. So, let me ask you again, are you free tomorrow?"

"Well, when you put it like that, I guess I am."

"Good, good. Listen. Stay by the phone for a few minutes. My Administrative Assistant will be calling with your travel arrangements."

"Okay."

"I'll see you tomorrow. Thank you." The line went dead. Grady looked at his wife who had a dumb founded look on her face

"Well?"

"I guess I'm going to Washington!"

"What? When?"

"Tomorrow."

"Do you even have a clean shirt? Do your suits still fit you?"

"I don't know, do I? I've got one suit that still fits. I don't know about the others. I haven't worn them in a while."

"Why are you going to Washington?"

"They are setting up some sort of task force, and I think they want me to run it."

"Oh Grady, what have you gotten yourself into?"

"I don't know." Just then the phone rang. It was the Administrative Assistant with the travel details. Grady's wife ran upstairs to see if he had a clean white shirt.

The next day, after a plane ride, taxi trip and an escort through security, Grady found himself sitting across form the Attorney General of the United States.

"So, Mr. Franklin, can I call you Grady?"

"Please do."

"Have you thought about what we spoke about yesterday?"

"Actually, I haven't thought about anything else."

"So, what are your thoughts?"

"Well, my first thought is that we are a little late to the party. If we're looking at things leading up to 2016, we're going to be bumping into the 5 year statue of limitations before too long."

"That's why time is of the essence, and you need to get started as soon as possible!"

"Secondly, I'm going to need four AUSA's assigned to the task force from the DC office on a full time basis. I would like two of them to be democrats and two to be republicans."

"You are looking to avoid the appearance of impropriety?"

"No, I'm looking to avoid impropriety. I don't want the task force to get tunnel vision or suffer from expectation bias. You know, every piece of evidence is either relevant because it supports your preconceived notion or it's irrelevant because it doesn't. I want the cases to be examined from an objective viewpoint and I'd like to see how the other side views the evidence."

"Interesting. You realize of course, that we've had nothing but the other side for two years, and the media has been less than friendly to this administration."

"Yes, but if I'm going to the court, I want to win! I want the cases examined from all angles before we go to the grand jury."

"Fair enough. What else?"

The Assistant U.S. Attorneys need to be dedicated, loyal. hard working and above reproach. I don't care if they were hired when a democrat U.S. Attorney was in power, but they can't be politically active or looking to advance their careers. Same way with the republicans. I want smart, hard working lawyers not politicians!"

"Done. What else?"

"I'd like to have two more AUSA's as liaison officers. One from Maryland and one from Northern Virginia , in case we have to go there. They wouldn't be on the task force on a full time basis but just available to grease the skids, in case we need them."

"Good idea.

"I would like eight agents assigned to the task force on a full time basis, two for each AUSA. Same criteria, dedicated, hard working, loyal, integrity, you get the drift. Political affiliation doesn't matter because they are not hired that way and it's really not relevant to them. I would like a Postal Inspector, an IRS agent, a DCIS agent, an Office of Professional Responsibility agent, a Justice Department Office of Inspector General agent and a U.S. Marshal. I don't think we are going to want any FBI agents since we are going to be looking at the actions of the FBI and the intelligence services. That's why I think the O.P.R. and the I.G. would be helpful because they are used to performing the function of internal affairs."

"OK, let me stop you right there. I agree with everything you have said and you are going to get exactly what you want. Believe it or not, I've been giving the matter some thought as well. I have an administrative assistant that is going to be handling these details. The evaluation and selection process has already begun. As a matter of fact, it has been going on for some time. All of the agents will need arrest authority in their current assignment. I don't want pencil pushers on the task force. My criteria is at least seven years experience as a federal agent, trial experience and a history of success as well as inter-agency cooperation. Each of these agents is going to be commissioned as a Special Deputy U.S. Marshal with the authority to make arrests for all violations of the U.S. Code, serve subpoenas, warrants and such other duties as the Attorney

General may require. Their credentials will be signed by the President of the United States, and they will be working under the authority of the U.S. Marshal. In reality, they will be working for me or more accurately for you."

"Wow."

"Yeah, wow. This is about to get real serious, real fast. Before you get too excited about those credentials and badges, they are temporary and will be turned in at the conclusion of the task force. We just want to make sure that these agents have the authority to do what we are going to be asking them to do. In that regard, after today, you and I will not be meeting again. Any administrative details will be coordinated by my administrative assistant. I don't want to hear from you unless there is a problem that my administrative assistant can't handle. You will be in charge. You will make all the decisions. You will decide which cases to take to the grand jury and which cases to ignore. Your task force has been dubbed the Rule 6(e) Plumbers Union Task Force. I know that's a mouthful, and you can rename it if you want. Every thing that you do will be considered Rule 6(e) material, that is grand jury material, and not to be disclosed. The Plumbers moniker is because you are going to be investigating unauthorized disclosures of classified information and hopefully plugging leaks of a government that has made feeding the media a national pastime. I don't care if you get a quote from the New York Times. If it is in your files, it is to be considered Rule 6(e) material, and it is not to be disclosed by your task force. Every thing you have may be submitted to a grand jury at some point, so nothing is going to be disclosed. Every one on the task force will sign a non-disclosure agreement to this effect, so there will be no confusion on this issue. You will be in complete control of where your investigation goes, and what you look at under the general parameters of irregularities of the 2016 election and corruption of government employees at the highest level. Do you understand the implications?"

"I think I do. The buck stops here. If this whole thing blows up, I'm expendable."

"And they said you were just another pretty face."

"What about the members of my task force?"

"They will be protected. None of them will suffer because of being on the task force. I will make sure of that. You on the other hand…Just don't let the whole thing blow up."

"Your confidence is overwhelming."

"Okay, what else?'

"You mentioned a grand jury. I think we need to impanel a grand jury right away. If we have a special grand jury just assigned to us, we won't interfere with any thing else going on, and there is less chance of leaks. They won't have much to do initially, but we need the subpoena authority right away."

"Okay. I'll set that up. What else?"

"What about office space?"

"That's being built out as we speak. There's a building not too far from here, a quick hop on the metro. There will be adequate space for agents, the lawyers, a conference room and evidence storage. We are going to start out with an administrative assistant and a clerk typist to begin with. We'll add more support staff as need be. That should be all ready to go by next week. I can have someone take you by there when we're done here if you would like."

"That would be nice. Thanks."

"Okay. What else?"

"What about compensation?"

"Oh, shoot. I should have covered that at the beginning of the meeting. I'm sorry. You are going to be paid as an independent contractor at the pay level of a U.S. Attorney. No benefits-no sick leave, no insurance, simply an hourly fee for the hours worked. Because you are retired, you don't need any benefits and this makes it nice and clean for us. Your title will be Special Deputy Attorney General with the pay grade level and authority of a politically appointed U.S. Attorney. You will receive per diem and lodging just like any federal employee on a travel assignment. We have an efficiency apartment reserved for you not too far from the office building. You'll check in on Monday morning and check out Friday afternoon. If you want to stay the weekend, you can. If you want to fly back and forth, you can. It's totally up to you. If your wife wants to come to D.C. with you, she can stay in the apartment. You just have to pay for her flight. Your administrative assistant will take care of all these details for you. You just keep her informed of your plans and your hours and she'll fill out all the paper work."

"Sweet."

"Yeah, having an administrative assistant is pretty cool. You're going to like it. It will free you up to deal with more pressing matters."

"Okay."

"There is going to be some added security around the building because this is a sensitive area. You probably won't even notice it, but I just want you to be aware that it exists. There is a guy named Mathews that is heading up the security. He may be contacting you at some point."

"Okay.'

"Any thing we haven't covered?"

"Well, I'd like to get a better handle on this. You've said this is our last meeting so I would like a better explanation from you as to what you expect."

"Fair enough. As I have said you are completely in charge of the investigation and where it goes. My concern and my reason for establishing the task force, is the appearance that individuals within our government used their positions of authority to try to influence a presidential election and possibly undo the results afterward. Now, I realize that such an investigation will also involve individuals outside of government who were participants, and I leave that up to you. How high this thing goes is totally up to you. You will have to evaluate those decisions based on the evidence developed and the strength and weaknesses of your case in co-ordination with the attorneys that will be trying the case, i.e. the attorneys assigned to your task force. This is not a hand it off situation. Once you step into this tar baby, it is yours. I only have one rule, other than the non-disclosure 6(e) status that we discussed earlier, and that is there will be no immunity granted to any subjects or targets of this task force. Either you have sufficient evidence to go forward with an indictment, or you don't. If you don't, you will keep your mouth shut and go home, and nobody will ever hear any thing about this task force. If you have sufficient evidence, you will go forward and seek an indictment and take the matter to trial. A jury will decide. I'm not saying that there can't be plea agreements. Any one who wants to plead guilty can do so. Just be mindful of D.O.J.'s policy that once an indictment is issued, the defendant must plead to the most serious count in the indictment. I don't want you using the indictment as a hammer to knock somebody in the head to get them to plead to some little thing. If you are going to use the plea bargaining process to get co-operation against others, do it before indictment. Before you say anything, I know there is an exception to the rule for extraordinary circumstances. So if you have extraordinary circumstances, apply to D.O.J. for an exception, and I'm sure something can be worked out. We are not trying to work our way up a drug cartel from low level dealers. These were very highly placed government officials and some very bad actors who tried to subvert our election process and destroy our democracy. They did so with the co-operation of the opposition party and a hostile news media, who is nothing more than an arm of that opposition party. Your job is not going to be easy. These people are arrogant because they have gotten away with it for so long that they believe their own lies. Your job is to ferret out the truth and to hold these people accountable. If there are indictments, I will hear about them the same time as everybody else. I don't want there to be any allegations that I interfered or controlled your investigation in any way. At the conclusion of your task force, a document will be prepared for my eyes only which lists each individual indicted or who pled guilty pursuant to an information, the results, the sentence and any information disclosed in open court pursuant to those proceedings. There will be no other report. All documents, field notes, evidence and any thing used by the task force will be sealed and stored in a locked vault at D.O.J. unless and until a District Judge orders its disclosure."

"Well. I think that gives me the direction that I need."

"Good. Today's Monday. How about you start a week from today. That will give you some time to get your affairs in order, work out the details with your wife and hit the ground running. Like I said, your wife is welcome to come along for the ride. You might want to consider having her around for the next six months. This is going to be stressful, and she could be helpful. Totally up to you. I'll have my assistant, Betty, take you by the office to show you where it is and maybe swing by the apartment as well. She'll set up your flight for Monday and after that, she'll hand you off to your new administrative assistant."

"Okay. Thank you sir. I'm going to do my best."

"Good luck." Grady and the Attorney General shook hands and Grady went with Bev to see his new home away from home.

Matt

Colonel Bill (Matt) Mathews and Susan McCoy were sitting in her back yard enjoying the unusually mild weather when two men walked up. He was facing away from the house and she was facing towards the house. He saw the men's reflection in her mirror sunglasses. Her head was perfectly still. Deep down, both of them knew what it meant.

Colonel Mathews had been working on a temporary assignment at Bene Tech Corporation. He and five of his men had been inserted into the company in an undercover capacity as hardware engineers who were supposedly updating some of the company's equipment. In reality, they were looking for external threats by hackers trying to get into the company and internal threats by employees who were stealing and selling technology. Bene Tech had a huge contract with the D.O.D. They didn't make the things that went "boom", but they made those things work, the laser guided technology, the smart bomb brains, the stealth technology and a whole range of computer assisted weapons technology. Colonel Mathews was some sort of computer genius in his own right, but the men who worked for him were down right scary. They had finished their work at Bene Tech and his men had moved on, but Colonel Mathews had stayed behind to finish some administrative details.

Susan McCoy was the Chief Financial Officer of a major biotech manufacturer. She had started out as a C.P.A. and worked her way up to the company's top financial spot by a combination of hard work and some lucky breaks along the way. Her husband had been killed by an I.E.D. in Iraq. He had been a lieutenant in Colonel Mathew's unit. Colonel Mathews had not been the one to deliver the news, but made it a point to come to see her and offer his condolences. She saw in his eyes a sincere sense of loss as deep as her own. They immediately became fast friends. He was completely honest with her and told her everything that he could. His own wife had died of cancer during the first year of their marriage. Susan's two daughters called him Uncle Matt, and they adored him because he filled the void in their life, but he never tried to be their father. Over the years, he had been in the States as much as he had been deployed, and whenever he showed up, he always brought them presents. If they needed anything, he was there for them.

The two men approached the couple slowly and a bit stiffly. Everyone knew this wasn't a social call.

"Colonel Mathews?"

"Yes."

"I'm Mr. Smith and this is Mr. Johnson. We're from the Department of Defense." Both men showed their D.O.D. id cards with their pictures in a credential pack.

"Okay."

"We need you to come with us, sir."

"Okay, can you tell me where we are going?"

"No sir, I'm not at liberty to disclose that information."

"Okay, can you tell me if I'm going to be coming back?"

"No sir. I'm not privy to that information. Do you have a 'go' bag?"

"Yes, in my car."

"I would suggest you get it and bring it with you. If you don't need it, we can bring you back here. If you need it, someone will retrieve your car and get it to you."

"Okay, let's go." Matt said goodbye to Susan and told her this was just some hotshot officer throwing his weight around, and he would call her when he could. They drove for almost an hour and arrived at some nondescript office building. The driver stayed with the car and the passenger took Matt through security and up to a third floor conference room. He knocked twice on the door and let Matt in and closed the door behind him. Matt found himself in a large room with tables and chairs for a large group, but a single man was seated at one of the tables.

"Colonel Mathews, come in, please have a seat." The man looked vaguely familiar, but Matt couldn't place him.

"Can I call you Matt?'

"Sure. All my men do when we are undercover. It avoids complications. Them calling me Matt is the same as them calling me colonel as far as I am concerned."

"Do you know who I am?"

"No sir, I can't say that I do."

"I'm General Joseph Sizemore."

"Deputy Chief of the Army? In charge of Special Forces, Clandestine Services and all non-conventional warfare programs for the entire army? That General Sizemore?"

"One and the same."

"I'm sorry sir. I didn't recognize you out of uniform. I don't know that I would have recognized you in uniform. I don't think we have ever met, but technically you're my boss."

"Technically, I'm a lot of people's boss."

"Well yeah, like half of the U.S. Army."

"Okay, now that we've gotten that out the way, let's get down to business, shall we?"

"Okay."

"I hope it's not lost on you that we are meeting out of uniform and in private."

"No sir, it's not lost on me."

"Your unit is being reactivated."

"The whole unit?"

"You're going to need all of them."

"They've been scattered all over since our last deployment."

"Well the gang's getting back together again. They are staying at Ft. Belvoir. There's a Special Forces compound there used for staging and training of special ops. Civilian style automobiles are being moved into position along with technical and surveillance equipment. This is going to be a large operation of indefinite duration and the unique skill of your unit was deemed appropriate. Nobody at Ft. Belvoir will ask any questions because Special Forces are in and out of there all the time. Your men will be billeted there, but their base of operations will be elsewhere."

Matt's mind was spinning. He was having a difficult time understanding what he was hearing. His work at Bene Tech had been undercover, but he had been detailed on a TDY to a defense contractor to solve a problem, which he did. He hadn't brought his whole unit into play but simply used a couple of his men to do some computer snooping. They caught several employees who were stealing secrets on behalf of the Chinese and had plugged some leaks established by some Chinese hackers. That had been especially gratifying because every time they plugged a leak, they installed a "trojan horse" in the opposition's system.

The viruses became more and more severe until the Chinese just gave up. This was different. This was a full fledged op on American soil.

"Sir, the mere existence of my unit is a highly classified, top secret, Presidential Finding and all 60 members of my unit will fall on a grenade before they would reveal the existence of the Finding. Every member of the unit is highly trained in electronic, digital and street surveillance. They are experts in interrogation, rendition and all manners of sophisticated weaponry. We watch people, we kidnap them, we interrogate them and if necessary, we kill them. These are the fiercest warriors on the planet. We are the tip of the spear and the fact that nobody even knows we exist is what makes us so dangerous. You're telling me we are going to be operating on American soil?"

"It can't be helped."

"Why?"

"Because, you are the only ones we can trust."

"With all do respect…"

"Whenever a subordinate begins a sentence with that phrase, they are about to be disrespectful. So just stop and listen."

"Yes sir."

"A task force is being formed to investigate misconduct surrounding the 2016 Presidential election and thereafter by officials at the highest levels of our government. This includes employees at the F.B.I, the D.O.J, the C.I.A, the N.S.A. and the State Department. This investigation might ruffle some feathers and there may be an attempt to compromise the investigation. This team of four lawyers and eight agents will be housed in a separate office building and your unit will be charged with providing security for the building, the people and the investigation. The Army Corp of Engineers has finished out the building to our specifications, hardened walls, reinforced windows and doors, electronic locks, the whole bit. Your men have been busy installing surveillance equipment, camera systems, a security command post and a hardened perimeter.

The building has it's own underground garage and your vehicles will be staged there. There is also a building across the street that has an office on the top floor that gives you access to the roof. The task force will be on the second floor, your office will be on the third floor and there's another federal agency on the fourth floor. You will be providing security to that floor as well, but it will not be a major concern."

"Whose has been running this?"

"Lieutenant Mallory and Captain Oster. Oster has taken control of the details at Ft. Belvoir and Mallory has been coordinating the build out and installation of the office building. There's a couple of staff sergeants and a warrant officer at the building as well. The equipment all comes from Ft. Belvoir and is transported to the office building as needed. Everyone is in civilian clothing and we've even got a construction van ferrying personnel back and forth. All members of your units should be on site by this evening. We've been working on this for about a month, moving pieces around the chess board so as not to draw attention to the operation. All members of your unit have had their DD214's annotated to show TDY, Special Forces, Secret Classifications – mission details not specified. At the conclusion of the operation, if all goes well, their DD214's will show a return to whatever unit we hide these folks in, until we need them again. If things go wrong, their 214's will show a separation from service on that original date of their TDY. Employment records at All-Tech Security will be established. We have a prior relationship with All-Tech. All members of your unit will be provided with an undercover identification as All-Tech Security Guards. Also, all members of your unit will be issued a special U. S. Marshal credential to be used in the case of an emergency, but only in the case of an emergency." Matt sat quietly staring at the general for a moment and then slowly spoke.

"So, let me get this straight, sir. You are taking the most secret and lethal fighting force the U. S. Army has ever had and having them pretend to be security guards on American soil in violation of the Posse Commitas Act to defend a small group of lawyers against an attack by the F.B.I. and the C.I.A. and god knows what other group of law enforcement and intelligence agencies is out there. And if that weren't bad enough, we're going to be impersonating federal agents as well?"

"Pretty much."

"If this goes wrong, we are all going to go to jail."

"Yes we are, and I will be at the head of the line, so don't let it go wrong. Oh, there's one other thing, actually two other things."

"Of course there are."

"There is going to be another federal agency on the fourth floor and you will be providing security for them as well. We don't see them as target, but we would like a hard perimeter around them as well. They are going to be operating under the radar, but the details of that operation are not in your need to know. Just be aware that they are up there. Also, there is another operation on the west coast that may require some technical equipment. Your unit may be tasked with providing the equipment and showing how it works, but you won't be involved in the actual operation. You may be contacted by a Carl Lowenstein. You are to provide whatever technical assistance you can.

"Okay, well I guess I'm in. There's just one little thing."

"What's that?"

"There's a non-lethal weapon that has been developed at Foggy Bottom."

"You're not supposed to know about that. It's code word clearance above your pay grade."

"Well, specialized weaponry is kind of my area of expertise and with my access to computers…"

"Don't say any more. I don't want to know how you know. I will get you those weapons."

"Pistol, rifle and Flash bangs."

"How do you …never mind. Have your guy contact this person at this number and they can work it out." General Sizemore wrote a name and number on a piece of paper.

"Anything else?"

"No. When Do I begin?"

"You already have. You will be taken from here to your new office building. When you finish up there, you will be taken to Ft. Belvoir. Your car should be there by the time you get there. Just give your keys to one of my guys."

"Yes sir."

"Dismissed."

Matt was driven to the building on M Street, where he was met at the door by Chief Warrant Officer Chet Woginiewski.

"Wog."

"Colonel."

"Matt, for the duration of this op."

"Yes sir."

"Ok, tell me what we've got."

"As you can see, there is a security desk on the first floor. It's manned by All-Tech Security. They are actual All-Tech Security Guards whose job is to look like security guards, which is what they are. It's basically a three man rotation. One opens the building at 6:00, another closes it at 10:00 and a third works an overlapping shift in the middle. Anyone who doesn't work here has to sign in, get a visitor's badge, which they turn in when they leave. There's an office in back that we can use if we need to talk to anyone and the guards can use it as their break room. If there are any problems, they'll call us on the third floor, we'll come down and find out why the visitors are here. There are also small security offices on 2, 3, and 4, but they are just for show. Those offices will not be manned. If we encounter a visitor on one of these floors, we can use those offices to talk to them. They look like typical security offices.

The building isn't really set up to receive visitors, so if someone shows up, they will be turned away. The sign-in procedure is just for people who show up with an employee of the building. The security guards are officious pricks, like security guards everywhere. If they have to turn them over to us, we are just dumb bureaucrats trying to keep our jobs."

"Any traffic so far?"

"Not really, just the normal delivery drivers, construction workers, somebody looking for directions or a bathroom."

"Ok lets take a look." They walked to a bank of elevators.

"You call the elevator just like every other elevator in the world, but in order to punch in the floor you must first enter a code. This only works if the intruder is the only person on the elevator. If somebody else punches in their code, the intruder could simply follow them off the elevator. So it's an illusion of security not really security. The security guards on the first floor are really the first line of defense."

"How are they?"

"Pretty good. They know their job, and they want to do it. They are limited to the first floor, and that's fine with them. The task force will be on the second floor. We're on the third floor, and there's another outfit on the fourth floor. The fourth floor is some new federal agency that is also not receiving visitors. They are just getting up and running, so there is a lot of traffic, but everything seems authorized. Eventually we will be charged with making sure there are no unauthorized intruders, but that will be the extent of our involvement. Okay, here we are on the second floor. As you can see, it's not really open to the public. There are hidden cameras and motion detectors. The reception area has hardened glass and electronic locking devices. The walls are hardened as are all the doors and windows. The Army Corp of Engineers built this place out like a fort. The second, third and fourth floors are virtually impenetrable."

"How'd that work out?"

"Remarkably well. The guy in charge had been told he was to defer to us. He basically sat around and drank coffee while we told his guys what to do. They had a pretty good idea of what was needed before they got here, and he had a few suggestions."

"You don't anticipate any problems?"

"No. These guys build secret stuff all the time. They are in and out and on to the next project. They know how to keep their mouths shut. They hard wired everything. We put the secret stuff in after they left, and we'll take it with us when we go. Some federal agency is going to get a really nice facility some day."

"Okay tell me about the task force offices."

"Like I said, there's a hard perimeter, audio, video and motion sensors. Each office has its own computer and land line. All the computers are hooked into a network, but the network is not linked to the internet. There are four terminals in the conference room that are linked to the outside world for research, e-mail that sort of thing, but you have to move to the conference room to communicate with the outside world."

"That's going to make some people unhappy."

"Hopefully, it will cause them to think twice about how they communicate, and it will protect internal documents which is the primary concern. They will have a land line at their desk, but all calls will be logged in and out, number called and length of call."

"Welcome to 1984."

"It gets worse. There are encrypted cell phones that will be issued to members of the task force. These are to be used for official business of the task force only and are also tracked. We are not recording phone calls, but we can turn that feature on if we want. We will know where they're at, at any given time."

"What else?"

"There's evidence storage onsite which is basically going to be documents, transcripts, video and that sort of thing. That will all be logged into the system and anybody on the system can access the documents and work product can be shared. There is also the capability to maintain the document in a private file until they are ready to be shared, a draft copy if you will. We have complete access to every floor, every office and every computer at any time with our access cards. We will be downloading the contents of the central file on a weekly basis and transporting it to a remote location, a vault at Ft. Belvoir basically. If there's a crash, we can recreate the whole thing."

"Let's hope we don't have to explain that to the lawyers."

"Roger that."

"Okay, let's take a look at the third floor."

"Again, as you can see, no public access. No unlocked doors, cameras everywhere. If anybody gets to this floor which they shouldn't, there is no where to go." Wog waved an access card across a reader and a large door unlocked. Behind the door was a typical reception desk similar to the one downstairs. Wog pointed his thumb at Matt and said,

"Agnes, this is Colonel Mathews, who insists on being called Matt for the duration of this op. Matt, this is Agnes Frobush who is acting as our receptionist." The door buzzed and the two men entered the offices. Agnes Frobush stood up and offered her hand.

"How do you do sir? It is a pleasure to meet you."

"Likewise, Ms. Frobush."

"Please call me Agnes, all your men do."

"Okay."

"Agnes, I'm going to give the boss the ten cent tour. We'll all be leaving shortly."

"I'm going to stay and close up shop, just to make sure everything is buttoned down. Our guests arrive next week. I want to make sure every thing is ready." Matt was shown his office, the radio control room, the video monitoring room, the telephone trunk and the main computer work station as well as various storage rooms for tactical gear and the drone launching station. Finally he asked,

"We have a receptionist?"

"Well, technically she's not a receptionist, she's just acting as one. Think of her as your administrative assistant."

"I have an administrative assistant?"

"Well technically no, but it would help if you would see her that way."

"Wog, what the hell is going on?"

"I wasn't going to get into this yet, but I guess now is as good a time as any. She's a lieutenant colonel. She will be acting as your second in command. She will do whatever you tell her to do, but when you are not here, she will make the decisions and report them to you."

"I don't understand. Why was I assigned a second in command? I've got officers I've worked with for years that I trust. What's going on?"

"Well like I said, it would be helpful if you considered her your administrative assistant. She's here to help. That's the role she has been given. She knows how to get things done."

"If she is a lieutenant colonel assigned to my unit, she is subordinate to me, and I will assign her duties as I please."

"Well, technically she's not you subordinate. She reports directly to General Andy Andrews."

"What? She works for the Joint Chief? The Joint Chief has a spy in my outfit?"

"Calm down. It's not like that at all. The Chief doesn't know what's going on here. He doesn't want to know what goes on here. She is assigned to make sure everything runs smoothly. She is what they call an expediter in the private sector. She knows who to call to get things done. And the people she calls know to do what they are asked and to keep their mouths shut."

"What do they call her in the army?"

"An assassin. She's killed more people than you and I combined. Her husband was in Special Forces and killed in a classified mission when she was a second lieutenant. She went into a dark place and came out the other side as hard as metal. The head shrinkers saw her strength and sent her for special training. All of her missions are classified, and she won't talk about them, but I know what I am talking about. She is a stone cold killer. She's been on the General's staff for five years and she goes where he sends her. Her job is to make sure there are no problems. If she has to go to the General and report a problem, she is reassigned and so are you.
The unit probably gets disbanded and somebody else comes in to finish the job."

"And you were going to wait to tell me all this?"

"Well it's a lot to take in all at one time. I was going to try to ease into it."

"She looks so…"

"Frumpy?"

"Yeah, frumpy."

Did you notice her southern accent?'

"Yeah, I did."

"She's from Jersey. Studies have shown women with a southern accent are less threatening to men. How about the glasses, did you notice the glasses?"

"Yeah."

"They're clear glass."

"Let me guess. Studies have shown women who wear glasses are less threatening to men."

"You got it. Her clothes are bulky, but underneath she is pure muscle. She runs marathons as a hobby. There's a nine millimeter with a silencer in her desk drawer. Just so you know."

"Okay, what else?"

""The fourth floor looks just like this one. No public access. All locked doors. We have cameras and censors in the hallway but nothing inside. Those were our instructions. The stairwells lock once you exit. You have to go down to the first floor to exit the stairwell. We have keys, but nobody else does. We have direct access to the garage from the third floor with our private elevator. Nobody else has access to the garage. That can be changed and reconfigured once we leave."

"Are your guys ready?"

"Yeah, I don't anticipate any problems. We don't plan on deploying the drones, but we've got them if we need them. The plan calls for roving patrols, loose surveillance. With all the GPS stuff, we should be in good shape."

"Where is Lt. Malloy? I thought he was running the show here?

He is. He was here earlier. He took some of the guys out for a test run today. They've been doing some training and logistics. You know, figuring out how many vehicles we need here, how long it takes to get from the Ft. to here, traffic patterns, two man surveillance, walking surveillance, routes to various locations, that sort of thing. They're still ironing out some of the details, but we've got a few days before our guests arrive, so we'll be okay."

"Well, let's head to the Ft. and get this party started."

"We've got what looks like a work van downstairs. It's actually a passenger van and can carry seven. We can all fit in that."

A short while later, the van pulled up to the gate at Ft. Belvoir. An M.P. raised the barrier and waved Wog through. He obviously recognized Wog and the van. Wog drove on the base for awhile and came to another gate. He had to stop at this gate and the M.P. checked everyone's ID including the colonel's. Wog pulled up to a third gate. This one was manned by Special Forces operatives. They were less military in their bearing but more serious in their security concerns. They spoke to Wog for a moment and got the all clear signal. Suddenly fifteen men with automatic weapons materialized out of nowhere. They stood by as the van rolled into camp.

"What the hell was that?"

"They're getting ready to deploy. They won't be here tomorrow. They obviously heard you were coming, and that was their way of officially turning the camp over to you."

"Who'll be manning the checkpoint tomorrow?"

"There will be a new group rotating in tomorrow. Not to worry. Nobody's getting into the Special Forces compound without Special Forces authorization." As the van rolled through the camp, Matt saw the running track, the obstacle course, a work out facility, a mock up of a small town and other familiar Special Forces trade marks. He noticed his car parked in the lot as the van pulled up to the main building.

"If you'll come with me sir, I'll show you to your quarters." They walked down a long corridor and up some stairs. Matt's quarters consisted of a bedroom, a private bath and a small office. Lieutenant Malloy and Captain Oster had quarters on the second floor as well. The enlisted personnel had barracks on the first floor.

"Well, Wog if you will assemble the men in the ready room, I think it is time for me to address them. I'll be there in a few minutes."

"Yessir. I think they are probably already there. Word of your arrival probably spread pretty quickly."

As Matt walked into the ready room, the room stood up as one with no command being given. Matt looked over at Wog who was standing at attention with a slight smile on his face.

"At ease. Thank you for that. I would like you to remain standing for a moment as I explain the rules of engagement. We are being asked to provide security to a group of people, lawyers and agents, who are looking into corruption of our government at the highest level. We will be operating in violation of the Posse Committas Act, which prohibits the use of active duty military personnel from carrying out military operations on American soil. If we get caught, we might go to jail and we will probably be dishonorably discharged. You didn't sign up for this, and I am not asking any of you to do this. This has to be completely voluntary. If you cannot in good conscience participate, I understand, and I applaud your decision. There will be no hard feelings whatsoever. If you cannot participate, please remain standing. The rest of you sit down."

The room sat down as one. There wasn't a single man standing. Even Wog, who had been standing off to the side, had somehow found a chair.

"Wog, I didn't mean you."

"You're not leaving me behind." There was polite laughter throughout the room.

"It's been eighteen months since we were all together. Most of you in this room were involved in that last operation. We worked in the U.K. undercover as civilians and we rolled up the terrorist network in a matter of just a few months. We left the terrorists behind bound and gagged in a hotel room with a mountain of evidence, audio and video surveillance, interviews and a detailed description of the investigation. We made sure the locals had control of the explosives and we got out of Dodge before anybody even knew we were there. It's what we're good at. We go in, we do our job and we disappear. They don't call us the grey ghosts for nothing. We were so good at our job that the brass got scared. MI-5 and MI-6 were pissed. They had egg all over their face. We gave them all the credit and all they had to do was roll up the accomplices, but they were still pissed. We broke the rules. There was a big dust up at State, and the unit was disbanded. You've all been hidden at various bases until the dust settled. Well, now they've brought the unit back together and given us a different kind of mission. We will be operating undercover as civilians again only this time it will be on American soil. We don't know who our targets will be. They may be former or rogue or even active duty intelligence or law enforcement personnel. In this regard, we will be using a new secret non-lethal ordinance. I don't want to kill anybody that we don't have to. So everyone will be carrying this new ordinance for the duration of this operation. I've asked Wog to handle this, and he will be certifying each of you at the range. We will be operating undercover as security guards for All-Tech Security. This is a legitimate security outfit, and there are three All-Tech employees in the lobby of the M Street building. They don't know anything about us, and they don't want to know anything about us. They just control the lobby. If there is a problem, they will contact us. They've been told that they control the lobby and the rest of the building is our responsibility. . In addition to your undercover civilian id's as All –Tech Security guards, you will also be issued credentials identifying you as Special Deputy

U.S. Marshals. These are only to be used in the case of an emergency. If we have to make an arrest as a U.S. Marshal, chances are the operation is blown and we will all have to get out of town quickly. We will cross that bridge when we come to it. For the time being, we are all security guards working for All-Tech Security. You will be using your real names on your identification documents. If the shit does hit the fan, your DD-214's will be back dated to show a separation from service. I know it's a lot to keep track of. When you come on this base, you will use your military id. When you leave, you are All-Tech Security and you've got a third ID as back up. Just remember, if you use that third ID, you may be blown. Any Questions?" There were none.

"Wog, you got anything?"

"Just a couple Colonel, or rather Matt. From now on the Colonel will be referred to as Matt or Mr. Mathews, whichever you prefer, depending on you level of familiarity. We will refrain from using rank or military terminology. It is no longer 1800, but rather 6:00PM. Instead of saying 'Roger that' say 'ok' or 'got it' or 'whatever'. Get used to using civilian terminology when you are on base, so you don't slip up when you're outside the wire. Is Corporal Bradley here? Oh, there you are. Stand up Corporal Bradley. Oh, you are standing up. Sorry. There was light laughter around the room but only light, because everyone knew the diminutive Corporal Bradley was as deadly with a knife as they were with a gun.

"That joke never gets old Chief. Never gets old."

"Corporal Bradley, hereinafter referred to as Brad, is the unit's haberdasher. He is ordering clothing in bulk in various styles, colors and sizes. He is having the clothing modified with a zippered inner pocket for your third credential. Keep your All-Tech Security credential in you shirt pocket and you military id in your wallet in order to get on the base. We are going for business casual so you can blend in to the DC landscape. There will be a barber here tomorrow to give you civilian haircuts. Check with your squad leaders for your assignments tomorrow. We will be coordinating range times tomorrow on the new weapons just as soon as I get them. Okay, dismissed."

The Group

They could have been two rednecks sitting in a bar discussing the issue, but they weren't. They were two of the most powerful men in the country. They were seated around a conference room table with seven other individuals, all of who were powerful in their own right. They were all extremely wealthy. All of them had succeeded in their chosen fields. Some worked in government, some worked in the private sector, but all of them had one thing in common; an absolute love for their country. Those who worked in government had risen to the under secretary level. They could have risen to the top spot, but they chose to remain in the number two spot. Cabinet secretaries came and went, but it was the top bureaucrats that wielded the real power. Those in the private sector were exceptionally well connected both inside and outside of government. They knew how to get things done and they also knew how to stay under the radar. The group was nine members by design, so there could never be a tie vote. In reality, blue man chaired the meetings, and if he said no, that was the end of the matter. He rarely spoke except to direct the meeting to the next topic. The various members discussed the topics among themselves until the issue was completely vetted. The group had been in existence for over seventy years. No one knew for sure when it began. They only knew they had been recruited by their predecessor and handed a grave responsibility. Mr. Green spoke,

"Have you ever wondered why every prime time TV show has either a gay main character, a gay story line or a gay romance scene?"

Mr. Brown,

"I don't watch much TV."

"Seventy percent of all Americans watch between two to three hours of TV per day, most of it is in prime time."

"That seems like a lot, but you can always change the channel."

"Not if it's on every channel, but the question is why?"

"Well that's pretty simple."

"Humor me."

"Okay, they want to make you immune to it. If you see enough of it on TV, you'll get used to it and it won't bother you any more."

"Okay, why?"

"Because, if you get used to it, you will accept it and they will have abolished your homophobic tendencies."

"Keep going, why?"

"Because if they can change something so fundamental to your belief system, your religious foundation, your moral fiber, then they can change anything."

"One more step, why?"

"Because if they can destroy the moral fiber of the country from within, they can destroy the country. If the country had no moral fiber, no fundamental sense of right or wrong, then it can't stand up to an external attack."

"One final question, who? Who is this, "they" that you are talking about?"

"Wait a minute! Are you saying this whole thing has been orchestrated by some external force, some state actor?"

"Who? Who uses a campaign of disinformation to try to influence events and destroy societies?"

"Are you telling me the KGB was behind this?"

"Bingo!

"There was a college professor who was recently fired because he refused to teach that the human race has seventeen genders. He was not fired for teaching there were only two, but because he refused to say there were seventeen. Think about that for a minute and let the logic sink in."

"You guys knew about this and didn't do anything?"

"We heard rumors over the years, nothing definitive, just bits and pieces. It's kind of hard to get too excited about some college professor yelling about gay rights when someone has nuclear weapons pointed at your head. Communism gets replaced as the number one threat by terrorism, and then, son of a bitch, the terrorists are getting nuclear weapons. We've been kind of busy over the last thirty years."

"Okay, I'm sorry. Let's back up. What do you guys at the Agency know about this and what do you suspect?"

"We had a program a few years back, surveillance, undercover operatives, interviews, national coordination, the whole bit. When it was all said and done, nobody knew what to do with it. It was just too controversial. Free speech, rights of self-expression, all of that. So, the whole thing was put in mothballs. It was classified and locked away in a vault. As the deputy director for admin, I proposed that we destroy the file as it might come back to bite us someday. The decision was ultimately made not to destroy the file. It goes against institutional bias. You don't destroy any intelligence, it might come in handy some day. The file was given some kind of double secret code clearance and locked up forever."

"How does that help us?"

"Well in order to destroy it, I had to have access to it, so I could explain what was in it and why it should be destroyed. While I had access to it, I made a copy of it, which now resides in an undisclosed location. If any thing ever comes of this, I am on record as being the guy who said it should have been destroyed."

"You are a devious son of a bitch."

"Thank you."

"So what's in the file?"

"Well it took me a while to put the whole thing together. It's incredibly complicated, like I said, bits and pieces. The best I can figure, somebody in the KGB came up with this program in the late 50's early 60's and sold it to management, who ran with it big time. They recruited and trained agents extensively in the art of manipulation, recruitment and multi-level management. The agents were inserted into this country as twenty something year olds. They were a little older but pretending to be younger. Legends and ID's and phoney high school transcripts were created, and they all became college students."

"This was in the 50's and 60's ?"

"Yeah. It was a long range plan. They weren't your typical operatives. They didn't gather intelligence or take photographs or try to infiltrate the intelligence services or the military industrial complex. They had only one goal, and that was to rise as high as possible in academia or Hollywood, specially the TV industry. Someone in the opposition recognized that television would be the 'pane circe' of the modern age. The ancient Romans had a saying which loosely translated means bread and circuses, if you give the masses food and entertainment, they will be happy. Well a bowl of popcorn in front of the TV became the 'pane circe'. These operatives played the long game. They moved very slowly. The real genius behind the plan was the multi-level marketing aspect of it. They each recruited six people who each recruited six people and so on and so on. The essential element of the plan was to create fanatics who would in turn create other fanatics. The operatives moved up to positions of power in the universities and television industry to be able to employ the carrot and the stick method of motivation. If their protégés did what they wanted, they got promoted. If they didn't, they were cut off from the group. The approval of the group became like a drug. They had to have it to feel like life mattered. These operatives latched onto every liberal cause they could find: women's rights, civil rights, animal rights, anti-litter, anti-pesticides, zero population growth, anti-war you name, but these were all just a cover to get to the real issue, gay rights. They used their power to recruit, to train, to brainwash these people and turn them into fanatics who in turn could create other fanatics. Sure they got some mileage out of these other issues too, but they were all collateral benefits to the real mission which was to control the television industry. It was an absurd plan, one that never should have worked. There were way too many variables over too long a period of time. But it did work and remarkably well. If you look at just how much American attitudes have changed within the last five years, it is incredible. You've got drag queens reading to kindergarten students, because it is the inclusive thing to do. You've got military prisoners getting sex change operations at the taxpayers expense because it's an act of kindness. You've got boys self-identifying as girls so they can compete in girl's sports. There is no end to the madness because the Supreme Court let the genie out of the bottle."

"So how do we put it back?"

"We can't. There are all these cliché's, "how do you keep them down on the farm after they've seen Paree' 'you can't unring that bell' 'you can't put the toothpaste back in the tube'."

"So what are you saying?"

"We can't go backwards. We can't stop it, but we can slow it down."

"How?"

"We target these fanatics."

"The KGB Operatives?"

"No, they are long gone. They are either dead or in nursing homes drooling on themselves while smiling about how they destroyed the fabric of America. No we can't touch them, but we can go after their protégés, the ones they trained or the ones those people trained. We know who they are. We've identified the vast majority of the networks. We were able to work backwards and identify the original operatives. They only made one mistake. They used the birth certificates of dead children about the right age to get social security cards and then driver's licenses. You have to remember there were no computerized records back then. This wouldn't work today, but it was a common method back in the 60's. We identified 37 operatives who all showed up within a two year period of time. As far as we can tell, no others were sent over; seven went straight to Hollywood, the other thirty were dispersed to various universities around the country. They were "sleepers." They didn't do anything but try to succeed, so they could recruit, train and brain wash protégés. It took a while and a lot of legwork to identify the 37, but once we had the birth certificate m.o., things fell into place. We were able to identify the networks pretty quickly. The odd thing is that none of the networks are connected. They all operate independently."

"So what are you going to do?"

"We are going to 'sting' them. We are going to set up sting operations."

"On what?"

"Think about it. What is the one thing that is a bridge too far? What is the one thing they cannot do? Child abuse. You think mothers against drunk drivers are fanatics, try sexually abusing a mother's child and you will find out what 'hell has no fury' is all about. These people who are pushing this agenda are not paragons of virtue to begin with. They are not born again Christians. They are pushing the envelope on sexual perversion. There is a line you cannot cross. We're just going to nudge them over the line. It will be very subtle. They won't even know they're being manipulated, but it will be relentless. We will keep making offers until we find the one that triggers a response."

"Who are the targets, the writers, the actors?"

"No, the writers don't care about gay issues. They aren't the ones pushing this agenda. They just want to write. Same way with the actors, they just want to act. Now don't get me wrong, their attitudes have been adjusted just like everybody else's, including you and me, but they are not pushing this agenda. It's the executive producer, the studio head who stops by the writer's studio who suggests 'Why don't we make this character gay, it will make the series more interesting.' The writer says okay and goes along with the suggestion. It is all very subtle, there are no direct orders, just gentle prodding. We know who these folks are. We've got our targets. We've got an operational plan. We've got operatives ready to go, it's just a matter of flipping the switch and turning the program on."

"Wait a minute. Are you using child prostitutes?"

"No. We are using actors who are pretending to be child prostitutes. No child is going to be harmed by this program. No actor is going to be harmed by this program. Every actor will have a handler who will step in if things get out of hand. The actors are just going to give us a way in. Once we are in, we will use existing materials and the target's own words to hang them."

"How is this going to work?"

"It is all going to be fake. Fake prostitutes, fake friends, fake cops, fake prosecutors and fake defense attorneys. But it will be convincing. That is the key to the whole thing. We have to make the target believe that they are caught. We then turn them and use them against others, at least that's what they will think. The whole time they are working for us, we will be building a bigger and better case against them."

"What kind of time frame are you looking at?"

"We've got six months of work ahead of us, but you know how these things go. Nothing ever happens a soon as you would like. Realistically, we should be popping the cork on this thing somewhere between six months and a year down the road."

"What does that mean?"

"We've got fifty to sixty targets that we are building a case on. A quarter of them are in Hollywood, the rest are at various universities. There will a dozen or so that have rock solid cases with admissible evidence, no entrapment, no loose ends whatsoever. These cases will find their way to legitimate law enforcement, the FBI or local law enforcement, whichever works in the particular situation. These will be coordinated to hit all at the same time. Word will spread like 'wildfire'. Thus the name, Operation Wildfire. The rest of these folks will panic. They will be calling their lawyer, that we provided, only to find out he is unavailable. They will try to reach the AUSA that they have been working with only to find out he doesn't exist. Our whole operation will roll up and disappear. These people will know they have been had and will hire real lawyers and scream about entrapment and dirty tricks. The lawyers will tell them to keep their heads down and keep their mouths shut. They will be paranoid beyond belief. We will help out in that regard as well. A phone call, an e-mail, gossip, an anonymous tip to a university president, social media postings or even a comment from a colleague. We won't have to tell them to back off on their agenda. They will figure it out on their own. They will go to ground for five or six years. This isn't going to stop the assault on our fundamental values because it's already out there, and moving at its own pace. But this will slow it down significantly. And who's to say we only prosecute twelve? We may decide to go after 20 or 30 or maybe take them all. Remember these people are all protégés of the original KGB agents. They are fanatics. They believe in destroying America's fundamental values and using this issue to do it. They have been trained on how to do it, but they are not KGB agents. They have not been trained on how to handle an attack on them. This is the fundamental flaw in the KGB's plan. They are using Americans to do their dirty work. These people won't be able to understand how their country has turned on them for doing what they think is right. We will destroy the whole network in a year. Something it took the KGB 70 years to build. This will slow the advance for five or six years and give the opposition a chanced to grow."

Who is running the program?"

"A guy named Carl Lowestein. He's a former NSA Clandestine Service Operator. He was the head of a large unit of spy catchers. His unit was really good at what they did. They caught a lot of Russian spies. They were too good. They targeted and captured a high-ranking KGB Colonel. The Russians in turn arrested a low-level embassy clerk in a honey pot sting. The previous administration trades the Colonel for this twenty two year old kid who doesn't know anything. The Colonel goes back to Russia and two weeks later the NSA guy who headed up the investigation gets killed in a car accident. Hit and run by a stolen car, driver never found. The KGB, or FSB now, was sending a message. 'We can get to you anytime we want.' The NSA unit was disbanded. The head guy resigned and went to work for a private security outfit, providing bodyguards to the stars. He makes more money now than he did at the NSA. A lot of his people went with him to the security firm, some stayed behind in various other capacities. We've hired him through the security firm to run this operation. The security company doesn't know what's going on, nor do they care. They're getting paid for contracting this guy out. Carl and his people are all in. They've got a score to settle. If they can take down a program the KGB took seventy years to set up, it will go a long way to avenge the death of their colleague."

"Who is funding this?"

"The money is coming from a couple of foundations. They are set up to support community values, promote Christian values and support political candidates. The money goes through several PAC's and is totally untraceable."

"Ok, anybody else have any questions?" There were negative headshakes all around the table. Finally, Mr. Green looked to the head of the table, "Mr. Blue?" Mr. Blue nodded his head once and then he said,

"Let's move on to the plumbers. Ms. Brown, you have the floor." Ms. Brown, a striking woman in her mid fifties, rose and spoke from a standing position. As the Deputy Attorney General, she was used to commanding respect.

"As you know the Attorney General has appointed a task force to look into the improprieties surrounding the 2016 election and the misuse of power by our intelligence and law enforcement agencies. This investigation will focus primarily on the FBI, but there will be some spill over on the DOJ, CIA, NSA and State Department. The AG has appointed a man named Grady Franklin to head the task force. He's a retired Postal Inspector who worked for a year as a Special Assistant US Attorney. He has a reputation as a very hard worker and an honest shot caller. Most importantly, he gets the most out of the people who work for him." Mr. Green interrupted,

"So we've hired a boy scout to take on the deep state?" Ms. Brown looked at Mr. Blue, who in turn stared at Mr. Green. Mr. Green withered under the Blue Man's gaze.

"Sorry, please continue."

"Franklin was chosen out of a host of characters because of the traits I mentioned and because he is expendable; he knows it and is willing to do the job anyway. He is not looking to make a name for himself. He's been asked to serve and he is going to do the job to the best of his ability. It is refreshing to me that there are people who still believe in the value of doing the job right. We thought we could throw a disposable asset at this problem, make a big stink, and the problem would go away, but he has thrown a monkey wrench into the situation." Mr. Green's tone had become more respectful as he became the group's spokesman to question this program.

"How so?"

"He requested four Assistant U.S. Attorneys and eight agents."

"Seems a little light."

"I agree, especially in light of the fact that the Ronald Miller Special Counsel operation had twenty lawyers. But that is not the thing that bothers me. He wanted two of the lawyers to be from the opposition party."

"He wants to avoid the appearance of impropriety?"

"No. That's what I thought at first too. He wants to avoid actual impropriety. He wants an opposition force on staff to pick the cases apart, to point out weaknesses so he can combat them. If he is going forward, he wants to win."

"So he is smarter than you thought."

"Apparently. But you have to remember he has to play by the book. He can't leak to the media and run a smear campaign for two years. His job, as he sees it, is to fight against such things. His mandate is to treat this whole thing as a grand jury investigation. Either you indict someone or you don't. If you don't, you keep your mouth shut and you go home. That's the way it is supposed to work. What we've got now is an abomination of our criminal justice system."

"So, does he know what he is doing?"

"No. As far as he is concerned he is looking for leaks and liars. Those are pretty easy cases to make. There is a lot of recorded testimony and a lot of it is inconsistent. There were a lot of leaks and they were done intentionally. He doesn't know anything about the deep state or that it's destruction is our true goal. When we heard about the deep state, we all laughed. We thought they were amateurs, and in comparison to this group they are. But we are not laughing now. In two years, they have managed to completely turn the country upside down. Truth becomes fiction and fiction becomes truth. If the media tells a lie often enough and loud enough, the public believes it. There is a spin machine that allows these people to say one thing and do another and the public believes them. They are arrogant, but that will be their undoing. They created e-mails, text messages, a paper trail a mile long. They openly disclosed their plans and they sought out the limelight. They went on talk shows and discussed their opinions. If Franklin is successful in bringing indictments for perjury and disclosure of classified information, he will destroy the deep state. Those people who aren't indicted will see the error of their ways and think long and hard about attempting a silent coup in the future. Even if there are no indictments, the fact there was a grand jury looking into their actions, will make people think long and hard about their future actions."

"I would like to see some indictments."

"Me too. But this guy Franklin is the right guy for the job. By keeping the task force small, it will be contained, and it should be able to move fast. The people are all top notch, really smart, and once they are committed, I expect some results." She looked to Mr. Blue who said,

"Okay, keep us posted. Anybody have any questions?" There were none. He then said,

"Mr. Black, you want to tell us about the Southern Baptist Operation?"

"This operation came into being as the result of a recently reported statistic that 75% of all African American males under the age of twenty five are born into single family households. This is a huge statistic. These young men are bitter. The educational system has failed them. Their job prospects are dismal and they are doomed to repeat the cycle of fathering children that they do not support. This is a phenomenon that was created by our government. In the late 60's when the Great Society was created and aid to dependent children came into being, who could argue with the concept that children should not go to bed hungry at night. But almost as an after thought, a condition was added to this aid that it should go only to mothers in those situations where there was no father around. If the father was around, he should be providing support for his children. Well, the law of unintended consequences reared its ugly head, and the African American family was destroyed. When you're eighteen years old, and the rule is you can have as many children as you want, but you just can't stick around, life is good. But when you are forty years old, you feel you've missed something, but you don't know what it is, because you've never had it. The government did this. If you are raised in a two-parent household and the son comes to the father and says 'I can't find a job.' The father says, 'I don't know son, times are tough, but one thing I do know. As long as I have a place to live, you have a place to live.' It may not seem like much, but in reality it is everything. Chances are that father has worked his whole life, sometimes at more than one job. He's a role model. The African American community had a very strong family oriented culture, not just sons and daughters, but aunts and uncles, nieces and nephews, grandparents. Many times that culture was centered around the church, sometimes the neighborhood and even the place of employment. The government stole that, so we're going to give it back." Mr. Green again played devil's advocate.

"OK, we all get the back story, but how do you propose to do this?"

"It's simple really. We use the black churches. The black church has long been the dominant force in black culture. Granted, it has been radicalized and co-opted by many left wing ideals, but at its core it is still devoutly Christian and dedicated to Christian ideals, including the sanctity of marriage. We use that to our advantage. I say it is simple. The concept is simple. The execution is anything but. This will be a very complex operation involving secrecy at the highest levels and getting buy in from the black ministers will be the most difficult part of the operation."

"Ok, you've got out attention. Lay out the proposal."

"The President creates a new cabinet level position. Some innocuous sounding title like Department of Government Resources and Employee Development. The mission of the Secretary will be anything but innocuous. This department will be given a function similar to that of an inspector general, to ferret out fraud, waste and abuse. It will become know that this Secretary will cut every department other than law enforcement, intelligence and the military by ten percent. He will be the most feared and hated man in Washington. Every department head will be scrambling to figure out ways to protect his turf and try and take this man out. None of it will work because he will have the full backing of the President. Only the President will know what his true mission is. All of this turmoil and reduction in force and reorganization will just be a smoke screen for what is really going on. There will be an Under Secretary for Employee Development. He will be looking at those employees being displaced and select the cream of the cream for this new department. These people will be carefully screened, vetted and sworn to secrecy. They will be given the opportunity to change the world. Never doubt that a small group of people can change the world, because it is the only thing that ever has. These people will need to be salesmen who can convince people to do what they want them to do. They will also need to be operators who can co-ordinate non-government resources. The majority of these employees will need to be African American because they will be sent out to the field to convince black ministers to buy into the program. That's going to be the difficult part. Once we get that, everything else will fall into place. The program will be to provide day care to married couples to promote a married lifestyle in the African American community. All of these churches have a basement, which can be easily converted into a daycare facility. The facility will be run by the church ladies. They are the women who come to church every Sunday. They show up early and they stay late at every church function. They are the backbone of the church community. Once the black ministers are sold on the program, it will be their job to sell the concept to the church ladies. The beauty of this concept is not only does it promote Christian values, it also gives the black churches the opportunity to take back something that was stolen by white society. The church ladies will be given the opportunity to change the world one child at a time. Don't get me wrong, there will be some failures. A lot of the black ministers are going to tell our operatives to go take a hike. Our operatives are going to have a tough job ahead of them. Even if they get a 'yes' from one of the ministers, then they have to make the program work by pulling the strings behind the scenes. There will be no federal money going directly to these programs. There will be foundations and charitable donations, surplus food and corporate support for diapers and cleaning supplies. Contact will be made with the Christian Coalition to provide support for a mission, which supports the Christian ideal of the sanctity of marriage. It will be the job of the operatives to co-ordinate all of that to make sure the program succeeds. There will even be some reach out to employers to provide opportunity to these young couples. The program may even go so far as to provide training opportunities for one or both of the married individuals. The whole thing is based on the concept of changing the world. The employees of the Employee Development division have to be true believers, and they in turn have to make true believers of the black ministers. If we have one success in a city, the word will spread. The black ministers all know each other. The guy who has the success will talk it up. They will see the light in his eyes and they will want to be a part of something that is going to change history. The black man had his freedom stolen when he was originally brought to this country. He had his dignity stolen when the ADC program was created. We're giving him a chance to take it back."

"This is brilliant. Do you think you can pull it off?"

"Well, it's not going to be quick and easy. It will be a slow and tedious process. It took us sixty years to get where we're at. If we can turn the corner in six, that would be a major accomplishment. The program will have to be a complete secret. If the ACLU gets wind of it, they will shut it down, before it gets going. The one thing we've got going for us is that the very concept, separation of church and state, that would allow the ACLU to shut us down, would prohibit them from touching the program once it is up and running. Since there will be no federal funding and each day care is completely run by the individual church, there would be no grounds. The only thing we ask is that the day care only be provided to married couples. Everything else is up to the local church. Religious ed, if any, songs they sing, food they serve, hours of operation. Every thing else is up to the local church. There is a risk that a local church will want to expand its day care to single parent families because it is the 'Christian' thing to do. We can remind them of the reason for the program, to change the culture and bring folks back to Christian values. If they insist, there is nothing we can do. We will simply remove our support, and they can go it alone."

"Sounds like a real problem."

"It is, but our operatives have to make it clear from the beginning that this is the program, and it's the only thing we ask in exchange for all the help we hope to provide. If our operatives come through and provide all the help we think they can, them the black ministers will probably live up to their end of the bargain. That's not our real problem though. Our real problem is our need for secrecy. Our operation will be an ongoing never- ending saga. We will be constantly looking for new churches and means of support. Our end of the operation has to be performed completely in the dark. Our employees will have a cover story. They will be looking to find employment for displaced federal workers and there will be some of that to show in case they are challenged. If we can get six good years to set the program up, it may run itself. There is a back up plan where all these operatives get hired by a foundation, if the federal program gets shut down."

"Why not just do that in the first place?"

"Because it would be costly and time consuming. We are going to save the federal government a lot of money by trimming these departments and we are going to use a small portion of that money to run this program. Plus we use the resources of the federal government to get this program up and running immediately."

"Is the President on board?"

"Yeah, he got to him through his daughter. She loves the idea and even suggested our guy for the Secretary of the Department of Government Resources and Employee Development, the most hated man in D.C. He's a former business owner who knows how to get things done. As you know, it's not easy laying off government employees, but it can be done. You just have to follow all the rules. You have to follow the steps in the right order. You have to publish a Notice in the Federal Register of your intention to invoke the Reduction in Force procedures. There has to be a hiring freeze, a promotion freeze, a reorganization to try to limit the need for a reduction, an evaluation of needs and cost benefits and veterans have to be given preference. Employees know these things and they will see it coming a mile away. A lot of them will jump ship and go to the private sector. But this whole thing is just a cover to hide our real objective of the Division of Employee Development, ostensibly to help displaced employees but really to set up day cares."

"Seems like a lot of rigmarole to go through just to set up some day cares."

"It is, but trimming the fat out of the federal budget is a good thing and us getting to use some of that fat is an even better thing. Remember, we not just setting up day cares. We are changing the culture."

"Who is going to run the sub department?"

"We've found a guy. He's young, late thirties, energetic, charismatic, really will be able to build a young workforce. That is the key. He has to be able to get the most out of these young people he will be hiring. They have to be committed to the program, and they have to keep it secret. That's why we are putting them in the same M Street building as the Plumbers. That way the security force can keep an eye on them as well." Mr. Green looked at Mr. Blue and said,

"Somebody want to tell me about this security force?"

"Need to know basis, only."

"Okay."

"Any thing else? Then we're adjourned."

Plumbers

Grady Franklin walked in to his new office at 9:00 am Monday morning. He had been up for several hours working on his plan, but he didn't want to get to the office ahead of the staff. The security guards were expecting him and gave him his access card and the security code for the second floor. They told him to destroy the piece of paper once he memorized the code. The access code card opened an outer door, which put him in an inner office with a glass receptionist window. Seated at the window was a pleasant looking middle-aged woman.

"Mr. Franklin?"

"Yes."

"Come on in. I've been expecting you." She buzzed the lock and the door came open.

"I'm Beverly McIntosh. I'm going to be your assistant."

"Nice to meet you Ms. McIntosh."

"Please call me Bev, everybody does."

"Well, Bev it is, and you can call me Grady."

"Well, we'll stick to Mr. Franklin for now, until everyone gets settled. This is Carly Limon, she is going to be our clerk typist for now. She'll be doing all our typing and logging of evidence. If we need more help, we can get it, but I'll be helping out with the typing as well." Carly was a young blonde who looked quite earnest.

"Carly, why don't you man the front desk while I show Mr. Franklin around. Either Carly or I will be at the front desk during business hours, which are 8 to 5. If you need to come in outside of business hours, you use your access card to get in the lobby, then enter your security code to turn off the alarm and then your key to unlock the door. Every one on your staff will get one of these keys and a security code." She handed him a key and a piece of paper with another security code on it.

"You'll have to sign for that as will everyone on your team."

"Seems kind of excessive."

"You're telling me. I can't understand why we need someone at the front desk all the time when we are not expecting any foot traffic, and you have to be buzzed into the lobby anyway, but that's what we have been told."

Grady noticed that the front desk had monitors, which showed the lobby as well as the outside entrance. The front desk area was spacious and well equipped with typing stations, printers phone consoles, filing cabinets and a number of pieces of equipment that he didn't recognize.

"Pretty nice space."

"Yeah, the Army Corp of Engineers built it out. Those guys don't play. They are not your usual GSA contractors. A security outfit was here last week putting the final touches in place. Here is the conference room. As you can see, there are four computer stations over there. If you want to send an e-mail or do research, you use one of those stations. All the offices are equipped with a computer, but they are all hooked up to a private network. Let's say Carly types up a record of an interview. She then sends it to the agent for his review. He can then make changes or ask her to make the changes and once it is marked 'final draft', it gets filed in the central bank. Everyone on your team then has access to it, but no one outside your team has access to it. If a document needs to be filed electronically with the court, it will have to be done from the conference room."

"So you mean the document will have to be physically taken to the conference room, input into that system and then sent electronically. It can't be sent from our network to the conference room system?"

"Right".

"Seems kind of cumbersome."

"Well it is, and it isn't. The conference room system has some kind of super duper scanner that can scan in a 100 pages a minute. It can all be checked and then sent. It also has some kind of encrypted algorithm that can't be hacked. The whole point is we don't want anybody getting into our files. Nothing is hack proof, but if you have to walk down the hallway to send an e-mail, it will remind you that you are communicating with the outside world, and you should do so at your own risk. The security folks insisted on this system, and as you can see, they put is some pretty state of the art stuff. Ok, here's your office. As you can see, you have a direct line of sight to the front door.

You can see who's coming and going. The office is stocked with everything you should need. The documents your employees will need to sign are in that file. The creds for your agents are here. I'll take care of the keys and security documents and cell phones. Yours is there on your desk. Your team is due to arrive at 10:00am. I'll put them all in the conference room, and you can get started from there. All of their offices are marked with their names. We have randomly assigned offices with an agent on each side of an AUSA. If you want to change anything, now would be a good time. After you have met with your team, we can get together and take care of the administrative details. Any thing else you need? OK, I'm going back up to the front desk. Our guests will be arriving soon. I'll call you when everyone is assembled in the conference room.

Grady walked into the conference room carrying the folders and cred packs. He noticed there was assigned seating and nameplates with titles in front of everyone. This would help him get to know the names quickly. He supposed it would help them out as well. He would have to thank Bev for that later.

"Good morning, my name is Grady Franklin. I have been appointed Special Deputy Attorney General for the purpose of running this task force. We have all been assigned to this task force by the Attorney General, but make no mistake about it, the President has directed and approved the creation of this task force. So we all now serve at the pleasure of the President."

"The Attorney General has directed that we examine the appearance that individuals within our government tried to use their positions of power to influence the 2016 election and tried to undo the results afterwards. This investigation will be looking at the actions of some high-ranking members of the FBI, the Department of Justice and possibly the CIA, NSA and the State Department. There are two parameters of our investigation. The first is that we are a Rule 6 (e) task force, meaning everything we do is to be considered Rule 6 (e). Every scrap of paper, every transcript, every interview, even articles we clip from the newspaper, once it comes into the office, is considered grand jury material and cannot be discussed outside the confines of this office or the grand jury room. You will all be signing a document to that effect today to reinforce your commitment. The second parameter is that we are a law enforcement body. We will be examining the facts to determine if there is sufficient evidence to bring a particular matter before the grand jury for an indictment. If we obtain an indictment, we will be trying the case. There will be no offer of immunity here. I know this takes one of your tools out of your toolbox, but that's the way it has to be. This parameter comes from above. Either we have sufficient evidence to bring a case, or we don't. If we don't, then we go home and we keep our mouths shut. That's the way it is suppose to work. Unfortunately, that's not the way things have been working around here lately. We can still make deals and make plea bargains and all that. It's just that nobody gets a free pass. We are not dealing with drug dealers that will give us a big fish. All of these people were government employees who used their positions of authority for their own political agenda. We simply cannot have the political party in power using the tools of law enforcement and intelligence services to attack the opposition candidate. This undermines our democracy and if laws were broken in the process, it will be our responsibility to hold these people accountable who broke the laws. This will be the most important work that you do in your careers, but chances are that no one will ever know about it but you. Because we are looking at the highest levels of government, it is in our best interest to keep this matter quiet. If there are grand jury indictments, that will change. There will be some media buzz, but it will not be good media buzz. You will be attacked and portrayed as running a witch hunt, when in fact you are ferreting out those individuals who were actually engaged in a witch hunt. Our position will be, "no comment," even after a successful jury trial, we will not comment. The verdicts will speak for themselves."

"Before we get too far into the details, let me point out a few things. There are four AUSA's assigned to this task force on a full time basis. Two of them were hired under a Republican administration and two were hired under a Democratic administration. The purpose of that is to give the task force objectivity. I want an opposition force in place to question the investigation, to point out weaknesses and to tell us how the other side will see things. I want to pick the case apart so we can anticipate defenses and be ready for them. There are also two AUSA's who are only here as liaison officer's, one of them from Northern Virginia and one from Baltimore. If we need to go to those jurisdictions, it is hoped that they will be able to grease the skids for us and we won't have to jump through a bunch of hoops to get our job done. You two won't have offices here and we hope that we won't see you after today, but you'll be on the grand jury list and you'll have to sign the same nondisclosure agreements. There are eight agents from various law enforcement agencies. Two agents will be assigned to each attorney. This may change in the future and in all likelihood will change. The twelve of you are going to decide how this thing proceeds. I am going to establish a basic starting point as to what I would like to establish first, but where it leads from there is up to you. I would like to have a staff meeting every Friday at 10:00 AM. I am not a fan of meetings, so I would like to keep these meetings a brief as possible. I would like each AUSA to give a brief synopsis of what we have learned over the last week and what their plans are for the next week. The purpose of these meetings is to keep everyone up to speed, so nobody is left out of the loop. All of our work product will be in a central file and will be accessible to everyone on the team. If you're busy doing your own thing you sometimes don't have time to check the central file and see what everyone else is up to. I promise I will do everything I can to keep these meetings brief. If the attorneys want the agents to give part of the briefing as to a particular interview or some part of the investigation, then that's what should happen."

"While we are on the subject of computers, you will notice there are four terminals over against the wall. These are connected to the internet and can be used to do research or to send e-mails. The computers in our offices are connected to our internal network and are not connected to the internet. So if you want to send an e-mail, you have to walk down the hallway to do it. I know this sounds paranoid, but we are going against some very powerful people who are not above wire tapping phones or sending in spies. That's why we are investigating them. So, it is only prudent to protect ourselves. You will each be issued a new cell phone. This phone is only to be used for task force business. These phones will be collected at the end of the operation and become part of the permanent record. If you need to make a personal call, do so on the landline, which is also tracked or on your personal cell phone, which as you all know is not secure. The point is to be careful what you say over the phone or in an e-mail. As long as we are on the topic of paranoia, let's not make any new friends over the next six months. If someone approaches you on the soccer field, at your church or someone wants to take you out to lunch, just be aware that the opposition is not above using operatives to accomplish their mission. It doesn't have to be someone asking you how the investigation is going. It could be someone finding out some personal detail that could be exploited. Remember, in the trial of the century, the lead prosecutor's ex-husband suddenly had enough money to bring a custody suit against her. While she is trying to focus on her opening statement, someone is trying to take her kids away from her. All I'm saying is just be careful. When we finish up today, check out your new offices, get the lay of the land and check in with Bev. She has some administrative details to take care of. Go back to your offices and get what you think you'll need. Close out your pending assignments. If you have a plea or a sentencing, you should hold on to that, but anything else, if it hasn't been to the grand jury yet, turn it over to someone else. I understand that there are going to be some things that you just can't get out of. There are going to be situations where you have to testify because you are the one with the first hand knowledge. We will just have to deal with those on a case by case basis. You should let everyone who needs to know that you are going to be unavailable for the next six months. The only thing you can say is that you have been assigned to a special task force and it might involve grand jury material so you can't talk about it. All of you bosses have been told that you have been assigned to a special task force, but that is all they've been told, and that is all you can say. We hope to be finished in six months, but you know how these things go. That's it. That is all you can say."

"So let's talk specifics for a moment. There are things that we know, there are things that we don't know, there are things that we'd like to know and there are things we will probably never know. We cannot divorce the political implications from this investigation, because it is an investigation about political implications. There was a group of people who wanted one political candidate to win over another political candidate. Nothing illegal about that. Everybody is entitled to a political viewpoint. But this group of people tried to use their positions of authority to try to influence the election and subsequently undo the results of the election. In that, they crossed the line and brought us to this point in history. Did they act in concert with an inappropriate intent? That's one of those questions to be answered. Did they genuinely believe that their actions were justified as legitimate law enforcement endeavors, or did they use the cover of law enforcement to mask an ulterior motive? These will be ongoing questions throughout our investigation. We know there was no Russia collusion. There never was. This was a hoax that was perpetrated by a few influential people in the government. We will need to flesh this out in terms of the details that show it was a hoax, but the fact that it didn't exist at all has been clearly established after a two year special counsel investigation. The news media was a willing participant in this hoax and in many instances was more influential in driving this narrative than the government employees. But the news media is not a target of this investigation. They can't be. They have first amendment protection, free speech, absence of malice, all of that. We could spend six months to a year trying to get some news reporter held in contempt of court for refusing to divulge his source. For what? It is not what we are about. Sure, they were as much responsible for the destruction of our democracy as the bad actors in our government, but they are not the targets of our investigation. Neither are the elected officials who spin the facts on the House and Senate floors and on the nightly news to the point where you can't tell fact from fiction. That's what they do. They are politicians. They lie for a living. They have immunity. We can't touch them. Now that doesn't mean they can't be witnesses. They can be subpoenaed just like anybody else. If we've got video and audio of them saying things that support this false narrative, then they can testify to the fact that this is what they said. We can then present document after document that show what they said was untrue. They can be shown to be a part of this false narrative. Just remember that these people are not co-operating witnesses, and they may say something on cross that is more damaging than what you get on direct."

"What else do we know? Well, we know that there was some bias evidenced by text messages sent by people involved in the investigation. We know there were two investigations. One involving Hildy Claxton's e-mails and one involving the allegation of collusion. All the people who worked for Claxton got immunity and Jim Homey as much as gave Hildy field immunity. He went on national television and said she couldn't be prosecuted because she lacked criminal intent. While his legal analysis was faulty, he as much as established reasonable doubt by definition. But while leaking classified information may be off the table for Hildy, obstruction of justice is not. She wasn't given field immunity for that one. Thirty thousand e-mails were destroyed after they were subpoenaed by Congress. Why? What was she trying to hide and why? The two investigations were run by the same people and the divergence of methods and practices are striking by comparison and show at a minimum a negligence towards the truth and possibly a sinister motive. Again, those things will have to be fleshed out to determine if they have an impact on our investigation."

"We also know that the FISA Court found 17 instances of abuse by the FBI in applying to the FISA Court for a warrant to wire tap an operative of a presidential candidate. These 17 instances can be boiled down to six things that the FISA Court was not told by the FBI. The FISA Court was not told that Hildy Claxton and the DNC had paid for the document that became the basis for the warrant. The FISA Court was not told that the author of the document had lied, that the author had a known bias and that the evidence was unverified. The FISA Court was not told that there was exculpatory evidence suggesting innocence of the target of the warrant or that the wife of a DOJ official cultivated Claxton funded information. We know that Jim Homey and Suzie Bates signed the first and second warrant application. Jim Homey and Jana Renki signed the third. Denny McCoy and Rob Lowenstein signed the fourth. These people were in a position of power and they used that power to wiretap the campaign of a candidate for President of the United States. These facts are not in dispute. What is in dispute is whether they did so with a legitimate purpose or whether they had an ulterior motive. That will be your job, to look at all the discernible facts and determine a motive. We are looking at circular logic. There was no Russia collusion. There never was. If the people in power knew that, then their motives of using a wiretap in pursuit of something that they knew didn't exist, can't be pure. So the questions becomes what did they know and when did they know it? I come from a background of white- collar investigations, specifically mail fraud. It was said that the number one job of the con-man was to convince himself of the lie. Because once he is convinced, it makes it easier to convince others. The same thing applies here. Not only will you have to find the lies, but the timing of when they were exposed as lies will be critical."

"We also know that top government officials leaked classified information to the news media in order to further this narrative and lied about it. The Director of the CIA, Rex Brenamore, leaked details of the dossier and repeatedly lied about it. The Director of National Intelligence, Tim Dapper, leaked details of the dossier and lied about it. They both lied in their testimony to Congress about their use of the dossier in their assessment of intelligence. Hell, Jim Homey admitted on national television in his testimony before Congress that he leaked his notes of his conversation with the President to a college professor so they could get to the media. The I.G. decided that this matter should not be referred for prosecution, which is certainly not a grant of immunity and doesn't stop us from looking at it, but that old reasonable doubt thing rears its ugly head again. How can we prosecute FBI agents for leaking secrets to the news media when the Director sets the standard? Again, questions you're going to have to examine and flesh out the details. To the best of my knowledge, it has never been a successful defense to say 'Well Jimmy did it too'. "

"We've got leaking, we've got lying, we've got obstruction, we've got FISA abuse, we've got violations of the espionage act 18 USC 793, mishandling of classified documents 1924, destruction of government documents 2071(b), converting public documents 641 and conspiracy to defraud the United States, 371 and 1349. All of these areas of inquiry are open to you. There are no limitations on how high you go or how wide sweeping your investigation with the parameters that have been previously discussed. Members of the news media are not targets of this investigation, although they may be subpoenaed before the grand jury as fact witnesses. Elected officials are not targets of this investigation, but could also be subpoenaed as fact witnesses. There will be no immunity granted to any one and everything in this office is considered grand jury material."

"With all of that in mind, I would like to divide the task force into four areas of inquiry. I would like each of you to look into your area for the first week. After that, you can reorganize, restructure and combine your resources any way you see fit. I would like to get your initial read on each of these areas by our staff meeting on Friday."

"Kathy Solove, you and your two agents will look into the leaking of classified information and grand jury materials. Debbie Brinkman, you and your two agents will look into lying under oath either in depositions, before Congress or in sworn documents. Bob Williams, your group will look into obstruction of justice relating to the e-mails and Dale Brinkman, your group will look into FISA abuse. All of these areas overlap and may involve the same witnesses, so you will need to co-ordinate before you go forward with interviews so all our bases are covered. It may be a good idea to just do background research for this first week and hold off doing any interviews until we are all on the same page after our first staff meeting. I know this seems like a daunting task and is pretty overwhelming at this point, but there has been some investigative journalism done on this matter, not a lot, most of the main stream media were willing participants in this fraud perpetrated on the American public, but there were a couple of journalist who were paying attention and there are a couple of books out there that could be used as reference materials. I would caution you to stay away from journalists, at least at this point. They have a different agenda than you and they don't need to know what you're doing. You can read their books, but don't interview them, at least not yet."

"Okay, I'd like to have all the agents stand up please." The agents stood and looked around.

"Please raise your right hand and repeat after me: I do solemnly swear that I will protect and defend the constitution of the United States against all enemies foreign and domestic, and that I will faithfully carry out the duties of a Special Deputy U.S. Marshal and such other duties as assigned by the Attorney General of the United States, and I will abide by the terms of non-disclosure of any materials coming into my possession by virtue of being assigned to the U.S Attorney General's special task force. So help me God."

Okay, good. Take your seats. Here are your credentials identifying you as Deputy U.S. Marshals. As you can see, there is a badge and an appointment signed by the President of the United States. These are not yours to keep. They will be turned in at the conclusion of the task force. See Bev about getting your photo taken for the id portion of the credential."

"Here are the forms all twelve, excuse me all fourteen, of you are required to sign. I know it seems silly for people who have been dealing with Rule 6(e) issues their entire career, but this is different and it will prevent any misunderstanding. Read the form and if you are in agreement, sign the form." Kathy Solove raised her hand.

"Can we have copies of what we are signing?"

"No."

"Then I'm not signing the form."

"Then you are not working here. The originals will be maintained in a file here. If there is a problem with your disclosing information and you are subject to disciplinary action, you will be provided with a copy of what you signed. Otherwise, the document will be subject to the rules of this office, and nothing leaves this office. You can go back to your office and tell your boss that you were removed from the task force for refusing to sign a document prohibiting the disclosure of information. Your boss can then communicate that in formation through channels to the Attorney General. Now you can spin it such that, it wasn't because you refused to sign, but because you were denied a copy that caused you to leave the task force. But leave the task force is the operative fact and the one you will have to deal with." Grady let that statement hang in the air for a moment.

"Fine. I'll sign your stupid form, but you're a prick."

"I've been called worse. Look I was hoping I wouldn't have to make this speech, but I can see now that it is necessary. Anybody who doesn't want to be on this task force should leave now. You know what it is all about, and if you talk about it, the Attorney General will not think highly of you. If you leave now and keep your mouth shut, there will be no hard feelings. Anybody want to leave?" No one stirred, and Grady let the silence linger awhile to let everyone consider the ramifications of such a decision.

"Look, none of us wants to be here. None of us applied for this job. It is not a rung on the ladder of career advancement. It is not even an accomplishment for your annual performance review. It is not even something that anyone will ever know that you did except for you. You were selected for this assignment because of your knowledge, your experience, your success and your integrity. Of all the people they could have selected, they selected you. I don't know how the selection process worked, whether it was some kind of computer program or a manual vetting process. The fact remains they selected you. You have been asked to serve in an endeavor to determine if a group of people tried to damage our republic and to hold them accountable if they did, so it won't ever happen again. There is no glory in this job. There is no pot of gold at the end of the rainbow. There is not even any applause at the conclusion of a trial. The media will not be singing your praises. In all, likelihood you will be vilified because the media is part of the opposition. There is no cause for joy if we are successful because that will mean people at the highest levels did try to subvert our election process. You are being asked to serve out of a sense of duty and a belief in the system. It may sound naïve, but it is the only word I've got. Duty." Grady looked around the room and let the silence linger.

"Okay, I'm not going to put anybody on the spot right now. If you need to talk about this, come see me later today. My door is always open, unless it is closed, which means I'm in there with somebody and I need some privacy. There were a few nervous chuckles around the room and the meeting broke up.

A while later, Grady was sitting in his office and there was a knock at his door. He looked up and Kathy Solove was standing in the doorway.

"You got a minute?"

"Sure, come on in, have a seat."

"Everybody's gone back to their respective offices. I'm on the way out too, but I just wanted to stop by and say I think we got off on the wrong foot this morning."

"No, no. Not at all. You signed my stupid form."

"Yes, I did, but I called you a prick."

"Like I said I've been called worse. Let me tell you a story. When I was working in Detroit, I got called in on an IAD investigation. Not because I had done anything wrong, but because the guy I was with got into some difficulties later on in the evening. I was required to give a sworn statement and give specific details in that statement. I asked if I could have a copy of my statement. The IAD Inspector didn't know. He had to call back to DC to find out. No body had ever asked before. The answer was yes I could have a copy. If you think about it, of course the answer is yes. If you deny someone a copy of their sworn statement, after they have requested a copy of it, it makes you look bad. It makes it look like you are trying to pull a fast one. A position no body wants to be in, if you are going to any type of hearing. So you and I both know that you were entitled to a copy of a document that you just signed. This was about you challenging my authority to see if I was going to be serious about the non-disclosure of task force documents. If I was going to fold the first time the smartest lawyer in the room stood up to me, then the task force was doomed from its inception, and you and I both know it. But you had to call me a name just to save face. The fact that I let you get away with it, went a long way with the other members of the task force."

"The smartest lawyer in the room?"

"You are the most experienced, the most successful and regarded as the most intelligent attorney in your office. I've read your file."

"I have a file?"

"Everybody has a file. You and I both know that when this thing shakes out, if we are going to trial, you will be lead counsel. You are going to be in charge. You are going to be calling the shots. I'm the administrator. I'm going to be making sure everybody is doing what they are supposed to be doing. I will be looking over your shoulder, and I will have absolute veto authority, but you will be driving the boat."

"You act like I've already signed on."

"You made that decision in a nanosecond when you signed my stupid form. Saying yes to something like this doesn't help your career, but saying no, kills it. You figured that out when I stood up to you, and so did everybody else when you signed the form."

"I don't like Donald Trump. He's arrogant, a narcissist, a misogynist, he's crude and disrespectful in his tweets."

"You are not unique in that position."

"I voted for the other candidate."

"Again, not a unique position, about half the country did. Let me ask you a question. Did you at any time use your position of authority to try to influence the election?"

"Of course not."

"Does it bother you at all that others in positions of authority may have done just that?"

Well, I'm going to keep an open mind on that issue. I want to see where the facts take us."

'That's what I need from you. I need your open mind. I need your experience and your intellect, but most of all I need your open mind. I need you to tell me where I am wrong. I need you to point out what I am not seeing. If we go forward on this thing, I want to win. I don't want there to be any surprises. If there are defense, I want to be sure we are ready for them."

"You ask a lot."

"They wire tapped a presidential campaign. Doesn't that give you pause?"

"I try not to think about it, but yes it does give me pause."

"I think it was Ben Franklin who said, it is much easier to fool someone than it is to convince them that they have been fooled. The problem with that analogy here is, the people who were fooled wanted to be fooled. They hated this man so much that they wanted to believe he was a traitor and a spy for Russia. When it turned out that he wasn't and the whole thing was a made up story, they said 'oh well, it could have been true'."

"It gets back to those original questions that you posed to us: what did they know and when did they know it, were they acting in concert with an ulterior motive, did they have legitimate law enforcement motives or were they masking their true motives with a cloak of legitimacy? Just because an investigation doesn't find any wrongdoing, doesn't mean the investigation was not warranted."

"That's the type of thinking that I need. That is the defense that we have to be ready to counter. Can we show it was unwarranted from its inception?"

"I can see that you are going to be a pain in the ass to work with."

"Well, I've graduated from prick to pain in the ass. I think it was also Ben Franklin who said 'Neither a fortress nor a virgin can stand once they start to negotiate'. You and I have started to negotiate."

"Which am I, the virgin or the fortress?"

"I'm going to go out on a limb here and say fortress." They both laughed and the meeting broke up.

The Staff Meeting

Grady looked around the room. The agents looked bored and unengaged. The attorneys looked apprehensive.

"So, welcome to our first staff meeting. I know this one is not very compelling because we haven't done anything yet, but hopefully the meetings will get better as time goes by. Kathy, you want to go first? You were to look into leaking."

"As you suggested, we've just been doing research over the past week. The leaking has been substantial, but we're having a difficult time isolating the leaking of classified information. There is a ton of leaking of information to the media in order to gain a political advantage, but the information leaked is by innuendo and not specific. The media then takes that information and expands on it and uses sensational terminology to create a narrative. There are some large leaks that play a prominent role in this saga that, I guess, from a hindsight perspective could be woven together to show a conspiracy to defraud the American public. Looked at individually, the leaks don't seem like such a big deal. For example before the Donovan Stuhl dossier ever became public, the Director of The CIA, Rex Brenamore, wrote a letter to the then Speaker of the House, claiming there was Trump Russia collusion, and that letter got leaked to the media. The Director didn't leak it, but somebody in the Speaker's office did. The Stuhl dossier had been peddled to all the media outlets who had refused to publish it because the information in it couldn't be verified. Jim Homey meets with the President and tells him about the dossier and then leaks the fact that the President has been briefed. The news media now feels justified in reporting on the dossier in that the President has been briefed on it, not that anything in it is true. But once they report on it, the information gets repeated over and over to the point everybody believes it is true. This wasn't really the release of classified information because the dossier was bogus. The media ignored the lack of veracity and focused on the sensational aspect of the details, and that became the story. The media was the bad guy here because they didn't care about the truth, but they were played by the Director of the FBI to print a story, that he knew was untrue. The big leak came, when Homey was fired by the President. He leaked his notes of his meeting with the President through a third party in order to get them to the media. This led to the appointment of the Special Counsel, which was arguably his goal. When Homey made this admission before Congress, they all sat there with stunned looks on their faces, but nobody asked any follow up questions. Have you used this conduit before? Have you used any others? How many times have you leaked information to the press? Have you ever directed anyone on your staff to make a leak to the press? Is this standard operating procedure in the Bureau? I mean there is a litany of questions that could have been asked. It might not have done any good because the man seems to have a condition known as selective amnesia, but we'll never know. The IG, in his report of the matter, said he wasn't referring the matter for prosecution, because while improper, the classified nature of the documents were in question. Can you imagine a more classified document than one reporting a private conversation between the President of the United States and the Director of the FBI in the oval office? I can't, but maybe the plans and specifications of the Stealth

Bomber, but certainly not any conversation between government officials. At the very least, these notes did not belong to Jim Homey. They were government property, and his use of them constituted theft of government property under 641. The point is, it is difficult to tell this story in bits and pieces. It is all part of a bigger narrative. When you look at the individual leaks, they just don't seem to rise to the level of criminal prosecution."

"OK, Debbie Brinkman. You were going to look into the lies?"

"Yes. We also have had difficulty with the lies. We've been combing through transcripts and other documents. My guys are starting to turn green at the gills from reading transcripts and finding the lies. It's not what they normally do for a living. They want to go interview people, but we're not quite there yet. Close, but not quite. It is not that we can't find any lies, it's that there are so many lies we're overwhelmed. We have to look at inconsistent statements and cull through them with a test of materiality. What were the lies that really mattered? Those are the ones we have to focus on. We're going to have to establish criminal intent. What did they know and when did they know it? How do we show the incorrect statement was made for an evil purpose? In order to do that we have to show other statements that show a bias and prejudice by the people who were supposed to be fair and impartial. We have the same problems Kathy has. The lies were all part of the bigger story. In and of themselves, the lies don't seem like such a big deal, but taken in context of the big picture they all add up to support this false narrative. We've got the big lie that Trump colluded with the Russian government to influence the 2016 election.

That was untrue. It didn't happen. Now we know it didn't happen after a two year Special Counsel investigation. But even before that, there was a ten-month investigation by the FBI, which found no collusion. The problem we have as prosecutors is that these lies weren't told under oath. They weren't told in depositions, in Congressional testimony or in affidavits. They were leaked to the news media, and the news media then embellished the story and sensationalized the story and pretty much perpetrated a fraud on the American people. The news media lied for two years every night. They repeated the mantra of Russian collusion. The news media gets away with it because there is no body to hold them accountable. The media is supposed to report the facts in order to hold the government accountable. The media has been 'Dan Rathered'. They know the story is untrue, but they don't care because the story is too good not to run. That may be too harsh. It may be that they wanted the story to be true so badly that they didn't bother to look into it to determine if it was true or not. But at some point, the media changed from being a reporter of the facts to being an advocate for a particular point of view. It is now undeniably true that the media is firmly opposed to this President and anything that he wants to do and was a willing participant in the scheme to hang a false charge around his neck. You say the media is not a target of our investigation. Fine, I get that. We can't tell the story without referencing their participation in the scheme. Maybe the media was duped. Maybe they are an evil empire. It doesn't matter. They were involved, and their involvement needs to be part of the story in order to tell the story accurately. Rex Brenamore, Director of the CIA, wrote a letter to Larry Smead, Speaker of the House, alleging the Trump Russian collusion. The letter was a lie. It was leaked to the media. This wasn't under oath or in a deposition. Some time in June 2016, Donovan Stuhl is hired by Hildy Claxton and the DNC to do opposition research on Donald Trump. This research is to be funneled through Fission CVS, a research firm run by Ben Stinson who had been working with Claxton lawyers and the DNC since April. The first Stuhl memo is filed with Fission CVS around June 16, 2016 and claims Trump Russia collusion. Stuhl goes on to write 17 memos consisting of 35 pages over the next six months. These memos have become known as the 'Stuhl dossier.' This dossier was funded and paid for by Hildy Claxton and the DNC. Much of what is in the dossier is false and Stuhl admits in a deposition in April of 2017 that the information is unverified. On July 30, 2016 Stuhl meets with Bill Boar, a DOJ official and his wife Nancy Boar, who works for Fission CVS and gives them the first part of the dossier. Bill Boar immediately hands it over to the FBI. The next day the FBI opens 'Crossfire Hurricane' an investigation into the Trump Russia collusion."

"You can't fault them for that, they had some information that there was wrong doing and they opened an investigation. That's what they do. But the information was false. It was made up. It was opposition research paid for by the other political candidate for president of the United States. You would think the FBI would be smarter than that. You'd be wrong. They jump in with both feet. They ran with it and continued to run with it right up to the point when the Special Counsel concluded there was no evidence of Russia collusion. You have to ask yourself why. Why did the FBI continue to participate in the giant hoax on the American people? Why did they allow themselves to be used as a pawn in this political mud slinging? To answer that question you have to go back and look at the original motivations of the bureau. You have to look at the two investigations and the desperate treatment they received. Everybody who works for Hildy Claxton gets immunity even though some of them lied under oath. The Attorney General at that time is Dorothy Dench. She meets with Claxton's husband for 45 minutes on a tarmac in his plane. This was all while his wife is the subject of a criminal investigation. She didn't realize that created an appearance of impropriety? Did she skip that course when she was in law school? Two FBI employees are texting back and forth about their obvious bias against Trump and yet they are both involved in the investigation of his political rival. No appearance of impropriety there! But wait there's more. As soon as their boss, Jim Homey, clears Hildy Claxton on national television, they are both assigned to the Trump investigation. You can't make this stuff up, and we can't tell the story to a jury without showing the desperate treatment of the two investigations. And what about Jim Homey, who testifies before Congress, which is broadcast on national TV, and lays out all the things Hildy Claxton did with her e-mails. There are clear violations of the espionage act and the mishandling of classified documents act, but he concludes that no reasonable prosecutor would take this case because there is a lack of criminal intent. First off, the statute does not require criminal intent but rather gross negligence. Second, it wasn't his decision to make. This decision should have been referred to the DOJ and if the AG had to recuse herself, then her second in command at the DOJ should have made the decision. If you look at the two investigations, the only logical conclusion is that the FBI, certain members of the FBI, were biased against Trump. They weren't pawns in this giant hoax. They were the drivers of this hoax. They were arrogant in their power, and they thought they could get away with it, and so far they have."

"Now there were some lies told under oath that were in support of the big lie. Nancy Boar, wife of Bill Boar, lied under oath when she said she didn't send the opposition research to the prosecutors. Rex Brenamore, Director of the CIA, repeatedly lied under oath when he talked about Russian collusion and his use of the dossier. Tim Dapper, the Director of National Intelligence, leaked the dossier and lied about it and lied about whether the dossier was used to prepare the Intelligence Community Assessment. He later said some of it had been used. He later recanted some of his testimony when he said he didn't understand the question. Allen Stiff repeatedly lied about the timing of the bias in the dossier being exposed and about his secret knowledge of collusion when none existed. But he is a Congressman and not a target of our investigation. Bottom line, we're just getting started, and I am sure we will find more lies under oath by government employees. My opinion is we should be sifting through those lies with a filter of materiality. We should be looking for those lies that made a difference, that impacted the scheme to affect the election and to undo it afterwards. Every lie that we charge should be one that was in furtherance of the scheme to defraud. I don't want to grab the low hanging fruit and prosecute a couple of FBI agents or DOJ employees for an obvious lie that's easy to prove, and then go home and declare success. If we are going to do this, we should do it right. We should go after the big lie and call it what it is, a conspiracy to defraud the United States." Grady nodded his head in agreement and spoke.

"I agree with ever thing you have said, and I also don't want to just grab low hanging fruit. But let me play devil's advocate for just a minute. What if some of this low hanging fruit as you call it, can give us additional information about the 'big lie'? Suppose we can charge some employee with a lie that we can easily prove and after a conviction we can use sentencing consideration to get co-operation. Would you consider going after the low hanging fruit in that scenario?"

"Yes, of course. I think we have to look at every situation on a case by case basis. We have to seriously decide whether this is taking us in a direction we want to go, or are we just putting notches on our belt? It's a very easy trap to fall into, counting convictions and claiming success."

"Okay, I agree, but there is another aspect to this as well, and that is a strategic one. A few well-timed arrests could send a signal that this matter is serious, and people need to stand on one side of the aisle or the other. We'll need to take a look at this when we get there. Okay. Bob Williams, your group was going to look into obstruction of justice, what have you got?"

"It is clear that Hildy Claxton and agents working on her behalf destroyed 30,000 e-mails after they had been subpoenaed by Congress. What is not entirely clear is whether or not this is obstruction of justice. We can't find any instance where it has happened before. There is a ton of case law supporting obstruction of justice when evidence is destroyed after being subject to a grand jury subpoena or a trial subpoena. There is even case law supporting an obstruction of justice charge when the subpoena is in a civil case, but we can't find any for a Congressional subpoena. We don't know if this has never happened before or if the charge is simply not appropriate. There certainly is an argument to be made that a Congressional subpoena is not the administration of justice. It is a legislative function not a judicial one, separate branches of the government and all that. There is also an argument to be made that a Congressional subpoena is just as important as some civil case in podunkville. There are learned writings on both side of the issue, but we haven't found any case law. We are going to keep looking. There is something else about the e-mails. That is 'why'. Why did the Secretary of State use a private e-mail server to send and receive classified documents in violation of both the Espionage Act and the Mishandling of Classified Documents Act, 18 USC 793 and 18 USC 1924? The obvious answer is because she could. She was the boss of the State Department and nobody could tell her she couldn't do it. But there has to be a reason, and it is probably the same reason 30,000 e-mails were deleted after they were subpoenaed. Why? Again, because she could. Her lawyers went through the documents and decided what was relevant and what was not. That's not the way a subpoena works. The target of an investigation does not get to decide what is relevant and what is not. In the discovery process in a civil proceeding, the lawyers work every thing out behind the scenes. If there is a request for documents, the lawyers will get together and decide what is relevant. This was not a discovery process, but Claxton's lawyers were allowed to treat it as such. Again why? Why all this subterfuge? There is a reasonable theory that has been put forth that the former Secretary was conducting Claxton

Foundation business through her e-mail server, and she did not want that on a State Department computer. It's kind of like calling home on your government issued cell phone. They let you do it, but they ask you to limit your personal calls to five minutes a day. Have you ever tried to call home and limit your wife to five minutes? Good luck with that. So there is a reasonable explanation. She didn't want to conduct personal business on a state department computer, so she paid for her own computer server and could conduct whatever business she wanted. There is also a possible sinister purpose. It has long been alleged that the Secretary of State conducted a 'pay to play' campaign. If you donated money to the Claxton Foundation, you got access to the Secretary of State. You didn't necessarily get any favors from the Secretary of State, but you at least got access. Perhaps if the 'pay to play' scheme were exposed in these 30,000 e-mails, then favors might be as well. Let's say for instance the previous administration sells uranium to some Russian oligarchs and the Russian oligarchs make a substantial donation to the Claxton Foundation. That might be something that would trigger further inquiry. Is the 'Uranium One' deal something that this task force should be looking into? Grady frowned and said,

"I know that is something that should have been the subject of intense scrutiny prior to the 2016 election, but we are getting pretty far afield of our mandate. I know it sounds like it's related because it sounds like Russian collusion, but it really wasn't related to the 2016 election. The FBI's handling of the e-mail server investigation during the election is relevant. What Claxton did with the e-mail server while Secretary of State is not. We would need additional manpower, for that and we have a statute of limitations problem. So let's stick with the 2016 election, and what is relevant to that. I know I said there were no limitations to the investigation, but I don't want us going off on tangents. Okay, Dale Brinkler, you were going to look into the FISA abuse."

"Well our area of inquiry was pretty straight forward. We don't have the problems that everyone else has. There are lies by omission and they were sworn to. A FISA warrant is just like any other search warrant. You have to swear to the facts in the affidavit before the FISA court judge. The FBI was arrogant in their cavalier approach to the FISA warrant process. They rarely get turned down for a FISA warrant. This is an ex-parte proceeding, but all warrants are ex-parte proceedings. You don't bring a defense attorney into a hearing to decide if you're going to get a warrant for his client. That would be absurd. But the FISA proceedings are a secret tribunal and rightfully so. The Act allows spying on American citizens who are in communication with foreign actors in hopes of eliminating or preventing damage and or loss of life by those foreign actors. It is a sensitive matter and is treated as such. In this case, the FISA court proceedings were used by a few people at the top of the FBI and the DOJ to further a political agenda. While this is all part of a bigger picture, and we can weave that into the indictment, and the story we present at trial, this part of the investigation is simple. They lied and they did it under oath."

"Not many people know anything about the FISA Court. There are 11 FISA Court Judges. All are District Court Judges who are appointed for a term by the Chief Justice of the United States Supreme Court. They rotate one week at a time to serve on the Court in D.C. So on average, they spend five weeks in D.C. throughout the year. In 2016, each judge considered an average of about 28 applications for FISA warrants per week. Think about that. That's more than five a day, every day. That's a lot of applications to read and evaluate. The Chief Judge of the FISA Court has issued a scathing report of the FBI and its abuse of this situation. We'd like to put that report in evidence. There might be some problems with that. Hearsay, opinion evidence, relevancy, goes to the ultimate fact in issue, national security, the list goes on and on. Defense counsel will argue all of that in the hopes that one will stick. I think we can overcome those issues, but there is another consideration. The FISA Court should have caught this. After all, you don't get to be a FISA Court Judge if you are a high school drop out. There were four separate judges that approved four applications to spy on the Trump campaign. Granted the last three were just approving a renewal of the application. And it can be assumed that they relied on the first guy's evaluation. Still, this was a candidate for president and later the President Elect. This was an unprecedented use of this secret tribunal to spy on the President of the United States. Now granted the warrant was on Carson Pugh, a campaign worker in the Trump campaign. Does anybody doubt that this investigation targeted Donald Trump, especially in light of the information in the dossier? Is there any way the FISA Court didn't see that? As a matter of fact, this abuse by the FBI may damage the FISA Court to the point where it could be eliminated. The real damage here could be to our ability to track real foreign intelligence assets who want to do damage to our country similar to 911." There was silence around the room as the gravitas of that statement sunk in. Finally Grady spoke up,

"I think that's a strong argument and one we may want to make in our closing statement. We may also want to point out that the news media drove this narrative to the point that they may have put our country at risk. We can't indict them, but we don't have to let them off the hook either. I think bringing the Chief FISA Court Judge in to testify at trial is a decision we will make at the time, but I can't see any harm of putting her before the grand jury. Okay, we've all heard our teammates' positions. Let's go around the room again. Where do we go from here? Kathy, you go first."

"Well, I think you've had us chasing our tails for a week by dividing this thing into four separate inquiries. We can all see now that this thing is all part of one big problem. Did members of our government try to use their positions of authority to influence a presidential election and undo the results afterward? I think we should work together to focus on that big question. Forget about trying to pick off individuals on small crimes and focus on the big one. If people want to co-operate in exchange for sentencing consideration so be it, but we need to start preparing for trial now. That means proceeding to the grand jury in a logical manner and building our case from the bottom up. By the time we get to trial, our case should be rock solid." Grady suppressed a smile and thought to himself 'gotcha'.

"Debbie, your thoughts?"

"I agree with Kathy. I think we need to start working on the indictment now. This was a conspiracy on a grand scale. We can fill in the blanks as we go and make changes and modifications as the evidence demands, but it will give us a game plan and how to proceed with the grand jury. I think it is clear we need a time line. What did people know and when did they know it will go a long way to establishing the ulterior motive that will be so crucial in this case. Remember, these guys are all cops, and they are all going to claim they were just conducting a legitimate investigation. The ulterior motive will be the key." Grady thought to himself, another one on board.

"Bob, your thoughts?"

"Well my area of assigned inquiry didn't turn out so well. I think it's clear from what has been said here today that Hildy Claxton is not a target of this task force. Sure, she did some things that were questionable maybe even criminal, but bringing charges against her will be a distraction to the real focus of this task force. Her name is going to come up because of the disparate treatment and because things were done on her behalf, but she wasn't driving the bus. She didn't tell these officials at the FBI or the DOJ to do the things they did. So it's clear, at least to me, that Hildy Claxton is not a target. Well that begs the question, who is the target? It seems like we are going at this by process of elimination. Nobody in the media is a target regardless of how many lies they told or how often they told them. The media was clearly the driving force behind this fraud on the American people. The media has become an evil force that doesn't care about the truth. It only cares about presenting it's own political viewpoint and ratings. I'm not even sure ratings are all that important. We are not going to target any elected officials. Allen Stiff lied repeatedly at every chance he got in front of every TV camera he could find. We can prove he repeatedly lied, we can prove he knowingly lied and we can prove he did so with a malicious intent, but he is not a target. So, who is a target? That's a decision we are going to have to make and we are going to have to make it pretty quickly. Before we go to the grand jury, we need to know who's going to be offered a seat at the table." Grady thought, so he's not on board yet. That's okay, we need a devil's advocate.

"Dale, your view?"

"Well, I have to disagree with my learned colleagues. The FISA abuse stands alone. They lied, by omission, they knew they were lying, they did it under oath and they had an evil intent, end of story. Now all of these shenanigans with the Stuhl dossier and the bias and prejudice goes a long way towards establishing that evil intent, but that's all relevant evidence at trial. I don't think the FISA abuse needs to be a part of some grand conspiracy charge involving some Cecil B. DeMille gang bang cast of thousands. Keep it simple stupid. That's my motto. You know as long as we're talking about conspiracy theory, on January 5, 2017 there was a meeting at the White House with the previous administration. The meeting was attended by the Director of the FBI, the Director of National Intelligence, the VP, acting Attorney General Suzie Bates and also Sue Price. The very next day, Homey briefs the President Elect on the Stuhl dossier and leaks it to the press that he has done so. The press then runs with the story, not the dossier is true, but that the president was told about it. Once that happens, the press feels free to print the entire dossier and the Russian collusion delusion begins. Is it possible that the previous administration orchestrated this whole thing?" Grady interrupted the ensuing silence,

"Well, I think that falls into the category of one of those things we'll probably never know. Now don't get me wrong, if you want to put each of those five people before the grand jury and ask them if this was discussed at that meeting, then go right ahead. Before you do that though, you have to ask yourself, is this going to be beneficial to the investigation. The previous administration is not a target of this task force. I think we can all agree, that is just too much weight for us to bear. Did he know what was going on? Probably. Can we prove it? Absolutely not. So do we want to be the ones to bring up the issue and let the defense attorneys point to the guy not in the room and say, 'my guy was just following orders.' Or do we want to let the defense attorneys bring it up and let them be the ones to besmirch the reputation of the guy not in the room." Grady could see the wheels going around and from the frowns on their faces, they didn't like what they were hearing and didn't like what they were thinking. Dale spoke first,

"So, what happened to the sky is the limit. The investigation takes you wherever it takes you?"

"That's still true. The investigation takes you wherever it takes you. But there are limits. There is to be no grant of immunity, period. There is to be no leaking from this office, period. The media is not a target of this task force, period. And elected officials are not targets of this task force, period. Politicians make policy decisions, but those decisions are influenced by political considerations. We can't go after elected officials for making what could be policy decisions. To the best of my knowledge, the previous guy was an elected official. Look, I'm not saying you shouldn't ask certain questions. All I'm saying is your areas of inquiry should further the investigation, not take us off on a tangent. You guys are in charge of the investigation. You decide how you want to handle it. Just be careful."

"Okay, at this point I think it is clear we need to restructure. I knew this would happen. I just didn't think it would happen this quickly. So, at this point, we all need to be going in the same direction. The focus from this point on is on the attempt to influence the 2016 election and the attempt to undue the results afterward. This will include the disparate treatment of the two investigations, but only for the purpose of showing bias and prejudice on the part of the bad actors. Kathy, I would like you to start working on the conspiracy to defraud the United States and all of its component parts including overt acts in furtherance of the conspiracy. If any of these are individual crimes, consider charging them as crimes as well. Debbie, I would like you to work with her on this, but I'd also like you to begin putting a time line together. The dates of what happened, will be helpful to us to get a handle on this thing and could be useful at trial. In this regard, every time you put a date on the chart, document how you establish this at trial. I think several 'write boards' here in the conference room would be beneficial for all of us. Dale, I would like you to work with Kathy and Debbie on the conspiracy indictment, but I would like your focus to be on the targets of the investigation. I'd like you to establish a file on each of the targets. What did they do and when in furtherance of the conspiracy. This will be an ever changing file as we gather more and more information. What the final cast of characters will look like will be up to the three of you, and what you believe you can prove. I think at this point, we have to consider Denny McCoy, Paulie Ruck and Linda

Pugh of the FBI and Rob Lowenstein of the DOJ as our initial targets. This can change, but this is a good starting point. It is hard for me to envision a scenario where Jim Homey is not a prominent figure in this conspiracy, but before we indict a former Director of the FBI, we need to make sure we have our ducks in a row. Bob, you're on your own, at least for now. I would like you and your agents to focus on the FISA abuse and the Stuhl dossier. Determine how you want to proceed and who you want to put before the grand jury. Co-ordinate with Kathy so you are not stepping on each other's toes. Understand that your portion of the investigation might get blended into the conspiracy charge, because it's difficult to tell this story without mentioning the FISA abuse and the Stuhl dossier. We'll run the two parts of the investigation on separate tracks, but we may merge them later on. We're going to have to be mindful of a double jeopardy type argument, charging people for two separate crimes for the same conduct. I may not be using the correct legal terminology here, but you know what I mean, it looks bad. Also, I'd like you and Dale to get together and come to a determination whether Donovan Stuhl, the ex-British spy, and Ben Stinson, the opposition research marketing guy, should be targets of the investigation. It is clear they were the driving force behind this whole false narrative, but they weren't government employees. They were just making money off the FBI, the DNC and Hildy Claxton in order to promote this phony narrative. Is that a crime? I can't decide. It certainly looks like they were part of a criminal conspiracy, but I'd like you guys to look into it and come up with a reasoning on how we should proceed with respect to these two guys. Any questions?" Dale raised his hand.

"You've asked me to create a file of possible targets. Is the former Attorney General, Dorothy Dench, who had the infamous tarmac meeting and directed the FBI investigation of Claxton off the table?

"No."

"Is the former Director of the CIA, Rex Brenamore, off the table?"

"No."

"Is the Director of National Intelligence, Tim Dapper, off the table?"

"No."

"Is the former Special Counsel, Ronald Miller, off the table?"

"Yes. He was not part of the criminal conspiracy. He was brought in afterwards and appointed to do a job and he did it. You can question his legal reasoning (we can't prove he didn't do it so he must have done it). You can question his legal ethics (hiring all biased lawyers for his investigation). You can question his motivation for continuing to beat a dead horse (investigating for an additional year a crime that he knew didn't occur). These are all political decisions. To try to weave these into a criminal conspiracy, only weakens your case. It doesn't strengthen it. Now the people on his team who were involved in the criminal conspiracy, before, during or after being on his team are fair game. That would include Carson Steinman, who is by all accounts a dirt bag prosecutor who doesn't play by the rules. I believe he actually ran the Special Counsel investigation and made the decisions that were attributed to Miller. However, I don't think you'll find any evidence of his involvement in the criminal conspiracy. He is too slick. Okay, any thing else?"

"Okay, Debbie, see if Bev can get you some white boards to go around the walls of the conference room. Maybe Carly has good handwriting and can help you out with this. She's not too busy yet, since you guys haven't interviewed anybody yet."

A while later Grady was sitting in his office when the intercom buzzed.

"Mr. Franklin."

"Yes."

"There's a Mr. Mathews here to see you."

"Mr. Mathews?"

"Yes. He's from security."

"Oh yeah, Sure. I was told he might be stopping by. Send him on back." Grady went to his door and waited.

"Mr. Franklin, I'm Bill Mathews, but call me Matt. Everybody does."

"Sure. Call me Grady. What can I do for you?" They both sat down.

"Well, I just wanted to come by and introduce myself and let you know we are around. If you have any problems with security, just let me know, and we'll try to solve them. I understand you are involved in a pretty sensitive investigation and there might be some people who might try to interfere with your investigation, so if you have any problems, just give me a call." Matt handed Grady a business card with the All-Tech Security logo and several phone numbers.

"The office number is manned during business hours, and if you can't reach me there, you can always get me on the cell number. Our outfit provides security to the stars, so we are quite capable of providing body guard type services, if that becomes necessary."

"Oh, I don't think that will be necessary."

"I don't either, but I wanted to let you know it's available. If any of your people run into difficulty, you know people following them, a sudden interest by a casual acquaintance, anything that makes them feel uncomfortable, let me know. We can look into it for you. That way you can keep focus on what you are doing."

"You haven't asked me what we are doing."

"No sir. I don't have a need to know. My job is to protect you, your people, the building and any information stored here."

"I see. Why do I get the impression that you know more than you let on?"

"It's my poker face, sir. It's been my downfall my whole life. We installed your computer system. We are very good at computer security. It's kind of our thing. No system is hack proof, but your system is as close as they come."

"So you are the guys who insisted that we only have those four separate monitors connected to the internet."

"Yes sir."

"Seems like a bit of overkill."

"Like I said, your internal system is as hack proof as we can make it."

"So, do you anticipate some kind of problem that I am not aware of?"

"No. We just want to be ready in case there is a problem. So we will need you to keep us informed of any potential problems. That way, we can provide any security that you might need."

"That is kind of interesting because when I gave my briefing to my people on the first day, I told them not to make any new friends for the next six months. I told them to be wary of anyone who took a sudden interest in them. They all looked at me like I was paranoid. You don't think I am?"

"No sir. I think it was good advice. If something like that comes up, give me a call, and we will look into it. You know it could be nothing more than a distraction. You are looking into that, and it takes you away from your main mission. As long as you've got us taking care of the little things, you can focus on the big things."

'Sounds like a plan. You know what they say, just because you're paranoid, doesn't mean they aren't out to get you."

"I've heard that before. We prefer to think of it as 'better safe than sorry'." They shook hands and the meeting broke up. After Grady walked him to the door, he went back to his office and sat for a long time thinking, who the hell is that guy?

Targets

A couple of weeks later, Grady was sitting at his desk and looked up to see Bob Williams and Dale Brickler standing in his doorway.

"You got a minute?"

"Sure, come on in. Have a seat. What's up?"

"Well, Dale and I have been kicking this thing around and we'd like to get your thoughts."

"Which thing is that?"

"The Donovan Stuhl, Ben Stinson thing."

"Ah yes. I did ask you for your reasoning on that. So where do you stand?"

"Well, they are not government employees, so there is no abuse of their authority. These other folks abused their authority. So they come in with a strike against them. We have to hold people with authority to a higher standard of conduct. Otherwise they can abuse their authority with impunity. These two guys didn't abuse their authority because they had none." Dale jumped in.

"But that begs the question, do you have to be a government employee to be indicted by this task force? Of course not. Non-government employees can commit crimes as well. So what was their crime? The one guy prepared an opposition research memo, actually 17 different memos over a six month period, and the other guy marketed that product. Sure, these memos were full of lies and half-truths and they knew it. At least Donovan Stuhl knew it. He admitted as much in a deposition. Ben Stinson at least turned a blind eye to the truth, but isn't that what opposition research is. You take some lies, you sprinkle in a little truth to give the lies some credibility, and you sell it to a political candidate. The candidate can then use that narrative against their opponent. The problem is these guys didn't just provide it to the political candidate, Hildy Claxton and the DNC, who paid for it. They then went and peddled it to every body they could. They tried to give it to the all the news media outlets, but the media wouldn't run it because it couldn't be verified. They gave it to the FBI. They gave it to the Justice Department. They gave it to the CIA. They gave it to the Speaker of the House and they gave it to a Senator who forwarded it to the FBI. They made it look like the FBI got it from two sources. They used conduits and back channels. It wasn't until Jim Homey briefed the president on it and then leaked that briefing that it became a story." Bob spoke again.

"So, was what these guys did criminal? We think it was. They tried to defraud the American people of a fair and impartial election and to undo the results afterward. They used the FBI, the DOJ and the CIA. They interfered in our election process and they caused abuse by our government at the highest levels. We think they are just as much a part of the criminal conspiracy as those people at the FBI and the Justice Department who let their political bias cloud their judgment. Maybe more so. I think we can clearly show criminal intent on their part at trial."

"What does Kathy think?"

"She is ignoring them for now. She's focusing on the government employees who abused their power. She's kind of pissed off about this. She's been a prosecutor her whole life. She believes in the FBI and the DOJ. She feels betrayed. She's a liberal. She drank the cool-aid and she can't believe someone on her side of the aisle abused their power in this way. She sees Jim Homey as the mastermind behind this whole thing. If you look at all he did, and the way this thing played out, there's certainly an argument to be made for that position."

"Bob, you're a liberal. How are you coming down on this whole thing?"

"I was hired during a Democratic administration, but I was never a true believer. I just wanted a job. I just want to prosecute bad guys. It is all I ever wanted. I just want to be the best prosecutor that I can be. I have a lot of views that would land me on the left side of the aisle in any debate, but I would never abuse my authority to promote a particular candidate. I just wouldn't do that. I say I'm not a true believer, but that is not entirely true. I do believe in our system of justice. I don't care who you are. You don't get to break the rules. I am not pissed off about this. You have to be a disillusioned romantic before you can be a cynic. Like you say, I'm going to go where this investigation takes me. I just have one request."

"What's that?"

"Just don't let this thing take my prosecutor job away from me."

"That is not going to happen. I have assurances from the AG that the four of you will be protected. That was a condition of my taking this job. When this is all over, I fall on my sword, if necessary, and you all go back to your regular jobs, if that's what you want. I just have one request of you."

"What's that?"

"Keep questioning what we are doing. Let me know how the other side would see this. Show me the weaknesses, so we can shore up our case. Now back to our original question. Are these guys targets or not? I think they are, but they didn't lie under oath and they didn't leak classified information. I think we need to build a file on both of these guys. Everything they did and when they did it to further this narrative. I think the way to do this is to build a separate indictment against these two. Let's see if that will stand up on its own. Many of the same facts in the large indictment will be included in this one, but there may be things in this little one that don't make to the big one. Let Kathy know what you are doing and keep her up to date on what you've got. She may decide she wants to include this, and she may not. If she decides not to include it, we will have to decide if the case will stand on its own. There is one more thing. As you are building these target files, look for things that show a pure intent. Let's look at both sides of the issue so we can justify our decision."

"Aren't you afraid of creating Brady material, evidence favorable to the defendant that we will have to turn over?"

"No. That material is out there. They will already know about it. I want us to know about it too. Us giving it to them, isn't going to help them any. Especially in light of the fact that we know about it and will be prepared for it."

"Ok, we'll start working on it and we'll keep you posted."

"There is one other thing. This goes without saying, but I'm going to say it anyway. A conspiracy requires an agreement to engage in an illegal act and then followed by an overt act in furtherance of the conspiracy by one or more of the members. We've got a ton of overt acts. Everybody did something, but we need evidence of an agreement. When you're building these files on the targets of their overt acts, look for evidence of an agreement as well, even if it's only an inference from their actions."

"Sure."

"No problem."

As Bob and Dale were walking away, Bob whispered to Dale,

"I'd completely forgotten about that."

"Me too. We've been so focused on the bad acts, we ignored the agreement. That's conspiracy law 101. Every first year law student knows a conspiracy involves an agreement to commit an illegal act followed by an overt act in furtherance of the conspiracy."

"We need to do some research that A can agree with B who can than agree with C who can then agree with D. They don't all have to agree at the same time in the same place for there to be a criminal conspiracy."

"I am sure Kathy didn't overlook this element if she's working on the indictment. In our defense, we've been focused on the individuals and what each did. We weren't looking at the big picture."

"Yeah, let's not do that again. That was kind of embarrassing."

"I'm going to do some research on conspiracy. You start looking through the files for evidence of an agreement. Let's start a separate file on that, any thing that shows these people agreed to commit this illegal act, so we don't get caught with our pants down again."

A couple of days later, Debbie stuck her head in Grady's office.

"Hey, can I run something by you?"

"Sure. Come on in. Have a seat."

"I've got the time line established. I would say completed but, I don't think it will ever be completed. I think we will be continually updating it as we go along."

"Okay."

"It starts in April 2016 when Fision CVS is hired by lawyers for Claxton and the DNC to do opposition research on Donald Trump. It ends in March 2019 when the Special Counsel delivers his report, which finds no evidence of collusion. There is a lot that happens in that three-year period. The time line will help us keep things straight and help us understand the complexities of this situation."

"This conspiracy you mean."

"Yes. That is exactly what I mean."

"Well, let's start calling it that. If we think in terms of a criminal conspiracy, we will start looking for the elements we have to prove in a conspiracy case."

"Fair enough. That brings me to my question. There was a lot of stuff that did not get included on the time line. There were a lot of things that happened, but they did not seem like overt acts in furtherance of the conspiracy."

"For instance."

"Well, there were a lot of collateral players in the time period of this…conspiracy. The Special Counsel's office indicts some people, but it really doesn't seem to be related to the Russian collusion narrative. It kind of throws mud on Trump in a guilt by association kind of way. It also shows a disparate treatment of Trump associates and Claxton associates, which is a theory of our case. These details kind of take us off on a tangent, and I didn't include them in the time line."

"Okay, I agree with you. I don't think they should be on the time line Don't forget, the time line isn't just for our sake. The time line will help the jury understand the sequence of events as well. Let's keep the time line concise and clear with all the relevant dates but not clouded with extraneous stuff. If Kathy wants to add some stuff into the indictment, we can always update the time line."

"Okay, but that brings me to my real question. At the same time all this leaking and lying was going on, the Stuhl dossier, the FISA warrants and all that was involved in that, there was something else going on. The FBI, or the CIA, or both, were using human assets to spy on the Trump campaign. The FBI has denied this, and the CIA ain't talking. There were low level Trump associates approached by members of foreign intelligence services. There was at least one informant placed in the Trump campaign. This gets kind of murky, as we don't know what was really going on with these human assets. When you've got a document, a transcript, an affidavit, a memo, e-mails, it's pretty easy to establish an overt act in furtherance of a scheme to defraud. Undercover assets cutting across agency boundaries and international intelligence agencies is a whole other matter. We may never know what really happened with these. So do we put these details on the time line or not?"

"Man, that's a tough one. It think what we do is we leave them off for now. If Kathy wants to use some of this stuff as overt acts or even relevant conduct, we can always add them on. Let me ask you a question."

"Okay."

"How about if you prepare a second time line of extraneous dates. This would be things that don't get included in the relevant time line but might be of use later on. I'm not trying to give you extra work to do, but if you are doing the work anyway, why not create this document. That way if the issue ever does come up, you'd have the information right at you fingertips. You'd look really smart."

"I'm really sorry I came in here. I was looking to get out of work, and you give me more work." Debbie smiled.

"It's a gift. And no, you weren't trying to get out of work. You were trying to help the task force move forward, and I appreciate it. You might want to mention this to Kathy, as I suspect she might want to take a peek at the new time line at some point."

"Okay, one other thing. You wanted me to document how these dates were established for trial purposes. It turns out this is pretty easy. Almost everything in the overt action area has a date on the document itself or on some other record. So the time line has footnotes to explain how each of these dates was established."

"Good. Finally something that is easy."

A couple of days later, Grady stuck his head in Kathy's door.

"You got a minute?"

"Sure, I was going to come see you anyway. There's something I wanted to run by you."

"Sounds ominous. What do you got?"

"No. You go first. I need a minute to organize my thoughts."

"Well, I just wanted to bounce a couple things off you. When we are looking at this conspiracy charge, I think we have to be mindful of the multiplicity- duplicitous argument. An indictment that charges a single offense in different counts is multiplicitous and subject to dismissal. An indictment that charges separate offenses in a single count is duplicitous and is also subject to challenge. The bottom line is, no matter what you call it, you can't charge two crimes in one count and you can't charge a single crime in more than one count. Where you have a conspiracy that consists of individual crimes and each of those crimes are charged, there isn't a problem. The overt acts in furtherance of the conspiracy are crimes in and of themselves and they are part of the bigger crime of conspiracy. My concern is we have multiple conspiracies with multiple players with multiple motivations. The conspiracy started out as an agreement to stop Trump from becoming president. Once that didn't work, the agreement shifted to one of undermining his presidency and possibly removing him from office. So what I'm saying is, there was a changing landscape and a constantly changing cast of characters. It's a complex puzzle with different people doing different things at different times with changing motivation, which changes the agreement to do an illegal thing. I understand the absence of direct proof of the agreement in a conspiracy generally results from the secretiveness and complexity of modern day conspiracies. And the courts have held that a conspiracy may be inferred from circumstantial evidence that can reasonably be interpreted as participation in a common plan. That all having been said, we've still got this shifting landscape of what were these people trying to do and who was involved when. You see what I'm saying?"

"I do, but I don't think it's a problem. A conspiracy can have more than one illegal purpose, especially as it is here, those two purposes are part of a larger purpose. As long as we lay that out clearly in the indictment, I don't think there will be a problem with the duplicitous argument, charging two things in one count. As far as charging the same thing in multiple counts, as long as we are careful in the overt acts language, there shouldn't be a problem. As far as the participants are concerned, that's a different matter. Even under the 'Pinkerton Doctrine' a participant can't be held responsible for the actions of co-conspirators until he or she is a member of the conspiracy. There's kind of an 'ex post facto' reasoning there. Even though the 'Pinkerton Doctrine' imposes criminal liability on conspirators for substantive offenses of co-conspirators committed during and in furtherance of the conspiracy. You can't hold someone criminally responsible for the acts of others before they became a member of the conspiracy. So we will have to watch that, and the time line will be helpful in that regard. Was that it?"

"No, there is something else bothering me about the time line. It is more of as jury nullification issue than a legal issue. You know how jurors some times get hung up on extraneous details, the make of a car, the time of day, how many bags. Some little detail doesn't make sense to them and they quit listening to the rest of the case, because something doesn't make sense to them."

"Yeah. That happens. So what is bothering you?"

"Well, let's say I'm a cynical person. One who believes all lawyers are sum, the government can't be trusted and everyone acts in their own self-interest. Let's further assume I'm on the jury. Now we've got these three guys: the Director of the FBI, the Director of the CIA, and the Director of National Intelligence. If Hildy Claxton is elected, all three guys probably keep their jobs. If not, all three probably lose their jobs, which they eventually did. Once Trump was elected, these three guys should have been falling all over themselves to make nice to the new president. They didn't. They doubled down on the Russia collusion thing. Three of the four FISA warrants were issued after the election. The vast majority of the conspiracy occurred after the election. Dapper and Brenamore were making statements after the election that they had to know were untrue. That big meeting in the White House the day before Trump is briefed on the dossier occurred in January right before Trump is sworn in. So, if they weren't acting in their own self-interest, what were they doing? Did they really believe this nonsense? Did you? Did you want it to be true so badly that you swallowed this narrative hook, line and sinker? Will our jury attribute this honest intention to these three guys? These are professional law enforcement and intelligence officials at the top of the food chain. Is it possible that these guys could be so easily duped? Did they deceive themselves because they wanted to believe? If so, does this create reasonable doubt as to their criminal intent?"

"I understand your concerns, but I don't share them. The targets of this investigation are the people who had knowledge that the rest of us did not have. It has never been my position that these people were acting in their own self-interest. They were acting with a political motivation, and it may be worth mentioning that in our opening statement, so the jury doesn't get distracted. You ask, by implication, if I as a professional prosecutor, was so easily deceived. Of course I was, as was at least half of the country. That was the real crime here. It wasn't just an attempt to throw an election by people in power. It was an attempt to destroy our democratic process and undo an election by use of a false narrative. A few people in power used the media in an attempt to destroy a sitting president. The media was a willing participant. Unlike me, they didn't care if it was true or not. Their hatred for this president is so real that it cannot be denied and is an essential part of the story. The indictment must point this out, and the evidence at trial will leave no doubt about their part in this fraud perpetrated on the American people. We may not be able to indict them, but we can show them for what they are. As far as your concern about reasonable doubt is concerned as to criminal intent, that will be our primary focus, showing the bias and prejudice of all involved. As we work our way through this thing, we have to keep our eye on the ball, and that ball is criminal intent. Any other concerns?"

"Just one. There is something else about the time line that bothers me. The FBI officially opens its investigation of Trump on July 31, 2016, a day after Donovan Stuhl meets with Bill and Nancy Boar and gives them the dossier. They immediately pass it on to the FBI. But the FBI had an agent in London getting the dossier on July 1. Undercover operatives were meeting with members of the Trump campaign in April, May and early July. So clearly something was going on before the official opening of the FBI investigation."

"Well, let me ask you something. When you were working as a Postal Inspector, did you sometimes spend time on a preliminary inquiry before you officially opened a case?"

"Yes."

"And did that preliminary inquiry sometimes last weeks maybe even months before you could decide whether or not to move forward with an official investigation?"

"Again yes, but…"

"Wait. Sometimes when you opened an investigation, did you find that other agencies were looking into the same matter?"

'Yes."

"So since we are talking about foreign intelligence operatives and foreign countries, is it possible that the CIA or some other intelligence outfit was running its own operation against Trump?"

"In light of what we now know, it's not just possible, it's probable."

"There are going to be some wild hairs that we are just not going to be able to push down. We just have to be as honest and forthright with the jury as we can and rely on the jury's sense of duty to do the right thing."

"Okay, I'm glad I got that off my chest. What did you want to talk about?"

"I want to subpoena the current Director of the FBI before the Grand Jury."

"What? Why? He wasn't even there at the time."

"There was a State Department employee who met with Donovan Stuhl and noted errors in his dossier. Specifically, he mentioned the Russian Embassy in Miami and there is no Russian Embassy in Miami. This State Department employee figured out in one day that the Stuhl dossier was a pack of lies and she forwarded her findings to the FBI. Ten days later the FBI gets the first FISA warrant. This memo from the State Department has been classified by the current Director of the FBI and he won't give it up. I am going to request this memo through the grand jury and he's going to claim it's classified and refuse to provide it. At the same time I issue a subpoena to him, I am sending a request to the Attorney General, asking that this document be declassified. If the Attorney General is serious about this task force, he will provide us with the ability to do our job. If he thinks the memo should remain classified, that sends a signal to all of us, who are putting our careers on the line."

"Damn, Kathy! Not only do you call my bluff by calling me a prick, now you're going to call the Attorney General's bluff, to see if he is serious. Is there no other way to accomplish your purpose?"

"We can subpoena the State Department employee as well, which we intend to do. If the matter is classified, she's caught in the middle and won't be able to testify about it."

"So you intend to destroy the task force before it gets started."

"No I intend to find out if the Attorney General is serious about getting to the bottom of this. If he is, and the current Director of the FBI refuses to comply with a grand jury subpoena after being told to do so by the Attorney General, I will charge him with obstruction of justice."

"Jeez, Kathy, what's gotten into you?"

"The FBI stepped out of bounds, and if this guy is going to cover it up, he is part of the problem. I am sending a message. My side of the aisle has been screaming, nobody is above the law for 3 years. Everybody at the FBI and the DOJ will now know we are playing by the rules, and they need to as well. If we can subpoena the Director of the FBI, we can subpoena them too."

"Wait a minute! Let me think. Have you written the letter?"

"Yeah."

"Let me see it." Grady took a minute to read the letter.

"Ok, this looks good. Respectful, but shows a definite need. Do me a favor and mark it "6(e) material" and "eyes only."

"Okay."

"Before you throw this grenade, let me see if I can work the back channels. The AG told me he didn't want to hear from me unless there was a problem, and he didn't want any problems. He wants this task force to be completely autonomous. He wants us to make all the decisions about targets and charges. He doesn't want there to be any allegation that he directed the investigation."

"Well, if he's got a written request from us asking him to evaluate the need for classification of this document, it shows the direction is being determined by us."

"True, but look at it from his point of view. Some snot-nosed AUSA is telling him what to do."

"I'm not snot-nosed and I'm not telling, I'm asking." Grady just looked at her. After a long silence he said,

"You are planning on having this hand delivered by your agents?"

"Yeah. I figured they'd drop off the letter, then serve the subpoena."

"You have other subpoenas you're serving?"

Yeah. We're moving. Things are going to get cooking around here pretty quickly. We're subpoenaing the IG's complete file on the FISA abuse investigation. There's no need to reinvent the wheel. We may need to fill a few gaps, but we're going to have plenty of documents very shortly."

"You expecting any push back from the IG?"

"No. I spoke to them over there. The sense I got was they were surprised, but completely cooperative."

"Good. Ok. When you deliver the letter to the AG, you don't have to put it in his hand. His administrative assistant can accept it. When you serve the Director, actually put it in his hand, no matter how long it takes. Ask the agents to keep track of how long he keeps them waiting. If he wants to play games, we will respond in kind. Don't send them out yet. I'll get back to you." Grady walked down to his office and buzzed Bev.

"Could you come down to my office for a minute?"

"Sure. Be right there."

"Hey. What's up?"

"Shut the door."

"What'd I do?"

"Nothing. This isn't about you. Well, it's a little bit about you."

"Ok. What can I do?"

"Are you in contact with the Attorney General's administrative assistant?"

"Sure. Almost every day. Anything we need comes through that office: supplies, logistics, your payroll records, that sort of thing."

"I need you to get a message to her."

"Okay."

"Kathy is going to be subpoenaing the current Director of the FBI."

"Oh my."

"Oh my indeed. There is a memo from the State Department in reference to the Stuhl dossier. An employee of the State Department figured out the Stuhl dossier was full of lies and forwarded her concerns to the FBI ten days before the first FISA warrant. The Director has classified the document and isn't giving it up. It makes the FBI look bad. She's going to hold him in contempt, charge him with obstruction, I don't know what all she's going to do. Before she does that, she is going to send a letter to the Attorney General asking him to declassify the document solely for the purpose of the grand jury investigation."

"Oh my. You need to get control of your people."

"I'm afraid that ship has sailed."

"You know what this means?"

"It means we could all be going home at the end of the week. If the Attorney General gets mad, he could disband the task force. If the AG doesn't give the task force the document that they need to do their job, there could be a mutiny."

"That's the way I see it too."

"Three things can happen, and only one of them is good."

"Do you think Kathy is trying to sabotage the task force?"

"No. I think she wants to know if the AG is serious about the task force, and if they will all have jobs to go back to. If this goes her way, we're all going to be very busy around here. Make the call. Get back to me."

"Okay. You got it."

A while later Grady walked over to the coffee pot. He stopped by Bev's desk.

"Well?"

"I talked to her."

"And."

"She's going to get back to me."

"She knows time is of the essence on this thing."

"Grady, she's the Administrative Assistant to the Attorney General. She understands priorities."

"Ok, keep me informed." As Grady was walking back to his office, Bob asked for a few minutes of his time.

"We're building a target file, just like you asked."

"Okay."

"What we're doing is loading documents into the data base. We are then cross-referencing these documents into each target file. Evidence of bias, prejudice, lies, motive, overt acts and the like are listed in each target file and where the information can be found."

"Sounds good."

"This thing is growing by leaps and bounds. Carly is coordinating the input of the documents. The agents are helping her feed the documents into the reader. Then she is creating a master reference where each document can be found. As the agents locate evidence and want to reference it into each of the target files, they bring it to her and she makes those entries. This may change in the future with the agents doing their own entry, but for right now it seems to be working."

"So what's the problem?"

"The problem is the target file itself. We just keep adding targets. We aren't making any decisions. It's too early for that. The more we look the more we find. This thing could grow into that Cecil B.DeMille gang-bang production that you fear. The FISA abuse investigation has it's own separate section in the target file. There were five people who signed the four warrant applications. Jim Homey and Suzie Bates signed the first and second warrant applications. Jim Homey and Jana Renki signed the third and Denny McCoy and Rob Lowenstein signed the fourth. Renki and Bates have the thinnest files of the five, but the issue with these five targets is simple. Did they know about the lies by omission in the warrant applications when they signed them. It's clear that all of them did, at least as to some of the omissions. These people were the Director of the FBI, the Acting Director of the FBI and Acting Attorney General. This was not some low level schmuck who was told to sign something. Each of them was at the highest position of their agency."

"Okay. We can't infer knowledge to them about the lies by omission, but we can infer knowledge to them of the importance of what they were doing."

"Exactly. Homey, McCoy and Lowenstein had full knowledge of all the lies by omission. Bates and Renki had some knowledge. Dale's got his agents tracking down these two targets as to exactly what they knew and when they knew it."

"The problem is overlap."

"Right. Homey, McCoy and Lowenstein are also in the main target file of the big conspiracy. The FISA target file data is also in the conspiracy target file but there is also stuff in that file that isn't in the FISA target file."

"So you're worried that if we charge Homey, for instance, with lying on a FISA warrant application and then charge him with lying on the FISA warrant as part of a larger conspiracy, he will be twice placed in jeopardy for the same offence."

"Obviously, we can't do that. We either charge him separately in a separate indictment, and then just use the FISA stuff as an overt act without charging it as a separate crime. Or, we could lump it all together in one indictment and charge those overt acts that are crimes. My problem is this thing is getting unwieldy."

"Go on."

"The conspiracy includes Homey, Lowenstein and McCoy. They were the three main actors and the ones in charge. It also includes Paulie Ruck and Linda Pugh at the FBI with their numerous text messages and absolute bias. Moral of that story is don't be involved in a sexual affair at the same time your involved in a major criminal conspiracy. You add Stuhl and Stinson as the driving force behind the dossier and you're already up to seven."

"Doesn't seem to bad."

"Yeah, but we're just getting started."

"Add in the two others on the warrants and you've got nine. Nancy Boar funneled information through her husband at DOJ to the FBI. Rebecca Puller unmasked more people from the

FISA intercepts than anybody in the history of the entire program. Jim Goetta, an FBI agent was involved in getting the dossier. And then there's Rex Brenamore, the Director of the CIA and Tim Dapper, the Director at National Intelligence, both of whom lied, and both of whom drove this narrative long after it became clear it was a lie. That's what fourteen? The list just keeps growing.

"Okay. I see your point. At this point, we have to just keep going. If we need to add someone to the target file, we do so. At some point, we will need to sit down as a group and decide who gets included and who doesn't. We're not there yet, but we're not that far away either. I think that decision has to be based on what makes the case the strongest and not be concerned with how many targets there are. That brings up another question. What if all these people request separate trials? Are we going to have to try this thing ten times?"

"That's not going to happen. One, defense attorneys believe in strength in numbers. If one of them doesn't think of a question to ask, the other one will. Two, that eliminates the opportunity to point the finger at the other guy. And three, judges are very reluctant to break up a conspiracy trial. There's lots of case law on their side for denying such a request in a conspiracy trial."

"Kathy is on top of this?"

"No doubt."

"Okay. Keep me posted."

As Grady walked into his office, the phone buzzed. It was Bev.

"Yeah."

"She called back. The AG wants to see the letter before he makes up his mind."

"Sounds reasonable."

"Grady?"

"Yeah."

"Just between you and me, I think he's going to throw the Director under the bus."

"Whoa."

"Yeah whoa. Don't mess this up."

"Well, we're going to do our best." Grady walked down the hallway to Kathy's office and told her to send her two agents over to the AG's office with the letter but to hold off on the subpoena until the AG makes his decision. He walked back by Bev's desk and asked her to let the AG's assistant know they were coming.

Later that day the Attorney General contacted the Director of the FBI and told him the State Department memo was being declassified for the purpose of a grand jury investigation only. He was also told he should co-operate with any subpoena he should receive in reference to the memo. The Director was not happy and said he needed to protect the FBI. The Attorney General advised him to speak with private counsel with regard to the issue of obstruction of justice, misprision of a felony and contempt of court before he said any thing else or took any further action. The next day the Director was served with a grand jury subpoena and he turned over the entire file in reference to the State Department memo. This file would later become known as the 'smoking gun'.

Security

Matt walked out of his office and down the hallway to the video monitoring room.

"Wog, what are our friends downstairs up to?"

"I don't know, but they're up to something. Yesterday, two agents went to the DOJ building. They weren't there very long, and then they came back. We think they went to see the Attorney General, but we're not sure. That's where the beacon transmitter put them, but our guys couldn't get inside without raising suspicion."

"We just have one car on them?"

"No we had two. Two guys in each car."

"Seems excessive."

"Our guys just need something to do. They've been following these people to work and back, but that's it. They've been holed up in that office reading transcripts and making charts. Today all hell is breaking loose. The agents are out serving subpoenas and doing interviews. They've started using the tech room at the courthouse. There's an interview room just down the hallway from the grand jury room that has been dedicated to this task force. Our guys set it up with monitors, audio, video, the whole works. If the agents want to show the witness a document they can bring it up on the screen. Of course, they have to bring any file with them and our guy enters it for them and works the system. The agents take the file with them when they leave. Nothing is left behind, part of the security protocol. They think our guy is 'tech support'. He's in an outside room at a console. They ask for what they want on the intercom and he puts it on the screen. All they have to do is call and our guy is there to support them. He's gotten to know the 'blue coats' at the courthouse. As far as they are concerned, he's part of All-Tech Security. He's unarmed of course. He looks like a computer nerd which is what he is, among other things."

"Have our guys noticed anybody taking any special interest in our folks?"

"No, but it wouldn't hurt to remind them that we are following these folks to see if anybody else is now that this thing is starting to ramp up."

"Okay, I'll, have a word with Malloy. What about the new weapon, everybody qualify?"

"Everybody except you and Agnes. She refuses to go. She says she is not carrying a toy gun. I'm really not in a position to tell her what to do."

"Everybody do okay with the new non-lethal rounds?"

"Well, yes and no. Everybody qualified with the handgun. It's sweet. Shoots just like a 9mm. Looks like a 9mm, feels like a 9mm. Trigger pull is the same. Only difference is the lack of recoil. Every bit of force is used to seat the next round. It's weird. I don't know how they did that, but they did. And it's accurate. Everybody shot as well or better than they did with their regular handgun. It's dead on bulls eye at 25 yards."

"So what's the problem?"

"The rifle. No body can hit anything with the rifle. The round is the same, just a little longer. It's a combination of powder and compressed gas. The projectile is a disintegrating dart encased in ceramic that opens in flight. The 'top secret' aspect of this thing is the chemical in the dart. It knocks a person out within 30 seconds and keeps them out for an hour. They wake up with one hell of a headache. Think of the worst hangover you've ever had. This is worse. The beauty of this drug is that it's body centric. That is, the body only absorbs enough to knock a person out. Once a person is out, they don't absorb any more of the drug. So dosage is not a problem. The same round can be used on a 100 pound woman or a 300 pound man. It can't kill them, it just knocks them out. There's also a flash bang that will knock anybody out within a 50 foot radius. It also is very quick. The gas falls to the ground within a minute and the air is then safe to breathe. It supposedly becomes inert after being exposed to the air for 60 seconds. I don't know. I wouldn't touch the floor, and I'd probably clean my shows afterward, but that's just me."

"So what about the rifle?"

"No body could hit anything with the rifle. It was high, it was low, it was right, it was left. These guys are marksmen and they couldn't figure it out. I mean they were within a coffee can lid at 150 yards, but these guys are all used to shooting bulls eyes. All except for Ralph Simmons. I swear that kid is a freak of nature. He shot high right , then high left, then three straight bulls eyes. He shot five more times, five straight bills eyes. Five more, five bulls eyes. He's a freak. No body else even came close to that. He claims it has nothing to do with windage, weight of the projectile or propulsion. He claims it is all trigger pull. Because of the mix of powder and compressed gas in the rifle cartridge, the trigger assembly has been modified. It's very delicate and needs to be pulled in a soft manner. That goes against all training protocols and makes no sense. The smaller pistol cartridge doesn't have this problem and shoots just like any other gun. In any event, he was the only one who could shoot the damn thing with any degree of accuracy."

"Well, I guess he's our designated sniper then. Make sure he knows that."

"I think he has already figured that out, but I'll have a word with him. Every body else is kind of jealous, but if push comes to shove, and he has to save their bacon, they'll get over it.'

"Okay, I'll get out there today and get qualified on the weapon. Everybody is carrying these things and are all clear on the rules of engagement?"

"Absolutely. No body wants to be the guy who gets shipped out of town and becomes the cause for operational failure."

'Okay, tell me about the E.S."

"Well, as far as electronic surveillance goes, we've got audio and video capabilities in the hallways, the lobby and the offices on the second floor. The audio is turned off on the second floor offices. We are not listening to what they are saying in the offices, but the video is on. We can see them moving about. We can turn that audio on any time we want, but pursuant to your instructions, we haven't done that yet. The audio as well video is up in the hallways of the second, third and fourth floor. We have no audio or video inside the offices of the fourth floor, just in the hallway. This was the instruction we were given when we set it up."

"Any problems so far?"

"No, everything is running smoothly."

"Computers?"

"Everything is working as planned. They've kind of accepted the closed system protocol and are using the terminals in the conference room for research and e-mail. We're monitoring all that, and no security concerns have arisen. Every Friday, the main frame file is downloaded and the duplicate copy is taken to Ft. Belvoir and locked in a vault there. Two guys are responsible for that at midnight on Friday, and they are taking their responsibility seriously. The computer system at the courthouse is also a dedicated system, and the agents have to bring any file with them they want to use during an interview. They take it with them when they leave. Our 'tech support' guy makes sure nothing is stored on site. This may cause some problems down the road as the interview room gets used more and more. There may be a desire to leave files there during the day for multiple interviews. Our guy is just going to be adamant that he could loose his job if he doesn't do what he is told. So the agents will have to take it up with his supervisor. He's going to be available anytime they need him to work the system. They really aren't going to have anything to complain about."

"Okay, how about the drones?"

"We haven't deployed them yet. They're here. We' got launch capability from the roof. We tested them a couple of time on practice runs. We put up four at a time to test multiple tracking scenarios. We've got audio and video capability, but the audio's not too good. There's too much background noise. The filtering device is good. We can hone in on certain conversations, but it goes in and out due to changes in background noise as the target moves. I really don't think we are going to need these things. We can put up a dozen if you want. We've got the capability to control and monitor a dozen at a time and our guys are good at it, I just don't see the need."

"Okay. I hope we don't need them. What about human assets?"

"That's being run down the hallway. Lieutenant Malloy, sorry Mal, is running that. Let's go see him."

"Hey Mal, how's it going?"

Oh, pretty quiet right now. We've got two sets of agents on the street. Our guys are close by, but there is really no need to close the gap. We've got twelve vehicles street ready at any given moment. One vehicle is assigned to each member of the task force. We follow them in, in the morning and back home at night. Mostly we're running two man crews. One to drive and one to watch the GPS signal. Most of the vehicles have a built in GPS tracker. Some are just using a lap top. The agents are starting to move around during the day, but the attorneys pretty much stay put. They go to court occasionally, but mostly they stay put. We jockey cars around a bit, and we rotate targets just to keep everybody fresh and familiar with all the routes of travel. As you can see, we've got a monitor for each GPS signal.

Franklin doesn't have a vehicle assigned to him, because he just walks back and forth to his hotel. We've got a foot patrol on him. Everything is monitored and controlled here. Everyone is on the same net, so it gets a little crowded at rush hour, but our guys are maintaining radio silence as much as possible during that time period. Agnes is helping out as well. She's got a GPS monitor at the front desk, but hers is a single grid that shows all the dots converging or leaving the building. She has a private line to me, and she also has the capability to break in to the main net if necessary. So far it's been working really well. If we have a problem, we'll see how well our guys respond."

"Let's hope that doesn't happen. It might be a good idea to remind your guys that their job is to see if anyone else is following the subjects not just follow the subjects themselves."

"Roger that, sir. I will remind them. Sir, there is one hole in the coverage that I wanted to discuss with you."

"What's that?"

"The two support personnel. They are not covered. They weren't issued cell phones. There is really no reason for them to have them. They just work in the office. We're not following them to and from work. We are not really paying any attention to them at all. Are they vulnerable? Are they subject to attack? Could they be a source of a leak? I just don't know what to do about them."

"It's a good point. Let me think about it for a minute. I think the agents and the attorneys are the face of this thing. If someone is going to make a run at it, they are the most likely candidates for an attack or attempt at compromise. The support staff is pretty much anonymous at this point. Nobody knows who they are. That's likely to remain that way. I'm sure they were vetted by the AG's office before they got assigned to this thing. I'll have Wog do a background check on them and build a file just in case we need to put them on our radar. Let's just leave things the way they are for now. If we need to make a change, we will. Good catch. Wog, let's go look at the drones."

"Okay. They're in a dedicated room back by the service elevator. The elevator leads directly to the garage and the roof. Nobody else has access to the elevator but us. Sergeant Maxwell is in charge of them. He's got four guys that are certified drone pilots and a slew of others who are capable in a pinch. Just don't touch any thing. He's a little testy about his babies."

"Wouldn't dream of it. Larry, how's it going?"

"Pretty well sir. We're just making some minor adjustments on the video feed. There's been some random microwave interference with our signal strength, and we're installing some filters that I am assured by the manufacturer will solve our problem."

"I understand you've done some test runs?"

"Yes sir. We've done several. As a matter of fact, we're pretty much testing all the time. We want to make sure everything is ready and operational at any moment. We're testing in various weather conditions and low light scenarios."

"How's that going?"

"As you might expect. Our infrared capabilities at night are superb on a clear night with no wind. Wind and rain are a problem. Not only with flight control but with the quality of the video feed as well. We're working on it, but it's a challenge. It takes two guys to launch these things safely, but we can have four in the air in a matter of minutes. We've got twelve on stand by. If you need us, we'll be ready."

"Good. I hope we don't need you, but it's nice to know you're on top of it. Let me know if you need anything. Oh, one more thing. Let's do a test during rush hour. I'd like you to co-ordinate with the GPS tracking and the human surveillance to see if we can use the two systems together. That way we will know if it is a benefit to Mal to have the additional information or not. Wog, let's take a walk." They rode the elevator down to the garage where Matt came and went every day but hadn't given it much thought.

"Tell me about the garage."

"Well, it's assigned just to us. That was part of the deal. It gives us anonymity to come and go as we please. All the tenants were given a free parking pass to the garage around the corner. Free parking pass right around the corner is quite a perk in DC, so they are all happy about the set up. They don't even know about this place or if they do, they don't care. All the vehicles here are ours. We've got twelve surveillance vehicles in use every day. They are all late model civilian looking vehicles so they blend in with DC traffic. We rotate them around to keep from getting burned. They're gassed up at the base, and they are ready to go at all times. We also have two ambulances that can be converted to prisoner transport. We have four large panel trucks that carry eleven each and two smaller work vans with various magnetic sign logos depending on the situation. We also have a few other vehicles available like the one you use and the one I use. Mal is in charge of coordinating the vehicles and making sure there are adequate vehicles at the Fort and here to get people back and forth. There is a cleaning crew that comes here every night. There are eight guys from the Fort. Captain Oster selected them from the base personnel. I think he put the fear of God in them. Charles Johnson is in charge of the cleaning crew. He brings them here at 10:00pm and they are out by midnight. I think they are scared of Charles."

"Rightfully so. I'm scared of Charles."

"Anyway, they don't mess around. Two men per floor and they clean the whole place in two hours. Half an hour here, and half and hour back for a total of three hours, and they are pretty much left alone the rest of the time. They don't know why they are cleaning this building. All they know is they've got a sweet gig, and they don't want to mess it up. Their cleaning carts are stored here in the basement. Everything works smoothly. The tenants don't know how the building gets cleaned. All they know is when they come in, in the morning everything is clean. It's a Monday through Friday deal. There's no cleaning on the weekends unless the second floor guys come in. Then Charles will bring in a skeleton crew on Sunday night for an hour. Let me show you the roof." They rode the freight elevator to the roof. There was a small section just outside the roof access that provided a perfect launch pad for the drones. It was blocked from view all around. They then rode the elevator back to the third floor and switched to the building elevator. They rode to the fourth floor and walked the corridor, which looked remarkably like the third floor corridor. They rode to the second floor and walked that corridor as well. Each floor had a small security room near the elevator, which could be used to interview uninvited 'guests'. There were no visible electronics in the room, and the rooms looked shabby. They rode down to the first floor, toured the lobby and then rode back up to three and Agnes buzzed them in.

"Agnes, I'm going out to the Fort to get qualified on the new weapon. I understand you haven't had an opportunity to get qualified yet."

"That's correct."

"I would like you to try to make the time to get out there and qualify with the new weapon."

"Yes sir."

"You're not going to do it, are you?"

"No sir."

"Damn it Agnes. I really don't want you killing anyone unless it is absolutely necessary."

"I promise you sir, I won't kill anyone unless it is absolutely necessary."

"You got your 9mm in your desk drawer?"

"Yes sir."

"Does it have a silencer on it?"

"Yes sir."

"How does that affect your aim?"

"Not at all."

"How can you see your sights?"

"I don't use the sights."

"How can you be accurate without the sights?"

"I have what they call muscle memory. I hit what I aim at, every time."

"What kind of distance?"

"Fifteen yards. At twenty-five yards, it's not quite as accurate. Four out of five. If I'm shooting at twenty five yards, I'll be slinging five rounds and I'll get four kill shots."

"You any good with a rifle?"

"I'm very good with a rifle. I'm rated as a sniper, but I don't get to practice that much. That's not where they use my skill set. They've got other guys for that. I hear your toy rifle isn't working so well."

"You seem to know an awful lot about what's going on around here."

"Begging the Colonel's pardon sir, but that's kind of my job."

"Okay, but I'd really like you to consider using the new weapon."

"Yes sir." Matt walked away thinking, man that's one scary broad. I'm glad she's on my side.

Summer

Grady stopped by Kathy's office, and she looked up from the papers on her desk.

"What's up?"

"I was wondering if you could do me a favor?"

"Sure, what do you need?"

"Well, maybe I should rephrase that. I was wondering if you would consider doing me a favor."

"What's the difference?"

"You could say no, which wouldn't be the worst thing in the world."

"You have a really strange way of asking for a favor."

"I would like to see if you could set up a meeting between your agents and Rey Rowdy. Not here of course, but wherever he wants to meet."

"Really?"

"I know we said we weren't going to interview journalists, because they have their own agenda, and they are like fly paper. Once they find out we exist, they'll be calling all the time wanting to know when something is going to happen. But Rey is not really a journalist. He's a Fox News contributor, which means he's somebody they interview occasionally when they want a particular point of view. He was a Congressman when all this nonsense was going on, and he was a prosecutor before he became a Congressman. He left Congress because he didn't feel like he was accomplishing anything. I found that weird, like maybe there was something in the works that I didn't know about like a judgeship or something. Anyway, he was very knowledgeable about the details of what we are looking into. He came across in some of the hearings as the only guy who understood what was going on. Since he was a prosecutor, he will understand the need for secrecy. And I think we can ask for his commitment before we talk to him."

"You think he would honor such a commitment if he could sell the story to Fox News?"

"I do. My impression of him is one of integrity. I think he has spent a lot of time looking at this, and he might have some details that we are missing. He might be able to point us in some new directions. He might also understand some pitfalls."

"It's a risk."

"More risky than subpoenaing the Director of the FBI?"

" Touche'. That didn't work out so badly though, did it?

"Could have gone either way, but no it didn't work out so badly. Well, give it some thought. The guy seems really intelligent and picking his brain may prove to be a useful exercise. Say, I was looking at some case law and there were some cases that were reversed on appeal where 1001, false statements, was used involving search warrants. The 1001 statute requires that the false statement be relevant to the functioning of a federal department or agency. The judicial system is not a department or agency. It's a separate branch of government."

"Yeah. I looked at those as well. Those are old cases. The statute has been amended since then to include a false statement in a judicial proceeding as well. We could charge 1623, perjury ancillary to a court proceeding, or we could charge 1001, false statement. We'll have to make a decision on that, whichever one fits the best. We certainly can't charge both. We would run into that multiplicitous situation you were concerned about."

"Okay. I was pretty sure that's what it was, but I wanted to check with you. I'm going to stroll over to the courthouse. There's a hearing on the Summer Dewdrop case."

"The porn star? What's that got to do with us?"

"Nothing. I just thought I'd sit in and see if anything interesting comes up."

"Okay."

"Think about interviewing Rey Rowdy."

"Okay. I'll think about it."

The courtroom was packed. There was a circus atmosphere, as if something exciting was about to happen. There were no cameras, but there were plenty of news people. Grady had been lucky to find a seat in the back. The clerk called out, "All rise."

"Hear ye, hear ye, hear ye. The United States District Court for the District of Columbia is now in session, the Honorable James O'Keefe presiding. All persons having business with this honorable court draw near and be heard. God save this honorable court."

Judge O'Keefe strode up to the bench and took his seat. The case had been transferred from the Central District of California to the DC District for some reason that Grady didn't understand. It had something to do with the venue and availability of witnesses. It had been a plaintiff's request and the President's lawyers did not object.

The judge looked around the courtroom and pointed to the blue coat bailiff. The blue coats weren't really bailiffs. They were security guards hired by the Marshal's Service to provide security in the courthouse. They wore navy blue blazers as part of their uniform, and everyone called them the blue coats. They were retired police officers and they were unarmed, but they maintained order.

"Mr. Underwood. Could you step up here for a minute please." The judge turned on the white noise machine so no one could here what was being said at the bench.

"Chester, in a few minutes I'm going to clear the courtroom of everyone except the parties and their lawyers. After you get everyone out, I want you to stand outside the door with the outer doors closed. This isn't because I don't trust you. It's because I do. I want you to maintain that post and not let anyone in. More importantly, I want to make sure that no one is sneaking up to the door and putting their ear up against it to hear what is going on inside. I want you to maintain that post for the remainder of the hearing. If you have to call upstairs and notify them of the change in rotation, please do so. If your superiors have a problem with you staying here, have them come see me and I will try to straighten it out."

"I'll notify them, but there won't be a problem."

"Good." As Chester Underwood made his way back to the doorway, the judge turned to the clerk.

"Please call the case."

"Summer Dewdrop aka Susan Clifton vs. Donald J Trump, case no. 18CV17820."

"The parties will enter their appearance for the record."

"Michael Abadabado on behalf of the plaintiff."

"Peter Daniels on behalf of the defendant, your honor."

"OK, as I understand it, there are two matters pending before the court this morning. The first is a motion to compel discovery on behalf of the plaintiff and the second is a motion to dismiss for failure to state a cause of action by the defendant. Is that correct?"

"Yes your honor."

"Yes your honor."

"OK, both of these are pretty routine matters in a civil suit, but this is anything but a routine civil suit. As I looked over the pleadings, it is apparent to me that this matter involves some sensitive topics. In order to prevent embarrassment to anyone and in the interest of justice, I am ordering a gag order on these proceedings. That means these proceedings will be conducted behind closed doors and the parties are prohibited from disclosing any information about these proceedings outside this courtroom. Is that clear Mr. Abadabado?"

"Yes your honor."

"Mr. Daniels?"

"Yes your honor."

"Mr. Underwood, would you clear the courtroom please?"

"OK, you heard the judge, everybody out." There was grumbling all around as the media was denied their big event. It took a few minutes to clear the courtroom and Grady was one of the last ones out.

"OK, I'm going to take some testimony this morning and create a record. The plaintiff will take the stand and be sworn in please." Summer Dewdrop walked up to the witness stand, was sworn in and took a seat in the witness box.

"Gentleman, before we begin, I want to make the record clear. Each of you has a continuing objection to any question that I ask, so your rights are protected on appeal. I want to move this matter along, so I don't want you jumping up and down making objections, so you have a continuing objection. There is no jury here, so there is no fear of misunderstanding. We are simply going to try to get to the truth. If you think my questions are immaterial, irrelevant, or improper in anyway, you will have an opportunity to make these arguments and your rights on appeal are protected. Do you understand?"

"Yes your honor."

"Yes your honor." The judge turned to the witness and smiled.

"Now Ms. Dewdrop, your real name is Susan Clifton, but you prefer to go by your stage name of Summer Dewdrop. Is that correct?"

"Yes."

"Now you have filed this lawsuit under the name of Summer Dewdrop with your real name of Susan Clifton listed as an alias. Would you prefer that I address you as Ms. Dewdrop?"

"You can call me Summer." She smiled at the judge.

"OK, if you would prefer, I will address you as Summer. Now I don't want you to be embarrassed or intimidated or the subject of ridicule. That's why I cleared the courtroom, so we can get to the truth with as little drama as possible. If at any time you get tired, and you need to take a break, just let me know, and we will take a break."

"Summer, how old are you?"

"I'm 33."

"Are you married?"

"No."

"Have you ever been married?"

"Yes, I was married when I was very young, but it didn't last very long, and we were divorced after a couple of years."

"Do you have any children?"

"I have a son."

"How old is he?"

"He is 18."

"Does he live with you?"

"No. He lived with his father for the last few years, but he's living on his own now."

"His father is your previous husband?"

"Yes."

"You are employed as an adult film star?"

"Yes."

"And the name, Summer Dewdrop, is the stage name you use in those movies?"

"Yes."

"Have you ever used ay other stage name?"

"No."

"How many adult films have you made?"

"Oh, I don't know, hundreds probably."

"More than a hundred?"

"Yes."

"More than two hundred?"

"No probably some where between a hundred and two hundred. I'm not sure."

"How long have you been an adult film star? I mean how long have you been making adult movies?"

"About thirteen years."

"About how long are these movies?"

"Usually about 15 minutes sometimes as long as a half hour but usually about 15 minutes."

"How long do they take to make? I mean are they weeks in production?"

"Oh no. Usually about half a day. Sometimes just a couple of hours. It takes more time to get dressed and undressed than it does to actually shoot the action." She smiles at the judge to get her meaning across.

"In these movies you are having sex with other actors?"

"Yes."

"Are they the same actors all the time?"

"No. They are all different. I have had the same co-stars on a few occasions, but usually it is somebody different."

"Do you have any romantic relationships with any of your co-stars?"

"No. Never. This is purely professional. We get the job done, and we go our separate ways."

"How are you paid for these movies? Do you get a fee per movie, or do you get a royalty off the profits?"

"It's strictly a fee up front. The more well known you are, the bigger fee you can demand. There are some really big names in the industry who can demand a royalty fee in addition to a contract fee, but most actresses would prefer a larger up front fee. I'm just now getting well known enough that I can get a larger fee up front."

"Would you say that your name has become more well known as a result of this lawsuit?'

"Objection. Relevance."

"Mr. Abadabado. I told you, you had a continuing objection. Please sit down and do not interrupt again."

"Summer. Is your name becoming more well known as result of this lawsuit?"

"Oh yes. I am getting several offers to do some movies. There is even a book deal that is being kicked about. I'm quite the household name right now. You've got to strike while the iron is hot as they say." She smiled at the judge again who nodded to show that he got it.

"When you are not making adult movies, are you employed in any other capacity?"

"I'm a dancer."

"A dancer?"

"Yes, you know in night clubs."

"You mean an exotic dancer in what is commonly referred to as strip clubs?"

"Well, we prefer to call them gentlemen's clubs, but yeah they're strip clubs."

"So you dance on stage in various stages of undress?"

"Yes."

"And do you sometimes take off some of your clothes while you are on stage?"

"Yes, sometimes."

"Do you sometimes perform what is commonly referred as 'lap dances' with customers of the club?"

"Yes."

"And the customers pay a fee directly to you for this service?"

"Yes."

"Do customers also give you tips if they like the way you dance ?"

"The good ones do."

"Have you ever worked as escort?"

"No."

"Never?"

"Never. I am not a hooker."

"It's my understanding that some men like to have the company of an attractive woman, such as yourself, at social gatherings or when out to dinner. It gives them a sense of power or prestige. It's a status symbol. Have you ever functioned in that capacity?"

"No. Never. It may be all status and prestige when they're out to dinner, but at the end of the night, the guy expects a happy ending. He may have to pay extra for it, but he expects it. Escorts are nothing more than high priced hookers and I am not a hooker."

"Okay. Let's turn to the facts in this case. You allege in your lawsuit that you had an encounter with the defendant at a hotel in Lake Tahoe in 2006. Is that correct?"

"Yes."

"Tell me what happened."

"Well. There was a convention there at the hotel and I was there networking my career. You know, meet and greet, try and make contacts to promote my acting career."

"This was a convention of the entertainment industry?"

"Yeah, mostly television but some film executives as well. I was trying to break into TV at the time. There have been some adult film stars who have gone on to TV, not many but some."

"So you were there trying to promote your career and you met the defendant?"

"Yes."

"What happened?'

"We talked for awhile. He had a couple of reality shows he was promoting and some beauty pageants. He said he might be able to help my career. We eventually went up to his room at the hotel. We had a couple of drinks and we flirted around a little bit. Then I left."

"Did you have sex with the defendant?"

"No. We messed around a little bit, but neither one of us ever took off our clothes. We didn't have sex."

"Did he offer you money?"

"No. It became clear to me that he wasn't interested in helping my career. He was only interested in one thing, so I left."

"Did you get the sense that if you had slept with him, he would have helped your career?"

"No. I got the sense that once he got what he wanted, he would have kicked me to the curb."

"So nothing else happened between you and the defendant at that time."

"Correct."

"So, moving forward in time, a few months before the election in 2016, you signed a non-disclosure agreement. Is that correct?"

"Yes."

"And as part of that agreement you were paid $130,000, is that correct?"

"No. I didn't get all that money. My lawyer kept a third of it."

"Objection. Attorney compensation is not a proper line of inquiry."

"Mr. Abadabado. Please sit down. I have told you that you have a continuing objection. I have warned you against interrupting the court. If you interrupt again, I will hold you in contempt. I will not warn you again."

"Okay, Summer. I'm sorry for that outburst. Let's get back to what we were talking about. You signed a non-disclosure agreement, which provided you were to receive a settlement of $130,000, but you didn't get all the money. You had to split some of it with your attorney. Is that correct?"

"Yes."

"Now what was your understanding of your responsibility under the agreement?"

"I was not to disclose any of the details of my encounter with Donald Trump at Lake Tahoe."

"You've previously testified that you did not have sex with the defendant and that he did not offer you any money for sex, so what was it that you agreed not to disclose?"

"The fact that we went to his hotel room and fooled around. He was married at the time, and it would have looked bad for his campaign."

"Do you understand that by filing this lawsuit you have disclosed what you agreed not to disclose?"

"Yes, but my lawyer said it was okay because it was a breach of contract and a defamation lawsuit."

"How was it a breach of contract?"

"Well, the agreement wasn't signed by the defendant. It was signed by his agent. So that was a breach of contract. So we can sue the defendant for more money."

"That's what your lawyer told you?"

"Yes."

"Okay. Tell me about the defamation allegation in your lawsuit."

"Well, in 2011, I was approached by a man in a parking lot in Las Vegas who said I could get in a lot of trouble for talking about Trump. I felt threatened, and I went to the police, and they had me work with a sketch artist to prepare a composite of the man."

"Go on."

"In April 2018, Trump said in a tweet that a sketch years later of a non existent man was a complete con job, and the fake news media was being played for fools."

"So that statement by the president damaged your reputation?"

"Yes."

"You feel you are entitled to damages as a result of the damage to your reputation?"

"Yes."

"Summer, you testified earlier that as a result of this lawsuit and the attending media circus, you have become somewhat well known. Is that an accurate statement?"

"Yes."

"You testified that there are several things in the works. Movie deals and possibly even a book deal, but these are all possibilities in the future. They might happen and they might not. Has your celebrity status already brought you any increases in income at all?"

"Oh yes. I'm having quite a bit of success. I've agreed to do two movie deals and I've received compensation for signing those deals. I am also headlining a nationwide tour dancing at clubs throughout the country. I'm famous at this point in time and I need to strike while the iron is hot." It was the second time she had used that phrase and the judge seemed to think this was getting repetitious.

"Fame is fleeting, but obscurity lasts forever?"

"Exactly, you honor."

"Okay, that's all the questions I have for this witness. Do either of the attorneys have additional questions for this witness?"

"Mr. Daniels?"

"No, you honor."

"Mr. Abadabado?"

"No, your honor."

"Okay, Ms. Dewdrop, you can step down. In light of the testimony received this morning, I'm going to give the parties an opportunity to file written briefs in support of their positions on the motion to dismiss. Mr. Daniels, I will expect your brief in two weeks. Mr Abadabado, I will expect your brief two weeks after that. We will meet back here 30 days from today at which time I will hear oral arguments in support of your briefs. Gayle, can you have this transcript prepared immediately?"

"Yes your honor."

"Good. Send a copy to each side with your bill. They can afford it. Gentlemen, let me remind you there is a gag order in place. You are not to talk about today's proceedings, and that includes your briefs. I will inform the clerk's office that these briefs are to be filed under seal and not to be released. Ms. Dewdrop, this gag order applies to you as well, as a party to these proceedings. You are not to discuss today's proceedings. Do you understand?"

"Yes, your honor."

"Good, this is for your protection as well as everyone else involved. Mr. Daniels would you remind your client that he is subject to the gag order as well and is not to comment on today's proceedings?"

"Yes, you honor."

As Michael Abadabado and Summer Dewdrop walked down the hallway, she whispered to him,

"I think the judge liked me."

"That old man just cut your legs off."

"What?"

"He got you to admit that the breach of contract allegation was just a way to get more money out of a non-disclosure agreement. He also got you to admit that you haven't been damaged at all by the President's statement. In fact you have benefited financially by the President mentioning your name. Our case just went in the toilet."

"You mean he played me?"

"Like a bass fiddle."

"What are we going to do?"

"I don't know. I'm going to have to work on my brief. I'm going to have to work some magic. Let me do some research. Maybe I can come up with something." As they approached the end of the hallway, the reporters mobbed them with questions.

"What happened at the hearing? Is the President going down? Did you have sex with the President? Does the President like kinky sex?"

"No comment."

"No comment."

As Grady walked back into his office, he passed by Kathy's door.

"Hey, what happened at the hearing?"

"I don't know. They kicked me out."

"What?"

"Well not me specifically. They kicked everybody out. It was a closed door hearing."

"Interesting. The judge didn't want his courtroom turned into a circus."

"I guess. Still I'm a little disappointed. I would have liked to know what went on. You are right. It was a circus atmosphere. It kind of tells us what we've got to look forward to if we return an indictment. Tell me, what is your opinion of cameras in the courtroom?"

"I am opposed to the concept. I know it's a balancing test. The public's right to know weighed against the defendant's right to a fair trial, but I come down on the side of a fair trial every time. I guess I am old fashioned, but I feel that a trial is sacred. To turn it into a TV show as entertainment for the masses diminishes it somehow. Witnesses, lawyers, even judges are more concerned about how they come across on TV than about justice. It can be a distraction. Trials are hard enough without adding an additional complication. How do you feel about it?"

"I agree with you, but apparently we are in the minority. For some reason that I don't understand, judges are granting more and more access to TV cameras in their courtrooms."

"Yeah, it is a strange phenomenon. Judges, in my experience, are old fogies and proud of it, except in this one instance. Anyway, I've been thinking about what you said about talking to Rey Rowdy. The more I think about it, the more I like the idea. We are a small group here, which is good in a way. We don't get pulled off on tangents. On the other hand, we could get caught up in group think. We are all pulling in the same direction and could miss an important detail. I think I would like to sit down with him myself. I mean, why filter it through an agent? He is not going to be a fact witness. I don't see him as being a witness at all. He is just someone to bounce ideas off of and perhaps point us in a new direction. Taking the agents along might be counterproductive, but having a second brain there might be helpful. I think I'll ask Dale to go along. I mean Rowdy might be a complete jerk. He certainly comes across in Congressional hearings as someone with an abundance of ego, but he might also be extremely helpful in his analysis. I should be able to get a read on the telephone of his attitude and if not certainly within the first few minutes of the interview. If he won't agree to confidentiality, we won't talk to him."

"Okay, Sounds like a good plan. Just curious, why Dale and not Debbie?"

"Optics. Two women showing up at his office presents one dynamic. A man and a woman present a different dynamic."

"I hadn't thought of it that way, but I see your point. Let me know how it goes."

Development

Roy Johnstone was a large man. He had a booming voice and a boundless energy. When he walked into a room, he owned it. To say he was driven, would be an understatement. He was one of those people who set goals, achieved them and then set higher goals. He played football on a full ride at Howard University. He'd been a starter all four years. He played tight end with a ferocity that frightened his teammates and intimidated the opposition. Not only did he block like a lineman, but he caught everything thrown to him. He wasn't exceptionally fast, but he was exceptionally strong. His running style was not to avoid tacklers but to run over them and keep going. He wasn't the star of the team, but everybody knew he was the guy who made the offense work. It took two guys to bring him down. That created openings somewhere else. He never fumbled the ball, not once in four years. He always gained seven or eight yards. Defensive backs hated him. They said it was like trying to tackle a truck. With that kind of weapon in your arsenal, it opened up a whole host of possibilities. The running back was the star, but only after Roy knocked someone to the ground and opened up a hole. The problem was Roy hated football and had no intention of playing in the NFL. The day he graduated he vowed to never play the game again.

He went to graduate school, got his MBA and went to work for a fortune 500 company. After a few years, he quit and started his own company. He was extremely successful and never looked back. He created his own business model of employee ownership of the company. He shared profits with his employees in a pension plan or a yearly bonus, whichever they preferred. He created a work force that was extremely loyal, dedicated and hard working. The harder they worked, the more money they made. It didn't take long for the concept to catch on. Those employees who didn't buy in to the concept didn't last very long. The company grew, and pretty soon he had two more companies operating under the same business model. He had two more after that and two more after that. He kept an ownership interest in all the companies, but 90% of all profits went to the employees. The problem was he could never sell any of his companies, because new owners would not be bound by his business model. He was just as loyal to his employees as they were to him.

He was married with three children. He had married his college sweetheart. She was a teacher for a while when he was in grad school, but became a full time mom once he starting making enough money for them to survive. She didn't understand exactly how it had happened, but her three children became her reason for existence. She loved her husband very much, but she understood that he was driven to some higher purpose. She supported him in his endeavors, and he loved her like life itself. By the time he was approached for the Cabinet Secretary position, he was thinking about retirement from his companies. He was restless and looking for something different. He hated the federal government with a passion. He thought federal employees were lazy, wasteful and got in the way of hard working citizens who were actually trying to do something or make something. The concept of downsizing the federal government appealed to him in a way that nothing had in a long time. The idea of being the most hated man in DC made him grin. He would run right at people and knock them down. It was explained to him that his function would be a ruse. The real job of his department would be conducted by the Undersecretary for Resource Development. He didn't care. He bought into the concept of providing daycare for married couples as well, and if he got to trim the federal government in the process, so much the better.

Samuel Parson was the complete opposite of Roy Johnstone. Other than the fact that they were both African American, they couldn't have been more different. Parson was recruited to be Undersecretary for Resource Development before Johnstone was picked to be the Secretary of Personnel and Resource Development. Parson was small, thin and quiet. He was extremely intelligent and had done a stint in academia, a stint in the government and a stint in the private sector. He had never quite found his calling. He was very good at managing people, but always felt he was destined for something more. He had become a conservative thinker over the years and wasn't very popular with the college crowd. He had become more and more disillusioned with the welfare state and felt that the socialist leanings of the left was the last nail in the coffin of the African American community. When he was approached with the opportunity to change African American culture and undo seventy years of destruction by the federal government, he felt he had finally received his calling. He was an instant convert and an immediate fanatic. He took the basic concept and began to lay out his strategies and structure. By the time Roy Johnstone starting sending him displaced employees from the various federal departments, he hit the ground running and was operational in no time. He originally met with the employees at an offsite location, their office or a coffee shop, some place where they could talk privately. Once he evaluated the employee and made a decision, he offered the employee an opportunity to proceed and required the signing of a non-disclosure agreement. They were told this was a secret government operation, and they were not allowed to talk about it, not even to the family. Johnstone had a knack for identifying talent and by the time they got to Parson, there were very few who got rejected. Johnstone's organization grew, but it took in mostly displaced human resource personnel, people who understood the personnel procedures and the Reduction in Force rules. Parson's organization grew as well, but his organization was staffed with operators. He was looking for people who could think on their feet, who were energetic and who wanted to succeed. There was extensive travel involved, but there was a good deal of planning ahead of time as well. There was staff meeting every Monday morning. This was a cumbersome affectation, but Parson insisted that everyone attend. These meeting brought everyone up to date on the status of the operation, the successes, the failures, the best practices, what was working, what was not and the growth of the operation. There was a certain fervor at the meeting. Everyone shared a common passion. They all wanted to succeed and the success of one was the success of all. There was almost a cult like atmosphere in that everyone felt they were doing something important. Some of the employees left on their travel assignment that day. Others left the next day, but all left with a sense of vigor. Not only were they doing something important, but the organization recognized their efforts. Parson was meeting with a potential employee. She had been vetted by

Johnstone, and Parson had conducted an initial interview, and he had like what he saw. She was bright, energetic, assertive and had that spark of youth that desired something more out of life. It was a hard quality to define, but he knew it when he saw it.

"So have you thought about what we discussed yesterday?"

"I've pretty much thought about nothing else."

"And what have you decided?"

"I've decided I want to know more."

"Well, it doesn't work that way. I need a commitment from you before we can move forward. I've told you this is a secret organization that you can't talk about even with your family. You won't be doing anything illegal, but you will be dealing with a sensitive matter that can't be disclosed. As far as anyone is concerned our department helps to find employment for displaced federal employees. We do some of that, but it is not our main function. You don't have to decide right now. You can think it over for a few days and get back to me."

"No. I don't want to wait. I'm not going to have any more information in a few days. I want to decide now. Okay. I'm in."

"Are you sure?"

"Yes. I am sure."

"Okay. Great. I need you to sign this non-disclosure agreement. It basically says anything I am about to tell you can't be disclosed to any person at any time for any reason. If you disclose this information, you can be prosecuted under the Federal Secrecy Act. Our department was created by Presidential Order, and he has the authority to classify the information, which he has done. Do you understand?"

"Yes."

"Okay. Sign right there next to the 'x'. I can't give you a copy of this document, because its very existence is a classified secret. If you are prosecuted for violating the terms of this agreement, you will get a copy of the document. Clear?"

"Yes."

"Okay good. Now that's out of the way, let's talk shop. As of today, you will be transferred to the Department of Employee Resources and Development. There will be no change in your pay or your level. There is no break in service. You are simply transferred from one department to another. We'll go over to the office and you will meet with the personnel people and fill out some paper work. It won't take long. When you're done, you'll go back to your office, clean out your desk and tell your immediate supervisor you've been transferred to a new department under the RIF procedures. He'll be sad. You'll be sad, but deep down he'll be thinking that's one less person I have to get rid of. Tomorrow morning you will be assigned a partner, and you will hit the ground running."

"Exactly where am I going to be running to?"

"Hold on. I'm getting to it. I've given this spiel so many times, that I'm starting to repeat it in my sleep. Currently, seventy-five percent of African American males, under the age of twenty-five, are raised in a single parent household. That is an astronomical number. The educational system has failed them, the job market has failed them and they are doomed to repeat this cycle. They don't have a father figure in their lives. They don't have a role model who takes care of his family. When the ADC system was created, it was decided that aid would only go to those dependent children who did not have a father around. It was designed to help the mother who was taking care of children on her own. Unfortunately, the law of unintended consequences reared its ugly head and the African American family was destroyed. Think about that. Our government destroyed the African American family. It took 70 years to get to this point, but here we are. You and I are going to change that. We are going to re-establish the African American family unit."

"How are we going to do that?"

"Well, I'm glad you asked. We are going to use the black churches to establish day care center for children of married couples who need to work. These day care centers will only be for married couples. That is the key. Day care is not the objective. It is a means to an end. The objective is to encourage the family unit. Free day care is simply a way to create a two parent family in the black community. There will be a strong temptation to extend the day care to unwed mothers as well because it is the Christian thing to do, but that temptation must be resisted. The black ministers have to be brought on board with the concept of re-creating the African American family unit. We are going to change history, and they are going to be a part of it. This is where you come in. You have to be a salesman for the program. You have to sell the idea to the black ministers. That's not all. Once you sell the idea, you have to administer it. Your only contact will be with the minister. He will have to sell the program to the church ladies who will actually run the program in the church basement. There will be no federal funds for this program, but you will help the church find foundation grant money and charity funding for supplies, food, paper products and diapers. There are plenty of sources out there. It will be your job to find them and put the church in touch with them. A large part of your job will be networking with charity organizations and finding the necessary supplies to make this program work, but you will do it from afar. You will be operating in the background and providing the resources and contact information to the minister who will actually run the program. The church will run the day care any way they like. They set the times, the food, the religious ed, the songs they sing and activities. The only thing we ask is that the day care is provided to married couples only. There are plenty of day care systems for unwed mothers. The fact that you are supplying admin services in the shadows will not be lost on the minister. You find the resources. He gets the credit. If the minister can't get behind the concept of providing day care to married couples, you have to move on and find one who can. The fact that we are providing day care is a good thing. The fact that we are re-creating the African American family unit is a great thing. We are going to change history and you are going to be a part of it. It won't be easy, and it won't be quick. There will be a lot of heartbreak and failure, but there will be some successes as well. I believe a spark will be created. Once one minister has success with the concept, others will follow. Once the ministers understand that we are not just providing day care, they will join in. We are taking back what rightfully belongs to us. The American government destroyed the black family unit with its well intentioned Aid to Dependent Children program. We are going to re-create it right under their noses, and they'll never even know what happened."

"Damn. This sounds subversive."

"It is, but it is authorized by the President of the United States. It is subversive to those forces within the government that have a vested interest in the welfare state. We are not going to end the welfare state. We are just going to re-create the family unit. They won't see it that way. They will see us as a threat. That's why this thing has to be kept completely secret. If they find out about it, they will shut us down. There will be lawsuits and congressional hearings and the ACLU will be screaming from the rooftops. The beauty of this thing is the very thing that would allow them to shut it down in its inception, will prohibit them from touching it once it is up and running. The separation of church and state will not apply. There will be no federal funding. There will be some foundation and grant money but not much. The ministers will be in control. You can't stop a church from running a day care for married couples, if that's what they want to do. Now there will be some hoops to jump through. There will be local ordinances and licensing and insurance requirements, and all of that. That will be part of your job to make sure that is all covered. Your job may also involve finding employment opportunities for the mom and dad or even training opportunities. You're going to be a one-man band. You're going to be balancing a lot of balls at the same time, and you're going to do it all in the shadows. No one except the minister will even know you exist. When it is all said and done, the minister will get the credit. No one will ever know that you changed the world except you, and the small band of fellow operatives. So, are you ready to change the world?"

"Yes, I am."

"Okay, let's go see your new office, and I'll introduce you to some people."

Judith Sam's head was spinning as she and Samuel Parsons walked the five blocks to the M Street building. This whole thing was surreal. A secret organization funded by the federal government that was going to reverse seventy years of policy. How did she get to this point? A couple of weeks ago, she was afraid she would be RIF'd and lose her job. Now she had just signed on to be a part of some brand new department that could blow up at any minute. Her whole life she felt she had some purpose in life. She worked hard in school and had dedicated herself to her job but didn't really find meaning in her life. It wasn't until she walked into the offices on the fourth floor and saw the people scurrying about that the hair on the back of her neck stood up. She suddenly realized that this was what she was meant to do. No matter what else happened in her life, at this point in time, she was meant to be here. She wanted very much to be a part of this and help change the world.

Rowdy

"Mr. Rowdy, I'm Kathy Solove and this is Dale Brickler. We're both assistant U.S. Attorneys from the District. Thank you for meeting with us on such short notice."

"Well, I have to admit I was quite curious why two AUSA's wanted to meet with me. You may have heard I have left public service."

"Yes sir. We are aware. We also know that in addition to joining your old law firm in South Carolina, you are teaching and working part time as a Fox News contributor. Before we begin, we need to clear the air so there is no misunderstanding. Anything that is said today must be in strictest confidence. We are appealing to your understanding of the grand jury secrecy rules as a former prosecutor. We are flat out asking for your commitment not to disclose to anyone for any reason anything that we say to you today. Can we have your commitment?"

"Well, let me see if I understand what you are asking? If you tell me something today, I can't disclose it for any reason. If I know something from some other source, and we discuss it today, I am still free to talk about that if I so choose."

"That is correct."

"Well, under those circumstances, you have my commitment."

"Dale and I, along with a few others have been assigned to a task force to look into the impropriety surrounding the 2016 election by government employees and others in an attempt to sway the election and to undo the results afterward. This inquiry includes looking into the FBI, the DOJ and the intelligence community. We've been asked to come talk to you because you seemed to have a pretty good handle on the facts when you were in Congress."

"Asked by who?"

"Our boss, Grady Franklin."

"Never heard of him."

"You wouldn't have. He's a nobody. He's a retired Postal Inspector, who has been asked to head up the task force. When I say he is a nobody, I mean he doesn't have any political ambition. If this thing goes sideways, he'll take the fall. He would only take the job on the condition that everyone on the task force would be protected when this thing was over with."

"I think I would like this guy."

"You probably would. I called him a prick at our first meeting, and he didn't fire me, so he kind of grows on you."

"I prosecuted a big case with the Postal Inspectors. They gave me some kind of award for grateful prosecution or some such thing. Anyway, I was impressed with their thoroughness."

"He's a pretty good administrator. That seems to be his strength. He gets the most out people. He praises people when they do a good job. He doesn't tell you to do something. He asks if you can help him out. That doesn't seem like a big deal, but it is. It's a trick he learned somewhere along the way. So do you think you can help us out?" Kathy smiled at Rowdy in such a way that said she had just walked him into a trap. He smiled back in a way that said he knew it.

"Sure, what can I do?"

"Well. We've pretty much got the big picture. There was a small group of people in the government that tried to use their positions of authority to influence an election, and when that didn't work, they tried to undo the results. What we were hoping for was that you could point us in the direction of some specifics that we may have overlooked."

"Okay. Let me catch up here. You're looking to bring an indictment for a conspiracy to defraud the United States involving members of the FBI, the DOJ and possibly the intelligence community. Have I got that about right?"

"Yes."

"First, let me just say you people are out of your mind. Second, let me just say thank God you are. This will be the biggest scandal in the history of our country. You will be reviled and ridiculed by the media. You will be accused of a witch hunt and working on behalf of a vindictive president. Every aspect of your lives will be turned upside down. They will be looking for anything to discredit you. Knowing all of that you're still willing to proceed?"

"Yes."

"Damn. Kind of makes me wish I was one of you. Okay, do you have the IG file with all the text messages?"

"Yes."

"What about the Congressional testimony of the major players?"

"Yes."

"Well you basically know everything that I know because that's what I had to work with. Beside the famous e-mails between Paulie Ruck and Linda Pugh, there were three other FBI agents who were involved in both the Claxton e-mail investigation and the Trump investigation who shared e-mails showing bias and prejudice against the president. What about the disclosure of classified e-mails by Claxton? Are you looking at that?"

"No. We looked at that and pretty much decided we couldn't make a case on that. With Homey giving her 'field immunity' on national television, he pretty much created reasonable doubt. I mean he didn't have the authority to do what he did, and his legal reasoning was flat out wrong. But when the Director of the FBI goes on national television and says what she did doesn't constitute a crime, that's pretty much the definition of reasonable doubt."

"True. I can see your reasoning on that. So you're looking at a lean mean fighting machine. You don't care if you catch them all, but you want to make sure the ones you do catch don't get away."

"Exactly."

"Well, you have to understand from my point of view, there was a constantly shifting landscape. You have the benefit of hindsight, that we didn't have. You now know there was no Russia collusion and there never was. Not only that, the people who were investigating it, knew it was all made up. There were so many lies being told by so many different people that it was difficult to keep track. I think that is going to be your biggest problem. Not that you don't have sufficient facts or you overlooked some detail. Your problem is going to be you have too many facts. This was a grand conspiracy on a grand scale that involves so many people that you run the risk of confusing the jury. It's just too complicated. What about leaks of classified information have you looked at that?"

"We have, but we decided, while the leaks may have been violations in and of themselves, we're only going to focus on those that were part of the big conspiracy. Like you say there was so much leaking and lying going on, that it would be real easy to get dragged down by the minutiae and not get anything done."

"I agree with you on the minutiae argument, but you are going to have some really hard decisions to make in deciding what to include and what to leave out. I once went to a seminar that was put on by one of the prosecutors on the Oklahoma City bombing case. The lead prosecutor on that case was a brilliant tactician who decided early on that they were going to limit evidence in the case. There were 17 federal agencies in that building that lost people in the bombing. They decided that only one person from each agency would testify. Seventeen victims from seventeen agencies were enough to give the jury the sense of the magnitude of this crime. It would have been tempting to put on a hundred victims to show the magnitude of the suffering caused by this crime. They interviewed them all, but they chose the best one from each agency."

"Your point being lean mean fighting machine."

"Exactly. I would not want there to be any chance of them getting off because the jury got confused or bored or lost interest. What about the FISA warrants? Are you looking at that?"

"Absolutely. That is a big part of this thing. We haven't decided if that's going to be a part of the overall conspiracy or if those will be separate charges. There are two schools of thought on this. One says keep it simple stupid and just charge the fraud on the FISA Court. The other school of thought says it's all part of the plot to overthrow the government."

"Have you looked at 18 USC 2381 or 2383?"

"No. No one has even brought those words up. It might apply, but I'm not prepared to go that far. It's a very serious allegation and treason and insurrection are not on the table at the present time."

"Fair enough. There are a couple of other issues to consider. The media is a huge part of this story. For three years they repeated the mantra of Russian collusion every night to the point where some in the media added editorial comment that became a part of the story. The media accused the president of conspiring with the Russian government to influence the 2016 election even when there was no evidence to support that accusation. The media had leaks from government officials and they ran with those leaks as gospel without doing any fact checking. The media was complicit in this fraud on the

American people. You can't tell the story without exposing the media's involvement."

"Our boss has set the parameter that the media is not a target of this investigation."

"Rightfully so. It would be like trying to shoot cockroaches. There's too many of them."

"That's not his concern. He's concerned about their first amendment protection and 'absence of malice' standard for suit and all of that."

"He's absolutely correct, but that doesn't mean you can't use their comments against those who are targets. You allege in your indictment that members of the media were used, wittingly or unwittingly to promote this false narrative to the American people. That simple little sentence allows you to bring in any member of the media you want, play a video clip of what they said and ask them if they said it. That's all you need. No matter what they say on cross about how they believed it and the president is unfit, all they are doing is digging a deeper hole showing their bias and prejudice. There's an archive service used by all the media outlets that can retrieve video footage, I believe for up to two years. You can go back further, but it takes a little more work. It's kind of like searching the old microfiche in the county courthouse. It's there, it just takes awhile to find it. Anyway stuff within the last two years is almost instantaneous. Not quite, but close. All the media outlets have their own archive, but if they want something from another network, they can get it from this archive service. You could subpoena this archive service and get all the video footage you want to use at trial. You'll have to structure your subpoena request carefully in order to limit what you get. If you simply ask for any video with the search terms Trump collusion, you'll have a thousand hours of video to go through. It might be a good idea to have your agents go over and talk to the computer geeks to find out how best to structure your subpoena request."

"Okay. We can do that. You said a couple of issues. What was the other one?"

"The politicians. They were as much a part of this false narrative as the media and there's not a damn thing you can do about it."

"Again, our boss has said elected officials are not a target of our investigation. They have immunity."

"Again, your boss is right, but that doesn't mean they can't be a part of the story. They made themselves part of the story. Your indictment alleges that elected officials were used, wittingly or unwittingly, by members of the conspiracy to put forth the false narrative that could then be repeated by members of the media. This one is a little more tricky, because these folks have an agenda and they are going to do everything they can to harpoon your case on cross examination. The media is supposed to be objective. They're not, but they are supposed to be. Their attempts to justify their actions will just show how prejudiced they are. Politicians on the other hand are supposed to be biased. They are the opposition party. They can lie on the floor of the House. They can lie on the steps of the Capital. They can lie on the Sunday morning talk shows and there is nothing you can do about it. I still think there is a way to use their lies to your advantage. I just think you have to be careful how you structure you case in your trial prep. Bring them in, put them before the grand jury, tie them down to their story. Then decide who is least likely to wiggle off the hook on cross examination. There is always a temptation to put the real jackass under oath, but you have to decide what is best for your case not what's best for your ego."

"We'll have to look at that. Like you say, it's a little tricky."

"Okay. Let's talk specifics for a minute. Any conspiracy indictment has to include Paulie Ruck and Linda Pugh. Their e-mail's show an agreement to enter into this conspiracy. The two famous e-mails, 'he won't be elected we'll stop him' and the one referencing 'the insurance policy' aren't the only ones. There are at least six others showing bias and prejudice. I think these need to be set forth in the indictment as they show the basis for the conspiracy charge. They have to be shown in context to what else was going on and actions that were being taken. There are several other documents that show Ruck was taking official action at the same time he was showing this bias and prejudice against the president. You may also have to go back and show the disparity of treatment between the Claxton investigation and the Trump investigation. Clearly, Paulie Ruck was the main bad actor of the two and Linda Pugh went along for the ride, but that's how conspiracies work. Homey was involved in everything and was part of the plot. Rob Lowenstein and Denny McCoy were intimately involved in the plot, and there is plenty of evidence to show their involvement. So that's a five-person conspiracy. That's manageable and provable at trial. If you expand your core group much further beyond that, you're going to get stuck in the weeds. Tim Dapper, as Director of National Intelligence, and Rex Brenamore, as Director of the CIA, were involved in this conspiracy just as sure as the sun is going to rise, but you will never prove it. They lied repeatedly to the TV camera but told the truth, for the most part, when they were under oath before Congress. You make that part of your conspiracy, that a large part of the conspiracy was a smear campaign against the president in the eye of public opinion. The term 'unindicted co-conspirator' has fallen out of favor with the Justice Department, because it looks like you are trying to throw mud on somebody that you don't have the goods on. So you don't call them that. You simply state in the indictment that members of the intelligence community made false statements in the media regarding Russia collusion. That way you can get your evidence in because it is in furtherance of an allegation contained in the indictment, but you haven't called anybody a name of 'unindicted co-conspirator'."

"So you don't think Dapper and Brenamore should be indicted?"

"Should be? Absolutely they should be to soothe my moral outrage over what they did. But from a tactical standpoint of what you can prove at trial, I think it would be a mistake. I think it weakens your case to have a couple of defendants who might or might not get convicted. You have to mention their names because they are a part of the story, but making them defendants may be somewhat iffy."

"Okay, interesting point."

"There is another thing that I am sure you have thought of, but it is essential to your case. All of these people have a built in defense. They are all going to claim they were performing a legitimate law enforcement function. They were simply investigating an allegation of wrongdoing. That is what law enforcement does. Jim Homey laid it out in an interview with SNN news when he said 'we weren't spying on the president. We were simply conducting lawful surveillance activities. That's what law enforcement does. You have to knock this defense down from the very beginning. You have to knock it down in your opening statement. You have to knock it down in your case in chief. If you have to knock it down every chance you get with every witness you put on. You have to show that this was not a legitimate use of their law enforcement power but an abuse of their law enforcement power for political reasons. You have to show the jury how and why they abused their powers. You have to be specific. You have to smack this notion down from the very beginning. You have to show the jury what dirt bags these people were. You have to show their utter disrespect for the rule of law and their arrogance that they could get away with it. And that they have gotten away with it until now. By the time the defense attorneys bring this defense up, it will be so crushed into the dirt that the jury will just be shaking their heads in disbelief. The key to your entire case is motive. There is no doubt what they did. The question is why did they do it. You have to focus on that throughout the entire trial from beginning to end." Dale spoke up for the first time while Kathy was scribbling some notes.

"Okay, there are a couple of things we are toying with. There are pros and cons on both sides of the argument. The first is

Donovan Stuhl and Ben Stinson. They were the driving force behind this false narrative. Donovan Stuhl wrote what has become known as the Stuhl dossier and Ben Stinson marketed it through his company Fission CVS. They didn't just do opposition research and get paid for it. They pushed this false narrative everywhere they could. They pushed it to the media. They provided it to congressmen, senators and the FBI and the DOJ. They even used a conduit to get it to the DOJ who could provide it to the FBI so it looked like it came from two sources. They were active participants in this scheme to defraud the American public. So the question becomes should they be part of the indictment even though they were not government employees and didn't abuse their authority?"

"That's a tough one. You said there were two things. What's the other one?"

"Kathy, you want to talk about the FISA warants?"

"Yeah, they lied to get the FISA warrants. They were lies by omission, but they were lies, none the less. Homey, Lowenstein and McCoy signed these warrants under oath and failed to disclose pertinent facts to the FISA court. Homey signed the first three. McCoy and Lowenstein signed the fourth. These cases stand alone. They are simple and easy to prove. So do we present a separate indictment to the grand jury or roll this up into the larger conspiracy?"

"Okay. That one is simple. The FISA situation has to be part of the larger conspiracy because it is. You can't tell the story without talking about the FISA abuse. It is all part of the same scheme to take down the president. You can't get caught up in the legalese of trial tactics and carve off this nice little piece because it would be an easy trial. You are not going after low hanging fruit. You are confronting a threat to our democracy. There is nothing wrong with charging the false statements to the FISA court in a separate count of the indictment and making these overt acts in furtherance of the conspiracy. You just have to make it clear in the indictment that Homey

is charged in three counts for the warrant applications that he signed and McCoy and Lowenstein are charged in a separate count for the one they signed."

"There are a couple of problems, but we think we can overcome them. There are a couple of others who signed the applications as well but don't appear to be major players and probably won't be indicted."

"In the history of the world, the legal argument that "jimmy did it too', has never gotten anybody off. Let them make that argument. Just be prepared for it."

"Exactly. The other thing is the IG said in his report that he was not referring this matter for criminal prosecution. That is not 'field immunity' like Homey gave Claxton and it is not even reasonable doubt, but it is a hiccup, and I expect to hear about it at trial. Just because the IG doesn't refer somebody for prosecution doesn't mean they can't be prosecuted. I'll just have to get the IG to say that at trial."

"I'm sure that won't be a problem. When Homey tried to claim that the IG report exonerated him, the IG was quick to point out that no it did not."

"We're going to have to put the IG before the grand jury, whether he likes it or not. He's in the middle of this thing and will probably be a prominent witness at trial. The IG has a different function than we do, and it will be important to point that out at trial."

"I agree with you. It's a hiccup but not a major problem As a matter of fact, I think the more the defense tries to make of this issue, the deeper the hole they will dig for themselves. I think the IG will prove to be a formidable witness on cross-examination. But getting back to your original point of Stuhl and Stinson. That's what they like to call in merry old England a 'sticky wicket'. There are very strong reasons for coming down on both side of the equation. Stuhl and Stinson were the driving force behind this false narrative. They didn't just create opposition research and market it to the DNC and Hildy Claxton. They pushed it everywhere they could. They'd already been paid for it by the DNC and Claxton, but they continued to push it knowing it was false because of their political agenda. On the other hand, it was the FBI that used this phony baloney dossier to get warrants. You probably know this, but it is worth emphasizing. On January 5, 2017, there was a meeting in the White House with Homey and Dapper and a few others and the previous administration. The very next day Homey briefs Trump on the existence of the dossier and then leaks it to the press that the president elect has been briefed on the dossier. The press is then justified in reporting the details of the dossier because the president has been briefed. It doesn't matter that the details are untrue. It's news because the president has been briefed. After the details get repeated over and over again by the media, the details become true, because the media says it is.

It was a brilliant plan, and it worked flawlessly. We'll probably never know who came up with the plan, Homey, Dapper or the other guy. Regardless of who came up with the plan, you can show definitively at trial that it happened. This should be laid out in the indictment because it was a turning point in this whole thing. Once the dossier becomes public, the medias treats it as gospel, and that is a big part of this whole narrative. The media changed public perception, and you've got to show that, but you've got to be careful to focus on the truth. Something that you may not know is around the same time the FBI got the first FISA warrant, October, 2016, it offered Stuhl $50,000 if he could provide any evidence verifying the claims in the dossier. That's odd in and of itself, because he'd already been paid as informant, but consider the timing. Stuhl was never paid the money, because he couldn't provide such evidence. The dossier was used three more times after that in three subsequent warrant applications with the FBI claiming under oath that the information was verified. Shortly after the second renewal of the FISA warrant, Stuhl admits under oath in a deposition in England that the information is unverified. I don't know how you solve your hearsay problem on that one absent Stuhl as a witness or a defendant. He was paid by the DNC and Claxton for creating the dossier. He was paid by the FBI as an informant. He was fired by the FBI for lying to them about his media contacts. So yes Stuhl is an intimate part of this story. Without him, there is no story. Does that make him criminally liable in a conspiracy to deprive the American public of a free and honest election and to undo the results afterwards? Turn it around. If the FBI and the DOJ had not abused their power the way they did, would the creation of the Stuhl dossier be a criminal offense? Probably not. It's still phony and sleazy and underhanded, but there is no lack of that in Washington. If we indicted every sleazy politician, there wouldn't be anybody left. So no. I don't think Donovan Stuhl is a defendant. I think he is an important witness. It will be difficult to tell the story without him. It is not impossible, but it will be difficult. You may have a problem there. He's in hiding. He's an ex-spy, and the British government is protecting him. If you think it's going to be difficult to get Dapper and Brenamore before the grand jury because they are ex-spies, you ain't seen nothing yet. Ben Stinson is another matter. Him you can put before the grand jury no problem. He may not be cooperative and he may want immunity. It depends on how you handle him as to how much you get out of him. He may be able to give you some of the Stuhl details."

"He's not getting immunity."

"Why not

"Our boss has said nobody get immunity."

"That's kind of harsh. It takes one of the tools out your toolbox."

"Agreed, but I kind of think it comes from above. Either there is evidence to indict or there is not. If there is not, keep your mouth shut and go home."

"Ah, the aftermath of the Hildy Claxton investigation where everybody got immunity so there was no one left to prosecute even those individuals who lied to the grand jury."

"Exactly."

"Makes it difficult but not impossible. You're going to have to finesse these people. Tell them they are not targets or subjects as long as they tell the truth."

"I agree. I think we use the grand jury to our advantage. Bring everybody in. Find out what they are going to say under oath so there are as few surprises at trial as possible."

"Sounds like a plan. If you have any more questions, you can reach me at this cell phone number. I'm only going to be in town for a few more days. I'm going back to South Carolina. I'll give this matter some thought, and if anything occurs to me I'll give you a call."

"One more thing."

"Sure, what is it?"

"Would you be willing to sign this non-disclosure agreement? It's just a written record of what we verbally agreed to."

"Shouldn't you have had me sign that at the beginning of the meeting?"

"Yes, but I was afraid you wouldn't sign it, and then I couldn't talk to you."

"What happens if I don't sign?"

"I'll just go back and tell Grady you refused to sign."

"And then I'm going to get a phone call. Aren't I?"

"At least one.'

"Give me the paper."

"Thanks."

As they were walking away from the building, Kathy turned to Dale and asked,

"What did you think?"

"He was kind of long on advice and short on specifics."

"Yeah. I got that too, but he did point out a few things. The archive service, the motive aspect, the intelligence community only lying when they were not under oath, the offer of the $50,000 and the January 5 meeting. I think I kind of knew about all that stuff, but he put it in perspective for me. His concept of a lean mean fighting machine made a lot of sense."

"So you have decided to limit it to five defendants?"

"No. I haven't decided anything yet. I think we keep an open mind, and we keep looking at everybody involved. We've got two others who signed the warrant applications. We've got FBI agents and other DOJ lawyers involved. Let's just see what shakes out. But his concept of a lean mean fighting machine makes a lot of sense. If we can get an indictment against these five people and get convictions at trial, that would be huge. These were the top people at the FBI and the DOJ."

"You're going to steal my FISA warrant case, aren't you?"

"I'm not stealing anything. We're simply including the FISA warrant applications as part of the overall conspiracy. You'll be sitting second chair in order to cover those counts at trial."

"I thought Debbie would be sitting second chair."

"Why'd you think that?"

"I don't know . You guys have been working pretty closely on this thing. Bob and I have been off doing our own thing. I just assumed you guys were kind of a team."

"You think Debbie thinks that?"

"I don't know."

"Crap. I really haven't thought about that aspect of this thing. We can't all four sit at counsel table."

"Why not?'

"It doesn't look right. It gives the jury the impression that the government is ganging up on the defendants."

"There's going to be five lawyers on the other side of the room."

"True enough, but it's still bad optics. I don't even know if the judge would allow it. They don't like tag team prosecutions."

"Yeah, I could see how it could get out of hand."

"I'm going to have to talk to Grady about this and see what he thinks. One thing has just dawned on me. I've been focusing on the big picture and trying to structure the indictment so I can fill in the gaps. I've got a lot of work to do on the specifics. I need to put some people before the grand jury. I've ignored the leaks, because I've shifted gears to look at the big picture. The leaks were a big part of this thing. It was the leaks that allowed the media to do what they did. A lot of the leaks were lies. In fact most of the leaks were lies, and the media didn't fact check. The leaks were coming from law enforcement and intelligence sources, so they were assumed to be true. We've now gotten to the point where the media makes up its own lies."

"Whoa, you're starting to sound like a convert."

"No, I'm just tired of thinking what we're going to be up against."

When they got back to the office, Kathy walked straight to Grady's office.

"How'd it go?"

"I don't know. He's got me thinking about a lot of things."

"Such as?"

"Did you send me over there to recruit him to be a member of our task force?"

"No. Why, did he want to be a member of our task force?"

"I don't know. Something just seemed off, like he was already a member of the team. He's pretty full of himself. I think if you put him on the team, he'd be in charge in about two days."

"Whoa. Slow down. What happened? What's got you so riled up?"

"Oh, it's just something Dale said on the way back. All four of us can't sit at counsel table. Somebody has to take a back seat, and I don't want to hurt anybody's feelings."

"Is that what this is all about? You don't want to hurt anybody's feelings?"

"Debbie is really good. She's one of the best trial attorneys I've ever seen. I'd just assumed she'd be sitting second chair, but Dale was assigned the FISA warrants. If they are going to be part of the overall conspiracy, it makes sense for him to be sitting second chair."

"Have we decided that the FISA warrants are part of the conspiracy and not separate counts?"

"No. They'll be separate counts but part of a single indictment and also designated as overt acts in furtherance of the conspiracy. That's what Rowdy suggested and I concur. It makes so much sense. I don't know why I didn't see it before."

"Okay. What works best for the case? Debbie at second chair or Dale as second chair?"

"I don't know. I want both."

"You can't have both. Pick one."

"What about if Debbie sits second chair most of the time, and Dale takes over as second chair when we put on the FISA evidence?"

"Sounds a little cumbersome, but it might work. You explain to the judge at pre-trial in front of defense counsel that there will only be two prosecutors at counsel table at a time, but the prosecution team consists of four members and the other two will be sitting in the first row to help out with documents and make the trial run smoother. You then slip it in that one of them might rotate up to counsel table as needed. You put the focus on the trial running smoothly, and I don't think the judge will object."

"Okay. I think that's best. What about Bob?"

"I'll talk to Bob. Don't worry about hurt feelings. You just focus on bringing the case. Let me worry about the personality issues."

"Okay. Great. That's a relief. I'm starting to get a little overwhelmed at how big this thing is."

"Don't sweat the little stuff. Let me worry about that. You just focus on your job. Okay. What else with the meeting with Rowdy?"

"Well, he gave me a lot o think about.'

"Such as?"

"He thinks we should limit the indictment to the five defendants: Homey, Ruck, Pugh, McCoy and Lowenstein. These were the five main players, and three of them signed the FISA warrant applications. It paints a nice tight picture."

"What about Dapper and Brenamore? He doesn't think they're involved?"

"Oh, he thinks they're dirty as sin, but he thinks they might get off, and that would weaken our case."

"What do you think?"

"I don't know. I want to keep looking, but he makes a good point. We can describe the activities of the media, the intelligence community and Donovan Stuhl in the indictment without actually charging all those folks. We charge the five main people. The FBI is part of the Justice Department so these five people are the JD-5."

That's got a nice ring to it. I like it, but I don't think the media will. Let's not use that term outside this office. More significantly, if you indict the former Director of the FBI, the former acting Director of the FBI, the lead FBI agent, the lawyer for the FBI and the former acting Attorney General, you've pretty much accomplished the mission of this task force. You add in the fact that the indictment alleges the involvement of the media, the intelligence community and the dossier, the whole story gets told. Okay. Keep looking. If we need to expand, we can, but I think you're focused in the right direction now. Let's start cranking up the grand jury and start parading folks through there. You're going to have to start delegating some of this to the other three. You can't do it all. Just make sure to tell them what areas of inquiry you want covered. We should expect some push back, motions to quash subpoenas on the basis of national security, that sort of thing. Maybe put Debbie on that. She can do the research and be prepared to go for expedited hearings and arguments to the Court of Appeals. I don't want these people to be able to slow us down, but at the same time I don't want to just give up whenever they file a motion."

"Good point. I think the grand jury will be helpful to avoid surprises at trial, but we can't get bogged down in procedural issues. We'll get every thing we can and then move forward."

"Good. I'll talk to the other three and let them know how we're going to need their help. One other thing, it was never my intention to replace you on the task force with Rey Rowdy. You're here because you are the best person for the job. I have every confidence in you."

"Okay. Thanks."

Ellie

The intercom on Matt's desk buzzed, and Agnes' voice came across on the speaker.

"Matt, Susan McCoy is on the line. She's tried to reach you on your cell, but can't get through."

"Oh crap, I think the battery is dead."

"That is not allowed. She's crying. Something's happened."

"Put her through."

"Matt, they've got Ellie."

"What? Whose got Ellie?"

"I don't know. I don't know." There were sobs on the other end.

"Okay. Slow down. Tell me what's happened."

"I got a call at work. On my direct line. The public doesn't have that number. It's only provided to certain people. The voice was disguised. He said, 'We've got Ellie. Do exactly as we say and she won't be hurt. Do not call the cops. Go directly home and wait for our call. We'll be watching.' Matt you've got to get her back. You've got to!"

"Okay. Calm down. We'll get her back safe. I promise. I am going to send Stephen over to your house. He'll be there shortly. What's the name of her school and where is it located?"

"McKinley Junior High. It's on Douglas Street. I don't know the address. When I got home, Mrs Murphy was worried. Ellie always comes directly home from school. She has a half a glass of milk and a cookie and she does her homework. Always. You could set a clock by her. Matt you've got to find her."

"I will. I promise. What about Charlotte?"

"She's right here. She got here shortly after I did. She rides the bus from high school. She doesn't know anything."

"Okay. Steve will be there shortly. I'll keep in touch." Steve was Susan's brother and worked for Matt in the computer room. He was currently at the Fort off duty. Matt came running out of his office.

"Agnes, were you on the line?"

"Yes."

"Good. Call the Fort. Tell Captain Oster it's a red alert. He'll know what that means. Get Steve over to Susan's house right away. Tell him to take his tap and trace stuff. All we know at this point is Ellie has been kidnapped." Matt ran down the hall to the computer room. Wog looked up from his monitor.

"What is it?"

"Ellie's been kidnapped."

"What? Ellie McCoy?"

"Yes, Ellie McCoy."

"When?"

"Not sure. She never made it home from school. Probably somewhere between the school and her house. Could have been earlier, but I doubt it. The school would have called."

"What's the name of the school?"

"McKinley Junior High on Douglas Street."

"Okay. I'm on it. We'll grid the area for traffic cams and any others. I'll put everything on this. You want me to tell Larry to launch the drones or do you want to do it?"

"No. I'll go talk to him. You find me video of this."

"You got it." Matt ran down the hallway to the tech room and found Sgt. Maxwell tinkering with the camera on a drone.

"Hey boss, what's up?"

"Somebody kidnapped Ellie McCoy, probably somewhere between her school and her home, probably within the last 45 minutes or an hour."

"Where's the school?"

"In northern Virginia. McKinley Junior High on Douglas Street. It's in Fairfax, not too far from the Fort."

"Where's her house?"

"2715 Timbercrest in Fairfax, about a half a mile from the school. Susan drops her off in the morning, but she walks home in the afternoon. She could ride the bus, but she prefers to walk. She says it clears her head and helps her think. I don't know why I'm telling you all this."

"Every bit helps. What do you want?"

"I want to put a drone up in a grid pattern between the school and the home. I want you to hack any video in that grid looking for the kidnapping. Feed your data to Wog. He'll do the search. You just get the data. I don't care how many laws you have to break or how many systems you have to hack. Just find me something. Put two more drones up on either side of the grid in case we have to follow a trail."

"You got it." Matt walked back down the hall.

"Wog."

"Yeah."

"Susan's house is located at 2715 Timbercrest in Fairfax, about half a mile from the school. Max is going to feed you anything he gets from the drones."

"Good."

"I'm going to co-ordinate with Malloy. I'll be in the coms room if you need me." Matt walked to the back of the building where the communication room was located. Lieutenant Malloy was standing by.

"I just heard. What do you need?"

"Bring everybody in from the street. We're going to need everybody here."

"Okay. Hold on a minute." Malloy relayed the order for all units to return to base.

"Go ahead."

"We've got a slight problem. We're set up to run operations from here. We're not really set up to run an operation from the Fort. The problem is it looks like this thing is in northern Virginia. All our technical equipment is here. The drones, the monitoring system, the computers, the coms, the vehicles. Everything is here and we need it there. We're going to have to set up a com center at the Fort and we're going to need an open line between here and there. Maybe more than one. We don't have any data yet, but if my opinion of Wog and his people is correct, we will be getting some pretty quickly. That information will need to be relayed to the Fort. This operation needs to be run out of the Fort. I don't think they took her very far. In any event, the trail starts there, and we have to be ready to follow the trail from there. Get in touch with Oster. Have him set up a command center there. He's going to have to run the show from there. We will provide the information, but he has to direct the assets. Also, let's start moving vehicles and equipment from here in that direction. Keep anybody you need here. You're going to have to be in charge of coordinating the flow of information. All information goes through you. I'll tell Wog and Max."

"Got it." As Matt was walking out, Malloy was dialing Oster's direct line. Matt walked back and told Wog and Max to relay all information through Malloy, that a direct line was being set up with Ft Belvoir. Matt walked to the front desk where he found Agnes attaching a silencer to her weapon.

"What are you doing?"

"I'm getting ready."

"Getting ready for what?"

"I'm getting ready to use lethal force."

"No you're not."

"Yes I am. They kidnapped a little girl. That's out of bounds. By anybody's set of rules, children are out of play. They forfeited their right to live, when they crossed that line."

"If they hurt her, you are going to have to stand in line behind sixty guys who will hurt them back. Bill McCoy was a lieutenant in my unit who was killed by a road side bomb eight years ago. Ellie was only three years old and didn't understand. Her sister took it much harder and is just now coming out of her shell. Both of his daughters were adopted by my unit, and there is no lack of presents at birthdays and Christmas. Susan and I have become very close and I provide whatever support I can. She's not going to get hurt. We're going to get her back. My guys are the best there is at electronic surveillance, rendition and interrogation. That's what we do. We're going to find her, and we're going to get her back. Then we're going to interrogate the bad guys."

"Okay. What are you going to do with the bad guys, after you interrogate them?"

"I don't know."

"Well, there's a crematorium in Falls Church you can use if you need it."

"Good to know."

"Just saying."

"Okay, I'll keep you posted." As Matt walked away he thought to himself. Man that is one scary broad.

About fifteen minutes later, Wog looked from his monitor and whispered softly,

"Got you." Corporal Jennings asked,

"What do you got Chief?"

"Black panel van, no windows. It's about three blocks from the school. There's a kid on the sidewalk, can't make out the kid's features, but the van pulls up, stops for about 10 seconds, then pulls away. The kid is gone. It's got to be them."

"What's the time stamp?"

"3:10." Jennings called out,

"Okay everybody, black panel van, 3:10, heading north on Douglas Street. Everybody work out from there."

"Okay, I got it two more blocks north, still going straight."

"There it is, still going straight."

"Can anybody make out the plate?"

"Hold on. There. Virginia plate 7631MB.

"Run it."

"Comes back to a Martin Sims of Fairfax. Oh man. It was reported stolen two days ago."

"Anybody got the van?"

"Yeah, it turned left on Miller Street, but there's no traffic cams on Miller. I can't see it after that."

"Expand out from there. We've got to pick it up." There was silence for a few minutes except for the sound of the operators tapping their keyboards. They were hacking into any surveillance network they could find.

"There. He turned right on Mapleknoll at 3:21. I can't see him after that."

"Put a street map of that area up on the screen."

"It's a residential area. No traffic cams, no business surveillance systems. Mapleknoll is a through street, but it doesn't look like he's trying to leave the area. Looks like he is going to ground."

"Okay, everybody keep looking, maybe we can pick him up coming out of the residential area. Jennings grid off the area. Find all the closest surveillance systems. Make sure we box him in so there's no possibility that he can get out of the area." Wog walked down to Maxwell's shop.

"You got drones up?"

"Two are up. They're putting the third one up now. The first one should be over the area of the school in a couple of minutes. The second two are establishing a perimeter in case we need to expand the search. I don't have any data for you yet. I should have something for you shortly."

"We've got a black panel van turning on Mapleknoll from Miller at 3:21. We don't have anything after that. We're pretty sure it's them. They stopped next to a kid for about 10 seconds and the kid disappeared. Van was reported stolen two days ago. The plate is Virginia 7631MB. I need you to vaccum any surveillance footage you can find in the area. We're going to need your eyes in the sky and we're going to need boots on the ground."

"Okay, I'll send you anything I get." Wog walked down to the communications center and found Malloy and a couple of his guys studying maps on the monitor.

"We've got a black panel van at Mapleknoll and Miller at 3:21.We're pretty sure it's the guys. The van was reported stolen two days ago. Plate number 7631MB, Virginia plate. It stopped next to a kid for about 10 seconds and the kid disappeared. We need boots on the ground. Co-ordinate with Oster. Have him flood the area. We don't have an outside perimeter yet, but we should in a few minutes. What about vehicles?"

"Already done. Two ambulances and two tac vehicles are moving towards the area. Oster's got plenty of vehicles to put boots on the ground."

"Get Oster's people moving. I don't need to tell you time is of the essence on this thing. I have to go see Matt." Wog found Matt in his office suiting up with tactical gear.

"What are you doing?"

"I'm going out in the field."

"No you're not."

"I can't just sit here. I've got to do something."

"You can't go out there. You're too close. You'll just make everybody nervous. Let your people do their job. Oster, Malloy and Max, they're all on top of it. The operation is under way. Let it play out. They will find her. We need you here. You need to look at the big picture."

"What big picture?" Wog just looked at Matt. The silence stretched on for several minutes. Finally Matt said,

"Okay, let's assume you're right. This kidnapping is directed at us and our operation here. Two questions jump off the page. How and why."

"The why I'm not worried about. We're going to find out the why. When we catch these guys, they're going to tell us why they did this. I have no doubt about that." Wog looked Matt in the eye for a long moment. Matt shrugged and nodded in agreement.

"There's no R.O.E for this Wog. I don't care how many laws we have to break. The only thing that matters is getting her back safely."

"I understand that, and so does everybody else. These guys will walk through fire for you. Let them do their job. They are the best there is at what they do."

"Okay."

"That brings us to the how. I've been racking my brain trying to figure this out. We have a leak."

"In the unit?"

"No way. I refuse to believe that. Everyone of these guys know if you leak, you die. Not possible."

"The security guys downstairs?"

"Again, no way. They're retired cops. They've been vetted. They are way to smart to mess with us."

"The tenants? The group downstairs or the group upstairs?"

"Possible, but highly unlikely. We are protecting both of these groups and they know it. It just doesn't ring true."

"Who then?"

"Think it through. The group downstairs is taking on some pretty powerful opponents. The group upstairs is ruffling some feathers in the Washington bureaucracy with their reduction-in-force, downsizing, whatever you want to call it. Who do you think is more likely to stage an attack like this? Some bureaucratic geek who is loosing his job or a CIA agent who is facing criminal prosecution?"

"You think the CIA is behind this?"

"I don't know, but the real question is where's the leak? Let's assume it is the CIA. Let's further assume the CIA knows something is up. They always know when something is up. Suppose the CIA has contact at GSA who is told to be on the lookout for an unusual build out of a government building."

"The GSA leasing agent?"

"Perhaps."

"Man, who would have thought?"

"When all other possibilities are exhausted, yada, yada, yada…"

"You met the guy?"

"Yeah. He seemed a little too friendly at the time. He wanted to help out. He kept sending his people over. I didn't think anything of it at the time, but now that I look back on it. Maybe. There's something else."

"What?"

"Remember when we caught all those employees at Bene Tech who were selling secrets to the Chinese?"

"Yeah."

"Bene Tech made a big deal out of it and gave you an award."

"Yeah. I remember."

"Susan and the girls were there. They took your picture and put it in the local paper. They called you some kind of security specialist."

"Oh my God. You think that's how they got to Ellie?"

"It wouldn't take too much to figure out you're in charge of security around here. You put two and two together and you find a weak spot."

"Let's take a look at this GSA leasing agent once we resolve the current crisis."

"I'll put Ralph on it. He's really good at hacking civilian data bases. Matt, we're going to find her."

An hour went by with nothing seeming to happen. Operators came and went to assigned tasks. Monitors lit up with street grids as areas were searched. Keyboards clicked away. Data streamed in from the drones at an extraordinary pace. Oster directed the search from the Fort and Malloy coordinated the data and passed on relevant information. Vehicles and other assets were moved into position. Oster made contingency plans for potential prisoners at the Fort. Matt oversaw every detail and approved every request. At this point the officers were just being polite. They were in essence running the show, and Matt was just observing. Suddenly there was a squawk on the radio and everyone sat upright.

"We got it. The van's parked in a driveway behind a house located at 1602 Pineview. There's no garage so they had to park it in the driveway. It's a small culdesac almost hidden from view. The van is tough to see from the street. If you weren't looking for it you'd never see it."

"Man we caught a break. If it had been in a garage we would have had to use the heat signature profiles from the drones and that would have taken some time." All the monitors went blank for a split second and then came back up as everyone focused on that location. The data started to stream in. The drones were repositioned and given new instructions. Surveillance vehicles moved into position. Oster assembled a tac team, a back up tac team and a perimeter team. Roving teams moved into position to provide cover and support.

"It's a rental. I talked to the leasing company. I told them I had a rich client who was looking for a small quiet place to rent for a year. They said it was rented two days ago for a month. The guy paid extra for a one month rental."

"Heat signatures show two large bodies in the main portion of the house and a smaller body prone on the bed. Stand by I'm adjusting the angle…. Base be advised the smaller figure appears to be tied to the bed in a spread eagle position." All eyes turned to look at Matt who closed his eyes, took a deep breath and growled,

"Get on with it!"

"Captain Oster, what is your time table for assault?"

"Stand By." A couple of minutes went by and Oster's voice came over the speaker,

"The perimeter teams are in place. The back up tac team is staged one street over. The primary tac team is staged in a plumbing van. They will breach through the front door 60 seconds after the flash bang goes through the front window. That should give the gas time to dissipate. It shouldn't reach the back bedroom where the hostage is located. We've never used these things before, so we're hopeful it works as advertised. It's my understanding we want prisoners not bodies." Matt grabbed the microphone.

"That's affirmative Captain. Timetable."

"Oh sorry. We are waiting on the ambulances. They are about five minutes out. The plan is for the tac team to disable the hostiles, recue the hostage and then exit the area in the plumbing van. The ambulance will then replace the plumbing van in the driveway and the prisoners will be transported to the Fort for interrogation. The whole operation should be in and out before anyone even knows we were there. Ah Colonel. There's one other thing"

"What's that?"

"Agnes is here."

"Agnes is there?"

"Yes sir." Matt looked around and asked the room,

"When did she leave?" One of the techs looked up and answered,

"She left about a half hour or forty five minutes ago. She said to tell you she was headed in the direction of the Fort, if you asked but not until you asked."

"She's not going in with the tac team is she?"

"No. She's going to take the hostage home to her mother."

"Oh, Okay. That makes sense. I should have thought of that. Good. A female presence to calm things down. Although I can't imagine Agnes having a calming effect on anyone." The others in the room looked around, all thinking they were glad he said that and they didn't. It was the kind of thing that might get back to her.

"Stand by. The first ambulance is here. We're probably only going to need one. The second should be here shortly. We're ready to go on your command."

"Go."

A few minutes later, the plumbing van pulled into the driveway. The side door of the van slid open and a man carrying a short length of pipe exited. The pipe turned out to be a sawed off shotgun which put a projectile through the front window. There was a flash of white light and a soft pop. Sixty seconds later, five operators entered through the front door. They were in full tactical gear including gas masks and had "Police" lettering on the back of their gear. A shot rang out and one of them went down. Five projectiles darts hit the suspect. Two in the neck, three in the chest. After action reports would confirm that all five operators fired a single round and that all five hit the target. Even Jimmy who was shot in the arm got off a round as he was falling which hit the target. Apparently the suspect was in the kitchen when the flash bang went off and was out of the blast radius of the gas. Four of the operators left the unconscious bodies on the floor, helped Jimmy into the van and were gone from the area in a matter of minutes. Sgt Charles Johnson, Tac Force Leader, and the head of the cleaning crew, stayed behind. He walked into the bedroom where Ellie was fully awake. He removed his mask and Ellie was looking at the biggest black man she had ever seen in her life.

"Did Uncle Matt send you?"

"Yes he did."

"I knew he's come get me. I knew he would."

"Let's get you untied. Did they hurt you?"

"No. They threatened to, but they didn't. The fat guy was trying to scare me. He was saying what he was going to do to me after the other guy fell asleep." Sgt. Johnson had no sooner cut the last zip tie, when Ellie jumped off the bed, ran into the living run and kicked the fat guy squarely in the stomach. Sgt Johnson grabbed her from behind in a bear hug, lifted her off her feet and carried her back to the bedroom. He no sooner set her on the bed and she bolted for the door again. He was ready for her this time and grabbed her from behind.

"You can't kick an unconscious prisoner."

"Why not?"

"Because it doesn't do any good. We want him to be awake when we hit him. We want him to see it coming. We want him to feel it afterward. We want him to see the next one coming."

"So he'll tell you why he did this?"

"Exactly."

"Well hit him once for me."

"The first one is for you. The second one is for me." Sgt. Johnson looked up to see Agnes standing in the doorway.

"Hi. I'm Agnes. I'm going to take you to your mom. Sergeant, do you need a ride?"

"No. I'm going to ride with the ambulance guys. I've got some more work to do back at the Fort." He winked at Ellie and she smiled. Agnes had followed the ambulance guys in. As they were walking out, Johnson yelled at Ellie.

"Don't kick him again." She just smiled and walked out into the fresh air.

As they were driving away, Ellie looked at Agnes and said,

"You work with my Uncle Matt?"

"Yeah."

"I didn't know he had girls working with him. I've met most of the guys. I've never seen you before."

"I'm just on a temporary assignment. There are no females in Matt's regular unit, but that may change." Agnes pushed a button on the dash and a preset number rang at the McCoy household.

"Hello."

"Mrs. McCoy. This is Agnes Frobush. I work with Colonel Mathews. Your daughter is safe and sound and we're headed your way. Would you like to talk to her?"

"Oh yes. Please." Agnes handed her phone to Ellie and said,

"Push the green button to disconnect the hands free feature." Ellie pushed the button and said,

"Mom?"

"Ellie, are you okay?"

"Oh Mom. I was so scared." Ellie started crying and her mom was crying on the other end.

"I knew Uncle Matt would come get me. I just knew he would. He sent this big black guy to get me. I don't know what he did, but he took those two guys out." Ellie was laughing and crying at the same time. Agnes just focused on the road.

Back at the Fort, the two suspects had been taken to holding cells inside the special ops compound. The holding cells had been modified by Captain Oster as interrogation rooms. Each cell had a chair bolted to the middle of the room and the prisoner was strapped to the chair with a black bag over his head. Each prisoner was in a separate room. The rooms were equipped with monitors, which showed criminal history, mug shots and the like. Agnes had been to the base earlier and had muscled her way into the compound with her authorization from the Chief General of the Army. She scared everybody she came in contact with and reamed Oster for using "toy guns" when people were shooting at us with real guns. She told Oster he better damn well get some information out of these guys because that was the only reason they were alive. She had checked in on Jimmy to make sure he was okay. Oster had kidnapped a surgeon from the base hospital and brought him into the compound to fix Jimmy's arm. There was no real damage, just a nasty scar. The surgeon was told that this was a gun cleaning accident and no paper work was required. The surgeon balked at first but eventually relented. Agnes left in a huff and everyone was relieved when she was gone.

At the M Street building, the tension was gone and everything was getting back to normal. The drones had been recalled and were being recharged. All the surveillance monitors were back to focusing on the building. Matt and Wog were sitting in Matt's office.

"Wog, I've been thinking about what you said about the big picture."

"And."

"And we need to get everything back here now. All the vehicles, the ambulances, the tac vehicles, the surveillance vehicles, all the equipment that we moved, everything."

"Okay, hold on, let me go talk to Malloy. I'll have him start the process." When Wog came back, he said,

"So you think we're going to be attacked?"

"What else could it be? The kidnapping was a diversion. Like you said they picked up my picture in the local newspaper and thought I was some sort of security consultant brought in on this job. They figured I'd be distracted for 24 hours and this building would be unprotected. They didn't know what they were up against. Even so, it almost worked. They got us to move our assets. Our guard is down because of a successful op. Tell Oster to feed his people and then get them moving in this direction. Have your people harden the security perimeter. Tell Max we're going to need night vision capabilities on his drones tonight."

"Okay. What about the prisoners?"

"I have every confidence that we're going to find out what we need to know, but we need to start getting ready now. If they've done their homework, they know the cleaning crew is gone by midnight. I think sometime after that is the window. The front desk opens at six. There's no way they wait until five or even four. So sometime between midnight and four, I expect an attack."

"Okay. I'm going to send out for some food. It's going to be a long night."

"Wog, anything on our GSA guy?"

"Oh yeah, sorry. I forgot. Ralph picked his bones clean. It turns out he has a gambling problem. Owes money all over the place. Recently he came into some money and paid off some of his debts."

"Let's send someone to talk to him. They can use their Marshal badges. This constitutes an emergency as far as I'm concerned."

"Okay. I'll send Jennings and Parker. They've been chomping at the bit to do something all night. Malloy kept them here in case we needed them. It appears that now we do."

Back at the Fort, Charles Johnson removed the hood from the prisoner's head. He blinked a couple of times and said,

"Man, what did you guys hit me with? My head is killing me."

"Water will make it go away. Would you like some water?"

"Yes, please."

"You can't have any. You have to answer some questions first."

"What is this? You've got me strapped to a chair?"

"Well, let's get our facts straight. You kidnapped a little girl and you shot a federal agent. You're in a bit of trouble."

"We were going to let her go in the morning, and I didn't know they were federal agents. I just thought somebody was breaking into my house." Johnson reared back and landed a blow to the solar plexus. If the chair had not been bolted to the floor, it would have been knocked over. Two inches higher and the blow would have broken his sternum. The prisoner howled and almost passed out from the pain.

Now that we have the ground rules established, we are going to administer pain and you are going to tell us what we need to know."

"I want a lawyer." Johnson hit him again in the same spot. He howled again and slumped back panting.

"You don't get a lawyer. I'm sorry. I didn't make myself clear. You don't get a lawyer because you are not going to trial. If you were going to trial, do you think we would be hitting you like this?" Johnson reared back to hit him again.

"Stop. Stop. Don't hit me again." The prisoner was in tears.

"You are in a completely binary situation. Either you tell us what we want to know or you die a very painful death."

"Okay. What happens if I tell you want you want to know?"

"No deals. Either you tell us what we want to know or we continue to beat you. Have you heard of water boarding?"

"Yes."

"You're not going to like it very much."

"Okay, okay. I'll tell you whatever you want. What do you want to know?"

"Why? Why did you kidnap the little girl?"

"We were paid to. Me and Jason got $10,000 each. We were going to let her go in the morning. We weren't going to hurt her. I swear it. We were paid upfront, and we were only to hold her for one night. It had to be today."

"Who hired you?"

"Guy named Rex. Rex Gunderson. He works for the CIA. At least he claims he does. I think he's just some kind of bag man. Basically he moves money from one point to another. We've done jobs with him before. Never anything like this. We're just hired muscle. We protect him while he's got the money. This was going to be the easiest money we ever made."

"You might want to re-evaluate that position."

"Yeah. I rented the house using a phony ID. I gave them two months rent for a one month rental. They were happy to get it. The place had been vacant for a couple of months. Jason stole the van a couple of days ago. We keep the girl one day and let her go in the morning. Easy money. Could I have some water? My head is killing me."

"Sure." Charles took a bottle of water, inserted a straw and held it up to the guy's mouth.

"So let's get back to my original question. Why kidnap the little girl?"

"I'm not sure. I overheard some things, but it doesn't make any sense to me."

"Go on."

"Well, some how the little girl is connected to a guy who is in charge of security for a building downtown. I don't know how she is connected, and I don't know who the guy is, and I don't know what building it is. But if he's distracted looking for the little girl, then the building would be vulnerable. I think Rex intends to fire bomb the building. I heard him talking about some kind of fancy explosive that would make it look like a gas leak."

"And you think this is going to happen tonight?"

"Has to be. We were going to let her go in the morning. We left a message that we had the package. That was the only contact. So what happens to me?"

"I don't know. That's above my pay grade. One thing's for certain."

"What's that?"

"We're not going to beat you to death." With that Johnson put the bag back on the guy's head and walked out of the room.

Captain Oster had been watching on the monitor next door.

"What do you think?"

"I think he's telling the truth."

"So do I."

"You want me to call the Colonel or do you want to do it?"

"No, I'll call. He's probably expecting my call. I'll send the tape over so he can evaluate it for himself."

"Okay, I'm going to have a word with the other guy. I don't think we'll get anything more out of him, but I owe him one for Ellie."

"Really?"

"He told her he was going to have his way with her after this guy fell asleep."

"Oh Really? Well don't hurt him too bad."

"No I'm just going to hurt him a little, but I'm going to enjoy it. Captain, what are we going to do with these guys?"

"I don't know. We can't kill them, we can't let them go and we can't put them in the system. The longer we hold onto them, the bigger problem we've got. This is outside my realm of experience."

"Chances are, if things go the way we think they will, we are going to have some more guests this evening."

"I'm going to have to talk to the Colonel. We need a plan."

Rex

"Wog, what do you got on this Gunderson guy?"

"Nothing. No criminal record. No social media. Nothing. He lives in a condo in Georgetown, drives s nice car and is self-employed as a software consultant, what ever in hell that is. He lists income of about $150,000 per year. Just enough to make him look legit. If he's got $20,000 in cash to throw at those two dirtbags out at the Fort, we're missing something."

"What about those two guys, they got records?"

"Oh yeah. They've both got extensive rap sheets. Assault, theft, possession, mostly small time stuff. They've been in and out numerous times. They each did a two year stint over some kind of botched liquor store job. They're not what you would call first time offenders."

"Okay back to Rex Gunderson. How is it possible that he is the mastermind behind this thing, and nobody has ever heard of him?"

"Somebody is protecting him? I don't know boss. It's a mystery. There was one thing. A few years ago, there was a bank fraud, money laundering thing. A couple of guys got prosecuted, and his name came up in the investigation. There was a notation 'no further contact'. That seemed odd to me."

"You think he was a confidential informant?"

"Maybe. I don't think so. If he was a confidential informant, his name would have been scrubbed from the file. This was more like the cops were told to back up off, and they didn't like it. They left his name in the file as a warning to other cops."

"So you think he really does work for the CIA?"

"I don't know. It might just be that his involvement could have messed something up that they had going. It's all just speculation at this point. I'll keep digging. I had an idea, but you're probably not going to like it."

"Let's hear it."

"We have a complete duplicate file of what the guys downstairs are doing. It gets backed up every Friday and taken to the Fort. Oster could remove the file from the vault and document his removal, have a tech run the name against the file and then return the file to the vault. It would be a very limited examination just to see if the guy who is attacking them is being investigated by them."

"You're right. I don't like it. That duplicate file is for their protection in case they get hacked. If it ever came out, it could sink the whole case. That file belongs to the task force. We are just protecting it for them. It is not for our use. We are not doing that."

"Okay. Just thought I'd ask."

"There's got to be a better way."

"There is another possibility."

'What?"

"When we did the Bene Tech case, in addition to the employees who were stealing, we caught five Chinese nationals who were hacking the computers."

"I remember. We planted viruses in their systems That was pretty sweet. The viruses got more and more complicated and eventually they gave up."

"Not before they did a lot of damage to their systems back in China. We turned all the information over to the FBI, and they rounded them all up."

"Yeah, I remember."

"You gave all the credit to the FBI agent that was heading up the investigation."

"I was just trying to get the spotlight off of us."

"Well it worked and the FBI agent told me if we ever needed anything to give him a call. He's been promoted several times, and he's now the White House liaison with the intelligence community."

"You think we can trust him?"

"Absolutely. He's one of the good guys. We've stayed in touch, you know both having an interest in computers and that."

"Okay. Reach out. See if he knows anything about this guy."

"You got it." Matt walked down to Malloy's office. There were several guys in the office, and they were going over maps and building diagrams.

"Okay. What do we got?"

"Well, we figure if they are going to hit us, they will probably come in the back by the loading dock. That looks like the most vulnerable to the casual observer. If they know what they are doing, they can pick that lock. If they don't know what they are doing, they can blow the lock with thermite in a matter of seconds. They will probably have a digital device, which they can attach to the alarm to defeat the alarm. My guess is they plan to take that with them when they leave so as to not leave any evidence behind. Only they won't be leaving. Once they deactivate the alarm, we will activate steel doors which will descend from the ceiling, in essence locking them in a steel cage. They will be on our monitors the entire time."

"What if they come in the front?"

"That will be a little tougher. We don't have a steel cage trap on the front entrance. The elevators are locked down and they will have to use the stairwell. Once they get in the stairwell, we can electronically lock them inside. Same principle. They'll still be locked in a steel cage, just a tall skinny one with stairs. We don't know how effective the gas will be in that large a space, but we'll figure it out. The smart money is on them coming in the back. That's how I would do it. Get in, disable the alarm, set the charges and get out."

"Okay. I'm going to want to see how you deploy your resources. The building will be completely dark once the cleaning crew leaves at midnight. I'm guessing shortly after that is when we get hit."

"I'm still working out the details. I'll come get you when the plan is ready."

"Good." Matt walked back to Wog's shop. There was a steady drone of activity, cameras being repositioned, grids being set up on the monitors, not the frenzied activity of earlier but a steady preparation.

"Anything new?"

"Yeah, Jennings and Parker are back."

"And?"

"And the guy pissed his pants."

"What?" Wog laughed and said,

"The guy literally wet his pants when they showed their badges and said they wanted to talk to him about a kidnapping and an attempted murder of a federal agent."

"So did he spill the beans?"

"Well, there's not a whole lot of bravado left once you've wet yourself. So yes he spilled the beans. It seems he's been on this guy's payroll for a while. Gives him tips about what federal agency is moving where. Little tidbits of gossip about the federal government. Nothing sensitive, just keeping him in the loop about what's going on."

"Who's to say what is sensitive and what is not."

"Yeah, I guess you could say we were careless."

"So he told him about us?"

"Yeah, Gunderson came to him a couple of months back and asked him to be on the lookout for any unusual build out of a federal building. He told Gunderson that there was a private security firm involved in the build out of the M street building."

"What else did he tell him?"

"I don't think he knows anything else. They pushed him pretty hard. He swears all he told Gunderson was there was something unusual going on. He didn't know anything else about the building."

"What did he know about Gunderson?"

"Not a whole lot. He said when Gunderson first approached him, he implied he worked for the CIA, but that over time that implication went away. He just gave the impression he is some kind of hustler, trading information, always looking to make a buck. He thought the guy might be a little shady but had no idea any criminal activity was involved."

"Sounds a little self serving."

"Yeah. The guy's scared he's going to loose his job."

"How'd they leave it with him?"

"They told him if he keeps his mouth shut, he won't be prosecuted, but if he breathes a word of this to anybody, he's going to jail."

"You think we're okay there?"

"Yeah. I think his days of being a snitch for Gunderson are over."

"Man, a GSA leasing agent. Who would have thought that would be our weak link? This town is something else."

"There's one other thing."

"What's that?"

"Agnes is back."

"She's back? When did she get back?"

"Little while ago. She said she came back for the free pizza. I suspect she still wants to shoot somebody."

"Oh man."

"Matt."

"Yeah."

"She's not the only one. A lot of the guys are pissed off that Jimmy got shot. You're going to have to talk to them and explain the reality of this situation. We're balancing on a thread here, and this whole thing could dissolve in an instant."

"Yeah, you're right. I'll get everybody together once Malloy's got his plan drawn up."

Matt walked out to the front desk and found Agnes working on her monitor board. She had reconfigured the monitors for perimeter security and was checking various angles. Gone were the clear glasses, the frumpy clothes and the southern accent. She looked every bit the army colonel getting ready to go to war.

"So what do you think?

"I think you are in good shape. Malloy's drawing up you action plan?"

"Yeah."

"You going to use the drones with night vision?"

"Yeah, they won't give us a lot of detail, but we'll get heat signatures, numbers and locations."

"You think they're coming tonight?"

"Only thing take makes sense. I was pretty sure the kidnapping was a diversion. That's been confirmed by the prisoners. Speaking of which, how are things at the McCoy household?"

"Good. Mother and daughter reunited. Lots of tears, but tears of joy. They're good. You on the other hand, have a bit of a problem."

"Yeah, I know."

"You saved her daughter, and for that she will be forever grateful. On the other hand, you caused her daughter to be kidnapped in the first place. She can't forgive that. It will always be between you."

"Did you talk to her about it?"

"No. I'm just looking at it from a woman's point of view. I could be completely wrong, but I don't think so."

"No. I don't think you are either. I haven't called for just that reason. I'll touch base tomorrow after this is all over. I wanted to talk to you about something else."

"Okay."

"I need to talk to the Blue Man."

"No. You don't."

"I don't ?"

"No."

"Why not?"

"Because if you are talking to him, you can't do your job, and he wants you to do your job. Figure it out. Talk to me. That's why I'm here, to keep you from embarrassing the U.S Army."

"Okay. I've got these two prisoners, and I don't know what to do with them. I can't kill them. I can't let them go, and I can't put them in the system. Chances are I'm going to have some more prisoners before the night is over. There's a jail in Turkey that will take prisoners for six months, no questions asked, as long as you pay the fee. I'd have to get them to Turkey, which is no easy feat. I'd probably be breaking about sixteen international laws and be putting a whole host of people in jeopardy. We're just not equipped to handle a bunch of prisoners. We've got the space, but not the manpower. My guys aren't prison guards. It would take away from the mission."

"Okay. Let's think this through a minute. You've got two guys who kidnapped a child and attempted to kill a federal agent. If things go the way you think they will go, you're going to have some other guys who are attempting to fire bomb a federal building to obstruct a federal investigation into abuse by the FBI, the CIA and the Justice Department. This is all some giant conspiracy to obstruct a federal investigation involving kidnapping, attempted murder and fire bombing. If that's not domestic terrorism, I don't know what is. On top of that you can't trust the good guys. The FBI and the DOJ are the ones being investigated. So you ship them off to Gitmo"

"Guantanimo Bay in Cuba? Where we have all the terrorists we've captured from around the world?"

"Sure. Why not? There are separate facilities there. They don't have to come in contact with anyone else. You put bags on their heads. You ship them there. You keep them in isolation. You put bags on their heads and bring them back in six months and let them go."

"You think this thing is going to be over in six months?"

"Six months, a year, whatever. You tell them if they keep their mouths shut, they get out when the trial is over. They're getting off easy. They should get life and they know it. You don't care about trials and lawyers and due process and sentencing guidelines and all that nonsense. You only care about protecting the task force until it completes its job. That's your job."

"Can we do this?"

"I don't know. I'll make some calls tomorrow, see what I can set up. Since we are looking at a short term stay, six months to a year, I think I might be able to pull it off."

"Okay. Let me know what you come up with." As Matt was walking away, the thought occurred to him again "scary".

Awhile later, Wog walked into Matt's office,

"Hey, I talked with our friend over at the Bureau, well technically he's not at the Bureau. He's TDY at the White House as Intelligence Liaison Officer.

"Find out anything?"

"A little. This Rex Guderson is not on the CIA's payroll. Anything he is doing is not sanctioned by the Agency. He used to be a bagman for the Agency, moved money from one location to another. Some money turned up missing and they severed ties with him. He's basically a money launderer and he went free-lance. It's suspected that he works for organized crime, but nothing has ever been proven. Apparently he is pretty good at what he does, which is move money around. The way the guy explained it to me is, it ain't like in the movies with a guy walking around with a suitcase full of hundred dollar bills. There is a steady flow of small amounts of money going to lots of different people. This steady flow creates a steady flow of information into the Agency. Gunderson wasn't involved in the flow of information, only the dispersal of the cash. They expected him to skim a little, but he got greedy."

"What kind of money are we talking about?"

"Lots. You know casinos, drug money, government contracts, charitable contributions, political action committees. There are lots of organizations with lots of money that needs to be moved around. A million here, a million there and pretty soon you're talking big money."

"So we know who this guy is, but we don't know why he's attacking us."

"Pretty much."

"So I don't see how that helps us all that much."

"Well, it does and it doesn't."

"Explain."

"This guy has been living on the edge for a long time. He's got some pretty influential associates. He's smart. He hasn't gotten caught. He's arrogant. He's attacking us because he thinks he can get away with it. We still don't know his underlying motivation, but we know we're not up against law enforcement or intelligence operatives."

"Well, I guess that's good news."

"Good and bad."

"How so?"

"We're not fighting the government, but we might be fighting some pretty bad criminals."

"So let's not fight. Let's just put them down like the dogs that they are."

"Roger that."

"Let's go see Malloy and see what his plan looks like."

They found Malloy briefing his team when they walked in.

"Don't let me interrupt. I'll catch up."

"Like I was saying, Ralph Simmons will be the sniper on the roof with a spotter. There will be another spotter in contact with me here. The drones will be up, but we won't get a lot of detail at night. We will all be using the non lethal rounds, so the goal is to shoot first, and ask questions later. There is no 'Police, put you hands up, don't move, you're under arrest.' None of that. We put them down, so they don't have an opportunity to think about using their weapons. The goal is to let them get in the building and then take them down, so there is no question what they are up to. The goal is to take them down as quickly and quietly as possible. We remove them from the area. We take them to the Fort and nobody even knows they were here. The command will come from here when it is time to take them down. The bomb tech guys will be in the basement garage and will be responsible for removal of the explosives. The majority of our guys will be here on the third floor or in the basement garage. There will be a couple of vehicles outside to provide perimeter security, but we don't want to spook them. Tac Team Alpha will be here on the third floor and will come down on them from above. Tac Team Bravo will be in the basement garage and will come up on them from below. If they come in the backdoor, they'll be trapped and it will be over quickly. We'll gas them with the non-lethal gas and that will be it. If they breach some other way, front door or a window, we'll have to engage quickly. They may cut the power line, in which case we'll be dark until the back up generator kicks in. We'll just have to use the portable radios and night vision goggles to get the job done. Once the enemy has been subdued, everyone gets moved to the garage for transport to the Fort. Captain Oster is ready to receive prisoners for interrogation. The other two have been moved to isolation cells. The interrogation rooms are ready. Anything else?" He looked at Matt, who said,

"Sounds like a good plan, but you know what they say about plans in the Army?"

"Yes sir."

"Okay. Everybody stay loose and try not to engage until the command is given by Lt. Malloy. If we lose communication, use your best judgment. We need to catch these guys, but we need to not get caught ourselves. This is totally covert under the radar. Everybody clear on that?" there were nods all around.

"Wog, I need you to send a couple of guys over to his place. As soon as he is in custody, they need to break in and grab his lap top, hard drive, documents anything that will help us figure out what is going on. Also, before they are transported to the Fort, any cell phones, lap tops need to be turned over to Wog's people, so they can break into them. We're going to need that information as soon as possible for the interrogation. We can drag this out for a couple of days, but I don't want to. I want to know what we are up against as soon as possible. Wog, you think your guys can handle this?"

"Oh yeah. We're already on it. I told you we didn't have anything on Gunderson, but that was criminal record. We're building a pretty extensive dossier on him. My guys are not being very subtle. They're slamming every data base we can find. They're using brute force to search for his involvement. Now that we know we are looking for money laundering, the job got easier."

"No fingerprints leading back here, I hope."

"No. Some systems will know they've been hacked, but they won't know where it came from or why."

"Okay, get your people over there and get ready."

The cleaning crew was gone by midnight and the building went completely dark. The cleaning crew didn't know what was going on, but they knew something was up. Charles Johnson was especially unfriendly tonight. There was a buzz of activity on the third floor, but that office was completely concealed from the outside. There was tension in the air as the midnight hour came and went, but it was more of an anticipation attitude. This is what these guys did, functioning as a unit on an operation.

At 12:45 am, there was a transmission on the radio,

"Dark panel van traveling slow on M Street. Seems like dark panel vans are the vehicle of choice for criminals today."

"Save the commentary."

"Roger that. Okay it stopped in front of the building. A guy got out and the van drove off. He crossed the street and is laying down in the shadows with a wine bottle. Looks like he's the lookout pretending to be a drunk."

"The van's turned left on a side street. I can't see it any more."

"I got it. It's turned in the alley behind the building. Alright, it's stopped behind the building. Two guys are unloading stuff from the back of the van. A third is at the back door working on the lock. The van is pulling off."

"Somebody stay on the van. I want to know where it goes."

"Drone number one has it."

"The two guys are lugging stuff to the back door. Man that's a lot of stuff. They've each made three trips. The third guy is still working on the lock."

"The van has circled around and parked two streets over pointing at the back alley."

"The guy is having trouble with the lock. I think the one guy wants to blow it. The other one waved him off and is working on it some more. There. He's got it. The door is open. They're moving the stuff in. Wait one. They've got everything in. They are closing the door. NOW!"

In the command center on the third floor, Malloy gave the command and steel sheets descended from the ceiling creating an 18 foot by 18 foot steel cage. The transformation was instantaneous and the sound was deafening. Lights from concealed fixtures came on and a voice came through a hidden speaker,

"Drop your weapons and put your hands in the air." Each of the three had drawn a weapon and was frantically looking for something to shoot at.

"Drop your weapons and put your hands in the air." Malloy turned to the tech next to him and said,

"Okay, gas them." Two flash bangs dropped from the ceiling and a white light blinded the intruders. Within seconds they were unconscious and lying on the floor. The panels lifted back into the ceiling, the back door swung open and a fan pushed the inert gas out the back door. Shortly after that, the Tac Team from the basement loaded the intruders onto stretchers and moved them to the basement garage via the freight elevator.

"Okay. Let's roll up the other two. Can the driver see the lookout from his position?"

"No."

"Okay. Grab the lookout first." A marked car pulled up and put a spot light on the 'drunk.' Two armed 'officers' appeared out of nowhere and pointed weapons at the drunk.

"Come on out of there and keep your hands where I can see them." The drunk continued to play his part and pretended he didn't understand.

"Your three friends inside have already been caught so don't do anything stupid." The drunk stood up and came into the light. Just then there was a hissing sound as a rifle dart whizzed by the two 'officers' and struck the drunk in the left shoulder. He yelped and when down like a sack of potatoes.

"Come on Ralph! A little warning, if you're going to do that."

"Left wrist." The sniper replied.

"What?"

"Check his left wrist. He had a spring-loaded holster strapped to his left wrist. It shot a derringer into his left hand. He was just about to shoot you. I didn't have time to warn you. I just barely picked it up in my scope." The 'officer' checked the left hand and sure enough, there was a derringer from a spring-loaded holster. The 'officer' checked the right hand and there was another spring-loaded holster with a derringer that had not been activated. He removed both and loaded the unconscious lookout into the backseat. They headed towards the underground garage.

"Take the driver." Another marked car pulled up behind the van and turned on its flashers. When the driver looked up, a man with a pistol pointed at his head and a flashlight in his face said, "License and registration." The driver reached towards the glove box and was shot in the left shoulder. He yelped and said,

"I was just getting the…" He never finished the sentence and fell over unconscious. The shooter undid the driver's seatbelt, pushed him over to the passenger seat, buckled himself in and drove off. The marked car had turned off its flashers and left the scene. The whole thing took less than sixty seconds.

Back at the garage there was a mini convention going on with everyone gathered around looking at five unconscious bodies.

"Hey boss you want to transport them to the Fort in their own van? That'd be poetic justice." Malloy looked over at the van

"No. For all we know that damn thing could be stolen. Let's stick to the original plan. We'll transport them in the ambulances. Three to one, two to the other. Clean them. Everything from each prisoner goes in to a gallon zip lock bag, cell phone, weapon, ID, anything helpful. Get the bags to Wog so he can start building his profiles. Somebody photograph that plate and get it upstairs too. Everybody back to the Fort, except for the night crew. We'll leave here in five minute intervals, so as not to arouse any suspicion. Wog's people will probably be here for another hour or so transmitting data back to the Fort. Good job everybody. Let's finish up successfully."

Rex Gunderson woke up in the same interrogation room where the kidnapper had awoken earlier in the day. He was strapped to the same chair and had the same headache. Charles Johnson was not involved in this interrogation. He was being saved for later, in case Rex decided to take the long route. Sergeant David McGee was the unit's best interrogator, and he was prepared to spend some time with Gunderson. He was mild mannered and methodical but unrelenting. He could go for hours if need be and never forget a detail. He removed Gunderson's hood and sat back down in front of him.

"How's you head?"

"It hurts."

"Water helps. Would you like some water?"

"Yeah." McGee motioned to an assistant who brought over a bottle of water with a straw and allowed Gunderson to take as much as he wanted.

"You're not going to untie me, are you?"

"Nope."

"Afraid I'll make a run for it?"

"Where you gonna go?"

"I don't know, where am I?"

"You're in a bad place Rex. You've done a lot of bad things and made a lot of people angry. We know a lot about you and in the next twenty-four hours we will know a lot more. We have your laptop and your three cell phones from your place. We know you've been laundering money for the Jamaicans and the Mexican cartels. We know you double-crossed the Columbians, but they haven't figured it out yet. We know you laundered money for the Chinese. That one's a little troubling because it wasn't just drug money. It involved intelligence and gets into the area of treason. What we don't know is why you decided to fire bomb a federal building. We will find out eventually, but you will suffer a great deal of pain in the process. It will take some time and the consequences for you will be unpleasant. We will notify all your enemies of what you have done, and put the word out on the street that you are now a co-operating witness in an ongoing federal investigation."

"You can't do that. That's a death sentence and you know it. Look I made a mistake. Okay? Anybody can make a mistake. We can fix this."

"I'm going to leave now and give you some time to reflect on your situation. When I come back, things will be different. They're going to bring in the other guys. You know the ones who aren't as reasonable as me." McGee put the bag back on Rex's head and smiled at the camera because he knew.

"Wait, wait. Don't leave. I'll tell you what you want to know." McGee took the bag off and sat back down in front of Gundedrson. He waited for Gunderson to begin talking.

"You wanted to know why." McGee nodded.

"It's time. That's all. I just needed some time. It was going to take me two months, three tops, to liquidate my assets. It's not like in the movies where you grab a suitcase of money and run off to the Bahamas. I own bars, restaurants, strip clubs and various other ongoing business ventures that aren't easily liquidated. My partners aren't the type of people who sign contracts. Once people find out you're leaving town, they tend to take advantage of you, so it has to be done carefully. I know how to move money. It was just going to take a little time. That's all it was. Time."

"So you were going to fire bomb a building just to buy yourself some time?"

"Yes. If their records were destroyed, it would take them at least two months to reconstruct everything, maybe four months. By that time I'd be long gone."

"Why did you think they were on to you?"

"They weren't. Not yet. But they weren't very far away. They served some subpoenas on some entities that I was connected with, banks, cell phone companies, computer records. I moved money for a lot of people. Once they started pulling on the thread, my whole organization would have been exposed."

"So there were trip wires?"

"Yes. I have people on the payroll at various places to let me know if people start asking questions. I was getting heat from several directions and I decided it was time to get out of Dodge. I just need a little time."

"So the leasing agent, he was one of the trip wires on your payroll?"

"Yes, but that was different. I just asked him to be on the look out for any unusual security measures in a build out of a federal building. I knew there would be a secret grand jury investigation of this mess with the government corruption. He's on my payroll, but this was a special request. I didn't think the grand jury would move this fast. I got alarm bells from several sources. Look, I made a mistake. I panicked. So how do we fix this? There's always a way to fix things. What do you need?"

"I don't know. We'll talk again later." He put the bag back on the prisoner's head and walked out of the room. Captain Oster was waiting outside.

"What do you think?"

"I think he's telling the truth."

"So do I."

"He's smooth. He's strapped to a chair and he's trying to negotiate a deal. I've never seen anything like it. It could all be bullshit to cover up who he's actually working for, but I don't think so. I think he's all alone. He's a big time money launderer who saw his empire about to come tumbling down. He's probably got an exit strategy all set up. I wouldn't be surprised if he has a place on an island with no extradition treaty and a ton of money already there. He wanted it all, so he was going to stick around for a couple of months and liquidate his assets."

"Okay. Have a go at the other four. See what you can find out then come back at him. It doesn't look like he was working for any of the entities under investigation. He was just collateral damage."

"That's what it looks like at this point. We'll know more in a few hours, but my guess is the guys on the second floor don't even know his name. This was all some paranoid delusion."

'Keep at it. I'm going to give Matt our initial evaluation."

"Roger that."

Debbie

Later in the day, pretty close to noon actually, Grady was sitting at his desk when the intercom buzzed.

"Mr. Franklin?"

"Yes."

"Mr. Mathews is here."

"Send him on back."

"Matt, how are you doing?"

"Good. Mind if I close the door?"

"No. Not at all. What's up? You don't look so good. Are you alright?"

"I'm fine. I just didn't get much sleep last night. That's kind of what I wanted to talk to you about."

"Okay."

"Have you ever been in a situation where you are damned if you do and damned if you don't?"

"Yeah. I understand the concept."

"Well, that's where I find myself this morning. I've given this a lot of thought and come down on the side of the equation where I talk to you."

"Alright."

"Let me get through this in my own way. When I get through, you can ask all the questions you want, but I may not be able to answer them." Grady nodded his head in agreement.

"Last night there was a break in of this building and an attempted fire bombing. The bombing was prevented, nobody got hurt and all the suspects are in custody. Earlier in the day, there was a kidnapping of a young girl. The girl is the daughter of a woman with whom I have a relationship. The kidnapping was intended as a diversion, so I would take my eyes off this building while it was firebombed. The young girl was rescued unharmed and the two kidnappers were apprehended."

"My god, is everyone okay?"

"One of the kidnappers shot one of my men. In the arm, through and through, no permanent damage. He's going to have scar, but other than that he'll be okay."

"You said one of your men, not the locals, not the FBI?"

"There was no local law enforcement and there was no FBI." Matt let that sink in for a moment.

"This is a lot to process. I mean kidnapping, attempted murder, burglary, attempted fire bombing, a giant conspiracy to obstruct justice. This is huge. We can bring an indictment against these folks. This is going to be huge."

"No. You can't."

"We can't?"

"No. Think about it for a minute. My people, not the FBI, not local law enforcement but my people."

"You're security guards."

"Yes."

"How in the world?"

"I can't tell you that. Look, prosecution of this matter would be a distraction from your main mission. You don't need this distraction at this point in time."

"That's not for you to say."

"I'm afraid it is. My mission is to keep you, your people, the building and the records safe. That is what I have done. My methods are somewhat unconventional. You probably can't get a conviction on these people. The fruit of the poisonous tree and all that. I didn't have time to play nice. I had to save a little girl and prevent a building from being fire bombed."

"I don't like it. I play by the rules."

"I'm not asking you to break any rules. All I'm telling you is a crime was prevented. That's all you need to know. I am not law enforcement. I am security. I prevent crimes from happening. That's what I do. The FBI's main focus is gathering legally admissible evidence in order to prove each and every element of a criminal offense. My main focus was saving a little girl's life and stopping a building from being fire bombed. Due process is not my strong suit."

"Okay. I can live with that. I don't need to know any of the particulars."

"No. You don't. As long as we are talking about playing by the rules, it's my understanding that you can't tell me who or what you are investigating."

"That's correct."

"But technically, you could tell me if you're not investigating someone."

"I wouldn't want to get in the habit of playing 20 questions."

"Does the name Rex Gunderson mean anything to you?"

"No. Should it? Wait a minute. Let me run his name through our file." Grady turned around to keyboard behind his desk and punched in the name. After a few minutes he turned back.

"No. There is no mention of him anywhere in our file. Who is he?'

"Apparently he is a big time money launderer who was the mastermind behind yesterday's attacks."

"Why?"

"He panicked. Some of the subpoenas you issued got a little too close to home. He thought you were on to him. He decided to run. He needed time to liquidate his assets so he thought he'd slow you down a little bit."

"He was going to fire bomb a building just to slow us down?"

"Well, think about it for a minute. If you had showed up this morning and there was no building, just a smoking pile of rubble, how would that impact your investigation? You'd have to relocate, you'd have to reconstruct you files. You'd basically be starting over. Not to mention the psychological effect this would have on your team. Some might be angry. Some might be concerned for their families. What you tell your people is up to you, but I felt I had an obligation to talk to you."

"Well, I appreciate that even if I can't know all the details. So what you're telling me is, this wasn't sanctioned by some government entity or government employees. It was totally unrelated."

"That's what it looks like now. I'm pretty confident in that conclusion. If that changes, I will let you know."

"So where do we go from here?

"Couple of things. You might want to mention to your people to be extra careful. You know, the if you see something, say something speech."

"Okay. What else?"

"You might want to consider backing up your data, so you wouldn't have to reconstruct the whole thing if something happened."

"Good idea. What do you suggest?"

"My guys are pretty good with computers and security and secrecy. We could handle this if you wanted."

"No risk of disclosure?"

"Absolutely none."

"Okay, but let's play this pretty close to the vest. There is no need to mention this to anyone unless something happens."

"You got it." Matt got up to leave.

"Matt."

"Yeah."

"I'm sorry about your guy getting shot. Please give him my best. And I'm sorry about your friend's daughter being kidnapped. That's just unthinkable. Are you going to be alright?"

"Probably not. We'll just have to wait and see."

Several days later, Agnes stuck her head in Matt's office,

"I'm working with Oster, but it's pretty much a done deal."

"Really?"

"Yeah. Oster has gotten all he's going to get from these guys. They're all telling pretty much the same story. They were recruited by Gunderson, paid upfront, and it was a one time deal. There's a routine flight to Gitmo everyday taking supplies and such. They'll be on it tomorrow. They've been told if they keep their mouths shut and follow the rules, they'll get out in a year. They don't believe it, but they're willing to play along."

"You were able to get permission for this pretty quickly."

"Well, it wasn't so much permission as it was telling people what was going to happen. When you carry an authorization card of a four star in your pocket, people tend to get out of your way."

"So in a year, they all walk away scot free. Doesn't quite seem right."

"No. It doesn't, but it's not about justice. It's about protecting whatever is going on downstairs. The fact that it is only a year is what made this thing work."

"Yeah, I can see that. The army needs to protect itself."

"You talk with Mrs. McCoy yet?"

"Yeah. We had dinner the other night."

"And?"

"And we've mutually agreed it would be better if we didn't see each other for awhile."

"She dumped you, huh?"

"Pretty much." Matt smiled at the familiar tone taken by Agnes.

"I'm sorry Matt. I was hoping she'd get over it."

"Me too. I feel bad for the girls. They didn't do any thing wrong, and now they've lost another male figure in their lives."

"Give it time. You know what they say, 'time wounds all heels."

"Is that what they say?"

"That's what I say, 'cause I make it happen."

"Yes you do."

A week went by and Matt received a phone call.

"Matt, Mr. Franklin is on the line."

"Okay. Put him through."

"Grady, what's up?"

"Matt, I need to talk to you. Can I come up to your office?'

"That's not necessary. I'll come down."

"What, you don't want me to see your office? I thought we were buds."

"It's a mess up here. I'll be right down."

"Okay."

When Matt was seated in Grady's office, he asked,

"So what's up?"

"We had that little chat, you know if you see something, say something. Let's be extra vigilant and all that."

"Yeah."

"Well, one of my assistants, Debbie Brinkman, was over at the courthouse, and she ran into her old supervisor, the Deputy Chief of Criminal. He asked her how she was doing and when she was coming back, the usual stuff, but then he asked her to lunch. He's never asked her to lunch before. He's married, she's married. They don't socialize outside the office. It seemed out of the ordinary."

"How did she leave it?"

"She put him off. Said we were really busy, and if time allowed she'd get back to him."

"Good. When he calls, have her set it up two days in advance. That will give us enough time to set it up."

"You mean if he calls."

"No. I mean when he calls. He's going to call. That thing that just happened, that was unrelated to what you are doing? This ain't that. This is the other thing. The opposition is on the board. They're coming for you now."

"Oh man. I was hoping you were going to say this was nothing."

"Look. She doesn't have to do anything. She doesn't have to wear a wire. She doesn't have to try to draw him out. Just go have lunch and see what he has to say. We'll take care of the rest. It would be helpful if she picked a place that was quiet, not a lot of background noise. You want me to talk to her?"

"No, no. I'll do it. I want to keep this as casual as possible. I don't want her distracted from her job."

"Okay. Two days notice. Keep me posted."

Matt walked directly to Wog's office.

"We got something. I need you to get ready."

"What do you need?"

"Electronic surveillance and a lot of it."

"What's happened?"

"One of the assistants downstairs has been contacted by a coworker who wants to go to lunch."

"Doesn't sound like much."

"He's married, she's married. They don't socialize outside of the office. He's never asked to lunch before. He's her boss at her old office, he'll be her boss when the detail is over."

"Well, when you add in all those details, it might be something."

"It is something. I'm going to flood the restaurant with agents and listening devices. You're going to have to filter it all out and figure out what was said."

"It would be easier if she were wearing a wire."

"She's not doing that. She's just going to lunch and see what the guy has to say. She's not even going to know we're there. I'm going to talk to Malloy. He's going to run the operation. If it turns out to be something, you're going to have to get into this guy. I mean everything, phone, computer, laptop, e-mails, bank records, everything."

"What's his name?"

"I don't know. I'll get you that. It can't be too difficult to figure out. He's the Deputy Chief of Criminal for the D.C. District."

"Damn."

"Yeah, this just got serious."

Sure enough, a couple of days later, Debbie got the call, and she set up a luncheon date at a quiet place not too far from the courthouse. She was able to put him off for a couple of days, but he was persistent. When she arrived, he was already there nursing a glass of iced tea.

"Hey. How's it going?"

"Good. You drinking iced tea?"

"Yeah. I've given up midday drinking. There's too much stuff going on at the office."

"That's probably a good idea." After they had both ordered sandwiches and Debbie had her own iced tea, she asked,

"So how are things back at the office?"

"Same old, same old. You know Mick's got half a dozen people in jail, but Mick's always got a half dozen people in jail. Marty's got a big trial going on, several defendants and some big shot lawyers from out of town."

"That's the investment scam involving guaranteed returns?"

"That's the one."

"I can't believe they are taking that to trial. It seemed like a slam dunk."

"Nothing is ever a slam dunk when high price lawyers are involved. How about you? You guys getting close to wrapping up?"

"Who knows. They said it would be six months, maybe longer. I suspect the latter."

"Really, you don't think you going to be back in six months?"

"I don't know."

"I heard about you guys subpoenaing the Director of the FBI. That was a pretty gutsy move."

"How did you hear about that?"

"The requirement of secrecy runs to the grand jurors and the agents, not the witnesses."

"Yeah, but if the witness is also a federal agent, there is certainly an implied requirement of secrecy."

"I don't think so."

"Agree to disagree."

"Who exactly are you guys looking at?"

"You know I can't answer that."

"Debbie, I'm your boss. I'm automatically on the 6(e) list."

"Not this 6(e) list, and you're technically not my boss while I'm on this detail."

"You won't be on this detail forever. When you come back, I'll be your boss again."

"And when I do, I'll be happy to discuss anything I'm working on, but I can't discuss this."

"Fine. I just thought you might like to have an objective set of ears to discuss complications with. I'm just offering to be a sounding board."

"I appreciate that. I really do, but I can't talk about this outside the task force. That was kind of a condition of taking the job. No leaks."

"Okay. I get it. I can see why a task force investigating leaks wouldn't want to have any leaks." He smiled to try to diffuse the situation.

"If you can't talk about your targets, can you at least talk about the statutes you're looking at?"

"No. I really can't. So how are your kids? Are they both still playing soccer?"

"Yeah. They start up again pretty soon. Yours?"

"No. Mattie's decided she doesn't want to play soccer anymore. She has decided she wants to play softball. Too much running. I think she's lazy like her mom." The conversation veered away from the task force. He offered to walk her back to her office, but she declined saying she had some errands to run. As soon as they parted company, Matt's guys were on him with directional microphones hidden in briefcases and trap and trace scoopers in overhead drones. The guys in the restaurant headed directly to the M Street building and provided what they had to Wog. His programs downloaded everything, filtered out the background noises and within 20 minutes, he had a verbatim transcript of the conversation. Matt walked into Wog's office a few minutes later.

"Well?"

"You were right. He asked for targets. He asked for statutes. He even offered to walk her back. She put him off."

"Good. What about afterwards?""

"He made a phone call. We were only able to pick up his end of the conversation and the number he called. In the future, we can get both ends of the conversation, if you want."

"What do you mean if I want? Who did he call?"

"The Director of the FBI."

"Oh crap. What did he say?"

"Basically that he didn't get anything. I don't know what he was told to do next, but since it is a cell phone, I can find out."

"No. Don't do anything else. Let me talk to Grady and see how he wants to handle this. Is she back yet?"

"Yeah, she just got back. She doubled back on the metro. She wasn't followed. Our guy went back to his office."

"I'll give her a couple of minutes to talk to Grady, and then I'll go down."

"Grady, Mr. Mathews is here."

"Send him on back." Matt passed Debbie on his way to Grady's office. She looked at him like he was something on the bottom of her shoe.

"Come on in. Close the door."

"She doesn't look happy."

"Matt are you following my people?" Matt looked at him for a long moment then nodded his head.

"Yes."

"Why?"

"To see if they are being followed. We're not too concerned when they leave to go home, but we want to know if anyone is following them here from home or from the courthouse. So far we haven't picked up any tails."

"Debbie said she felt like she was being followed. She didn't see anybody, but she just felt like it."

"That happens. My guys might be getting sloppy. I'll have a talk with them and have them back off a bit."

"So you were right. This was a direct approach. He asked about targets. He asked what charges were being considered and he even tried to find out our location. But you knew all that, right?"

"Yes."

"Do I want to know how?"

"No."

"Okay."

"He made a phone call as soon as she was out of sight. Do you want to know who he called?"

"I'm not sure. Do I?"

"Well, in my line of work, knowledge is power. What you do with that knowledge demonstrates wisdom."

"Who did he call?"

"The Director of the FBI."

"Oh man. I knew that subpoena was going to come back to bite me. Sorry, I shouldn't have said that. Forget that."

"Forget what?"

"Thank you."

"My line of work involves a certain amount of discretion. Some times it is just as important what you don't say as what you do."

"So I can trust you?"

"Absolutely."

"Good, I need to talk this through, and I don't want to involve my staff."

"Okay. Tell me what you are thinking."

"Well, I can put this guy before the grand jury and ask him if he asked about targets, statutes and location. If he says no, he commits perjury. If he says yes, he's looking at obstruction. If he made a cell phone call, it's out there. We can subpoena those records as well."

"Let me play devil's advocate for a second."

"Okay."

"Your first instinct is to prosecute the bad guys. That's what you do. My first instinct is to stop the bad guys before they do something bad. That's what I do. Take a step back. Have any laws been broken yet? He asked some questions, but he didn't get any answers. I know you could argue that just inserting himself into the operation is an attempt to distract you from your mission. But is that a prosecutable offense? Probably not. How you react to this situation could be more of a distraction. You need to focus on your mission. The important thing is that we stop this attack not that you find more targets to prosecute."

"What do you suggest?"

"Let me send a couple of my guys over to talk to this guy. What's his name, Sizemore?"

"Yeah, John Sizemore. He's the Deputy Chief of Criminal for the D.C. District."

"We can talk to him on your behalf. Let him know there's a subpoena out there. Keep your people out of it. You can always up the ante if you want later on. Remember the goal is not to win this battle. The goal is to get the other guy to quit playing."

"That sounds smart. I need to go talk to the Director. It's not enough to get Sizemore to quit. I need to take the Director off the playing field as well."

"Agreed. Just be careful. It sounds like this guy is a snake, if he's willing to obstruct justice of an investigation into obstructing justice by his predecessor."

"Ironic, huh?"

"Yeah." As Matt was walking out of the office, Grady was telling Beverly to get him an appointment to see the Director of the FBI today. It didn't matter what time, but it had to be today. If she had to go through the A.G. to do it, that was okay.

Matt walked directly to Wog's office.

"Wog, who we got we can use as U.S. Marshals today?"

"What do you need?"

"I am going to send them to talk to this Sizemore character."

"Send Doyle and Simmons. They're both in suits and ties today. They look the part."

"Okay. Wog, I think our guys might have gotten burned today. We're getting sloppy. You need to have them tighten up."

"Have Malloy do it. They have to listen to him. They don't have to listen to me."

"Wog, when did anybody in this unit not listen to you, including me?"

"Boss, this casual civilian thing you've got going for our undercover identity is fine for a couple of weeks, but we're going to be here six months or more. These guys need discipline. They need a command structure. Everybody got a little jumpy when we got shot at. You need to reign them in. This is a long term op and we can't get caught."

"You're right. I'll talk to Malloy. He can reign them in, and then I'll have a meeting at the Fort to reinforce the message. I'll meet with the night staff here separately. I'll get Oster to institute more of a command structure at the Fort. That should help."

"Good. Boss, I don't think our guys messed up. From what I could tell, she got jumpy when the guy offered to walk her back to the office. She was fine up until then. She put him off like a pro, but after that she got jumpy."

"Okay." Matt went off to brief Doyle and Simmons on how he wanted them to play it. After he sent them on their way, he went to see Malloy about backing off on the surveillance. There was no excuse for getting burned when every target was carrying a cell phone with a GPS tracker and the drones were in play. Malloy had to remind his people that the object was not to follow the AUSA's and the agents, but to see if someone else was following them.

"Mr.Sizemore. There are two gentlemen here to see you from the Marshal's Service. They say they don't have an appointment, but only need a few minutes of your time. They also said they were willing to wait as long as necessary."

"Curious. Did they say what this is about?"

"No sir."

"Alright. I'll be right out." A few minutes later Sizemore appeared at the front desk.

"Hi, I'm John Sizemore, what can I do for you folks?"

"Is there somewhere we could speak in private, sir?"

"What's this all about?"

"We would prefer to speak in private, sir."

"Oh. Alright. Come on back." The door buzzed open and the two 'agents' followed Sizemore down a long hallway to a corner office with a spectacular view of D.C.

"So what's this all about?'

"Do you mind if we close the door, sir?"

"Fine."

"We've been assigned to a task force that is looking into irregularities involving the 2016 presidential election."

"Okay."

"Today you had lunch with one of the attorneys on that task force, Debbie Brinkman."

"Yeah, Debbie worked for me before she was assigned to the task force."

"Did you ask her the names of the people under investigation by the task force?"

"Look, there is nothing wrong with having lunch with a colleague."

"No sir, we didn't say there was. Did you ask her the names of the people under investigation?"

"Private conversations between employees of the U.S. Attorney's Office are just that, private. I'm not going to discuss the nature of my conversation with my employees."

"We only have four questions. Did you ask the names of the targets of the grand jury investigation? Did you ask what statutes were being considered and did you attempt to ascertain the location of the task force by offering to walk her back?"

"That's only three?"

"The fourth question was who sent you?" There was a short silence as the implications of those questions sank in.

"If you're not going to answer our questions, we won't take up any more of you time." The agent looked at his watch, made a note and they both got up to leave.

"One other thing, Mr. Franklin said to tell you if we came back, we would have a piece of paper for you. He didn't tell us what it was, but he said you would understand." The two 'agents' left his office, walked down the hallway and exited the building. Sizemore sat there thinking. I wonder if she was wearing a wire. If I call her, her phone is probably tapped. Is my phone tapped? We were probably under surveillance. Am I under surveillance now? That was less than two hours ago. How did they put this together so quickly?

While Sizemore was stewing in his own juices, Grady Franklin was sitting outside the office of the Director of the FBI.

"Mr. Franklin, come on in. This is Stanley Berger. He's chief legal counsel for the bureau. I've asked him to sit in on our meeting."

"That's fine. I just wanted to come over and introduce myself. I'm afraid we may have gotten off on the wrong foot, what with the subpoena and all."

"No problem. That has all been resolved to your satisfaction I hope."

"Yes. It was very helpful. I just wanted to make sure you understand we're all on the same side. We are just trying to make sure that justice is done."

"Of course."

"You know what they say, sometimes the cover-up is worse than the crime."

"So what can I do for you today?"

"I just wanted to ask you one question. Did you receive a phone call today from John Sizemore, the Deputy Chief of Criminal for the DC District?"

"I receive lots of phone calls every day."

"That's why I wanted to talk to you today while it was still fresh in your mind. This would have been about two hours ago, 1:17 pm to be exact."

The attorney noticing the deflection of the question by the director decided to step in.

"What's this all about Mr. Franklin. You come here demanding details of a phone conversation between two Justice Department employees? I think you may be acting outside of your mandate."

"I'm not demanding anything. I just asked a simple yes or no question. Did you receive a phone call from Mr. Sizemore, the Deputy Chief of Criminal for the DC District. You see the reason that I asked the question is because Mr. Sizemore had a luncheon meeting today with one of the Assistants assigned to the grand jury investigation of corruption at the FBI and elsewhere. This was a meeting he requested by the way. He asked the Assistant the names of the targets of the grand jury investigation. He also asked what statutes the grand jury was considering and he tried to ascertain the location of the task force. Immediately after that meeting, he made a phone call on his cell phone. You guys being with the FBI and all, probably know that if you know the date, the time and the location of the cell phone along with the cell phone number, it's an easy matter to determine what number was called. That information can be obtained with a subpoena, if necessary. What's not quite so simple is obtaining a transcript of the actual conversation. That would require the approval from the Attorney General. The same Attorney General that you two gentlemen work for and the same Attorney General that established the task force in the first place. So before we get our feathers too ruffled about me exceeding my mandate, let's stop and think a minute whether or not we want to bump this up to the next level and ask the Attorney General whether or not that question is outside my mandate." The silence was deafening as both men considered the implication of what they had just heard.

"Look guys, I'm not trying to be a prick here. If I were, I would have brought a subpoena with me. If I were, I would not have come here at all. I would have gone straight to the A.G. and sent somebody else here with the subpoena. I came here as a man to look you in the eye and say one thing. Stop! If you don't, you are going to see what me being a prick looks like. I don't want to take up anymore of your valuable time so I'll show myself out."

"Damn."

"I can't believe that idiot called me on his cell phone."

"What did you think he was going to do? Run over to a drug store and buy a burner? He's an AUSA not a spook. Everybody calls everybody on their cell phones. Paper trails are created on every conversation."

"He could have waited until he got back to the office and called on his land line."

"Coulda, woulda, shouda. I can't believe you sent him in the first place. Wait a minute. Don't say anything else. I don't represent you. I represent the Bureau. Anything you say to me regarding criminal conduct is not protected by the attorney client privilege. If you need legal advice in this matter, you need to obtain your own attorney. I will give you one piece of free legal advice. Don't mess with that guy. He is serious. Take his advice and stop. He came here with an olive branch, not a sword. I have no doubt that olive branch will turn into a sword in a heartbeat if you continue to mess with him. Somebody's going down. Just make sure it ain't you. Oh, one more thing. Don't call me to sit in on any more of your off the book operations. I'm not involved."

A short time later, the Director received a phone call from John Sizemore.

"I am sorry, the Director is not available."

"Did you tell him who was calling?"

"Yes. He said he is not available and will not be available in the near future. Would you like to leave a message?"

"No. No message."

Southern Baptist

"Matt."

"Yeah."

"We've got an intruder on the fourth Floor."

"What? How did he get there?"

"I don't know. I'll have to check the tapes, but he is definitely there."

"Send Bradley. He looks the least intimidating." Bradley wearing a blue Blazer and looking for all the world like a security officer stepped off the elevator.

"Excuse me sir. Can I help you?"

"I was just looking for an office."

"Whose office are you looking for?"

"I'm not sure of his name, but it is a government office."

"Well, come with me. Maybe I can help you out." Bradley led the way to a security office at the end of the hallway. Inside was a battered table and couple of chairs. Bradley took a contact form off a shelf as if this happened every day.

"So what is your name?"

"Martin. Jim Martin."

"Who do you work for Mr. Martin?"

"I'm pretty much free lance. I'm currently on assignment for SNN."

"You're a reporter?"

"Yes."

"Do you have any identification?" Martin handed over a press credential for Satellite Network News.

"You have a drivers license or anything with your picture on it?" Martin started to get huffy when Bradley took a picture of both on the id's with his cell phone.

"Look you said you were going to help me."

"I am. What government agency are you trying to contact?"

"Department of Government Resources."

"You say you can't remember the name of the person that you had an appointment with?"

"I didn't actually have an appointment. I just thought I'd show up and see who I could talk to."

"Do you have a card? Maybe I could have some one get in touch with you." Martin handed over a card.

"Can I give them any idea of what you want to talk about?"

"The Department of Government Resources is in the process of reviewing all areas of the government in anticipation of downsizing. I'm trying to get a handle on that for a story I'm doing."

"That department is located in a different building. Why are you here?"

"I've heard that some of those displaced employees are coming here. I was hoping to get their perspective for my story."

"I see. Well I'll see if I can get someone to talk to you on the record. The truth is these employees are a bit concerned about their future and they may not want to mess it up by talking with a reporter. I'll see if I can get someone to get back to you. Why don't we go down to the front desk and I'll have them take all your particulars for future reference." Bradley led the reporter downstairs to the front desk and left his information with the security guard. The implication was not lost on the security guard.

Matt, Wog and Bradley sat in Matt's office.

"So we don't know how he found out about this building?"

"No. I didn't want to push and make him any more suspicious."

"That was a good call. We'll have to look into that. We don't know how he got up there." Wog jumped in,

"That we do know. I reviewed the tapes. He walked in with a group from the second floor. He got off the elevator with them then turned around like he got off on the wrong floor. When they went in, he went to the stairwell and walked up two flights to the fourth floor."

"That door is supposed to be electronically sealed."

"Looks like somebody left it open, maybe to catch a smoke, and it didn't get reclosed all the way."

"We're going to have to fix that as well. Get your people on that so it closes properly and if it doesn't, an alarm shows here. I'll talk to the guards downstairs and I'll touch base with the tenants to ask them to be a little more vigilant. Bradley, you did a good job getting him out of here before any damage was done. But this is on us. Nobody is supposed to get to the fourth floor. What really concerns me is how did he know to come here?"

"You think our GSA leasing agent is selling the information more than once?"

"No. He doesn't know about the Office of Employee Development. All he knows is that there were some extraordinary security measures in the build out. He may know about the tenants on the second floor, but I doubt it. He damn sure doesn't know about us or the tenants on the fourth floor. This has to be coming from somewhere else. Send our guys back to talk to him just to be sure. I'm going to have to talk to the fourth floor." Matt went down to the front desk and assured the security guard that he wasn't going to be fired, but asked that he be a little more vigilant in checking visitors to the building. It was difficult, because the fourth floor had a constantly growing cast of characters. Matt touched base with

Grady and explained the situation to him. Grady was understandably concerned in light of recent events, but there wasn't much his people could have done differently. Matt then made the call to the fourth floor.

"Could I speak to Mr. Parson please?"

"Undersecretary Parson is in a meeting right now. Can I take a message and have him get back to you?

"Sure, this Bill Mathews. I'm the head of security and I need to talk to with him about a possible breach of security."

"Hold on."

"This is Parson."

"Undersecretary Parson, this is Bill Mathews. I'm…"

"I know who you are. You can call me Mr. Parson. My secretary has been directed to be officious when dealing with the government hierarchy. Sometimes lieutenants think they're majors, and majors think they're colonels."

"I understand completely sir."

"I'm sure you do. So what have we got?"

"There was an intruder on the fourth floor today. He was intercepted by one of my people and politely removed from the floor. He came in with a group from the second floor, got off the elevator with them and then turned around like he got off on the wrong floor. When they went inside, he ducked into the stairwell and walked up two flights to your floor. The door wasn't completely latched. We think somebody went out that door, maybe to have a smoke and left the door open so they could get back in. They changed their mind and rode the elevator up and never re-latched the door. The guy's a reporter with SNN. Name is Jim Martin, we have his card. He said he was looking for the Office of Government Resources, not specifically the Office of Employee Development. We told him that department was in a different building. He said he heard some of the displaced employees were ending up here. We told him we would try to get someone to get back to him."

"So, this is a lot to take in. Let me see if I've got this straight. The fact that your security protocols were breached is not my problem."

"No sir."

"The fact that one of my employees was able to leave the damn door unlatched is not really my problem either. Although I'm going to fix it."

"No sir, it's not."

"The problem is somebody knows we're here."

"Yes sir. That's the way I see it."

"So, you're the head of security. What do you suggest?"

"I'm not sure, but from the brief conversation that we had, it sounds like somebody from the other office put him on to you. It doesn't sound like this came from your people. He didn't mention the Office of Employee Development. He said Office of Government Resources. It could be a disgruntled employee.

You know one that you interviewed who didn't make the cut. Or it could be somebody at the other office who doesn't like the fact that you have 'favored nation' status."

"You seem to know an awful lot about my operation for a security guard."

"Not at all sir. All I know is I'm supposed to keep your operation secret and keep the general public off the fourth floor. I've talked to the guards on the first floor and they are going to be a little more vigilant, so your employees can expect more scrutiny. I've talked to the second floor and they will be a little more vigilant. I'm assuming you will talk to your people and they will be more vigilant. My people are going to be tightening the controls on the electronic locking devices in the stairwells. All of that doesn't solve the problem of how did this guy know, what does he know, who else knows, and where is the leak?"

"We're back to that?"

"What I suggest is that you send someone to talk to him. Not you, but one of your subordinates. Someone with a great gift for BS. Someone who can give him a great deal of words without really saying anything. Give him a lot of copy for his article or newscast or whatever but stuff straight out of the PR manual. Stuff he could have gotten if he bothered to read the literature put out by your shop. At the same time your guy is flooding him with information and becoming his best buddy, he slips in a few questions to find out what the guy knows and how he found out. Have you got somebody like that?"

"Oh yeah. I've got just the guy. I may get back to you on this if we need to kick it around some more."

"I'll help out any way I can."

"Okay. Thanks."

Samuel Parson went to find his guy and briefed him on what he wanted him to do. The importance of the mission couldn't be overstated because everybody knew if what they were doing was discovered, they would be shut down. He then returned to the office of Judith Sams, where he was receiving her briefing when he got the phone call.

"So where were we?"

"I was telling you about our efforts so far in Charlotte."

"The two of you are working the entire state of North Carolina?"

"No. We're working the northern half from Charlotte up. Raleigh, Greensboro, Fayetteville and Ashville. Another group is going to take the southern half, Columbia, Wilmington and Charleston. The plan is to focus on the larger population areas first and then spread out to the smaller towns."

"You are currently working in Charlotte?"

"Yes."

"And what are your results so far?"

"We've got one on board, two maybes and a fourth who we really like."

"Tell me about them."

"Well, the one who is on board is old. He likes the idea and we're going to work with him, but I'm not sure he can pull it off. He's old and just doesn't have the energy. The two who are on the fence are also old. They like the idea but aren't sure they want to get involved in something like this. The fourth guy is younger. He likes the idea, but hasn't committed yet. He's thinking it over. If he buys in, he will make it work. You know that fire in the eye that you saw in me? I see it in him. He wants to change the world just like I do. Mr. Parson, I'm not that religious. I went to church with my grandma, and I still go now, but I don't have the fire in my belly that some people have. I go because it makes me feel good to go. I feel a little bit guilty that we are using religion to change the social order. But not so guilty that I'm not willing to do it. The notion that a family should be a two parent proposition is a good one. I feel strongly that the government has stolen our African American heritage by promoting the single parent family. It's the carrot and the stick approach. We are providing day care to two parent families and not providing day care to single parent families in the hopes we can change conduct. Maybe it will work and maybe it won't. I feel like I have to at least try. This is something that will take twenty years before we know whether or not we had an impact. If it works, it will be the most moral thing that any small group of people has ever done. If it doesn't work, we will at least know we tried."

"So where is James with all of this?"

"He's the admin guy. He's doing all the research on state and county regulations for day care centers. The licensing requirements, insurance, fire and safety codes, all that. He is also locating foundation and grant money for diapers, food, cleaning supplies, whatever we need. I'm the people person. I work with the ministers and the church ladies who will actually be running the show. Although James seems to do well with them as well. They like him because he is shy, and for some reason they like that. They don't care about changing the world. They are just thrilled with the prospect of introducing a child to Christianity."

"Are they going to be a problem?"

"Maybe. The ministers are on board. They see the big picture. From their point of view, it is a win win. They are providing a valuable service to the community and they are changing the world. The church ladies just see the day care. They don't see it as a means to an end. Changing the African American culture is above their pay grade."

"How do we fix that?"

"I don't know. It's amazing to me how many people are invested in the welfare state. They expect it. The government owes them this and they are going to get it. They don't see that the government is giving them something with one hand and taking something away with the other."

"It's hard to overcome seventy years of institutional training. It's going to take time."

"I guess. Back to you original question, I think I have to work on the ministers. I have to convince them to convince the church ladies. If they preach to the church ladies that they are doing something special and he is counting on them, maybe they will get on board."

"Sounds like a plan. Let me know if it works and we'll try it elsewhere. What about you other cities?

"We've got a day care operating in Raleigh and one in Greensboro. They're just small, just a couple of kids each, but we expect them to grow. It took a lot of pounding the pavement and a lot of rejection just to get one. We thought just getting somebody to say yes was the hard part. Turns out there is a lot of work involved in coordinating these things."

"You're leaving today?"

"Yeah, we're going to make the rounds. We've kind of got a system set up. We touch base with the one on board, find out what they need, handle the admin details and try to contact at least two other churches. We then move to the next city. We try to do this all in a week, but we can see that's going to change. James and I have adopted a philosophy that it's more important to do this right than to have a bunch of day cares. Don't get me wrong. The volume will come, and we know that. We just want to grow slowly so we make sure the program works. We want to provide the backup services that these people need to be successful. That's why we're here today. James has some paper work to do on foundation and grant requests and some licensing requirements. A big part of what we do is teach people how to deal with government bureaucrats. If you make a bureaucrat feel like he is the most important person in the world, he will leave you alone. If you challenge their authority, they will have to prove how powerful they are. The trick is to convince the bureaucrat that you are partners. You want to run the safest and most compliant day care in the world, and you need their help to do that."

"You're creating con artists."

"What's that old adage? The two biggest lies in the world: when the inspector says 'I'm here to help' and the person being inspected says 'and I'm glad you're here'. We like to think we're changing the narrative and making both of those statements true. The fact that we're getting what we want, is just a side benefit."

"Maybe I should have you two put on a seminar for some of my less successful operatives."

"No. We don't have any magic formula. You just keep trying and see what works. The key is the minister. If you can get him on board, everything else just falls into place. It seems to me the most important thing is identifying the right minister. It is difficult to define, but you'll know it when you see it. They all know that we are right, that reclaiming the African American family is a righteous cause. Not all of them are willing to participate in that cause. Everyone has their own vested interest. Some are reluctant to listen to outside influence. Some are stuck in the status quo. Some are just too arrogant to listen. Others are afraid to buck the system. Every once in a while, you see a spark, as if the guy has been waiting for someone to have this idea. There's a light bulb that comes on. Yeah, we can change the world and I can be a part of it. There's no glory in it. It will be slow. You can't change seventy years of institutional entitlement mentality overnight. We don't have to change the minds of the masses. We just have to let the ministers change the minds of a few. It's a start. It will grow. Word will spread that if you get married, there's free day care in the basement of the Mt. Auburn Baptist Church. Some will scoff at it. Others will think about it. We can't change what has already happened, but we can affect what is about to happen. Our market is the 17 to 20 year old group. Those people who haven't yet become addicted to the welfare handout. It's easy to say I want to support my family. It's hard to turn down free government money."

"You realize there is a sense of urgency. Even though this is a long term plan. Twenty years before we see any results. We have to plant the seeds before we are discovered. Once the churches are running the program, the government won't be able to shut them down. The same principle that would allow the ACLU to shut us down, will protect the churches from attack. If they want to provide day care to married couples, there is nothing the government can do about it. That is why it is so important that we follow all the licensing and regulation requirements and establish a relationship with these people. That way white society won't be able to shut the day cares down on some technicality."

"The beauty of this is we're doing this right under their noses and they don't even know we're doing it."

"That may be a motivating factor for you, but I have to look at the big picture. If we get caught, we have to dismantle the organization and move to a foundation. It will slow us down immensely and we'll be starting from scratch. A foundation just won't have the resources and structure of the federal government. We'll have to build it. We can get the money from foundations, but I would rather spend it on diapers and formula than salaries, hotel rooms and per diem."

"Well then let's not get caught. What about lawyers if the churches face legal challenges?"

"I'm working on that behind the scenes. We have a cadre of pro bono lawyers that have provided research and legal memorandums supporting the churches right to run day care for married couples only. It would be better if the lawyers were local and supporting their local churches, but we can't ask them to work for free and we can't burden the churches with legal bills. We will have to funnel some money to the attorneys through some innocuous sounding foundation. We're hoping it doesn't come to that, but we have to be prepared if it does."

"What about legal challenges to us? Are you prepared to go to court to defend the Department of Employee Development?"

"No. If we are challenged, we fold up our tents and run away. If we are discovered, the department will be dissolved. We'll form later as a foundation and try again."

"Sounds cold."

"It is."

"All of these people that you recruited will be out of a job."

"You knew that coming in. The government can't support Christianity."

"If we succeed, we will be working ourselves out of a job in five years or so."

"Hopefully. If the program is successful, the day cares will run themselves. There will be some foundations pop up that will help out, but our mission of getting it started will be over. The goal as you well know is to have the success of one day care generate other day cares. The idea that is being promoted is not day care but the Christian ideal of a two parent family. That's why the pastors are so important. Once they realize that young couples are joining their congregations, they are going to be thrilled. Young people aren't going to get married just so they can get free day care. Young couples who are married, who can get free day care are going to take advantage of it. The word will spread and there will be some whose decisions are influenced by the program. That is the ultimate goal. To change the mind set."

"I can't believe that I am part of this. It seems so overwhelming what we are attempting to do. So risky."

"What's the down side? All these people have to go find another job? So what? They'll all land on their feet. I'll make sure of it. What's the up side? We get to change the world. We get to start the process that allows the African American community to reclaim its family heritage. That's pretty heady stuff. When you get to the end of the journey, and you look back and say I did that, you've got to be pretty impressed with yourself. I've got some ideas that I want to run by you in the future. I want to set up training programs, employment opportunities and networking programs in the local communities. My goal is to goose this program a little bit to make sure it works. You'll have to find out what is available and what is needed. You'll have to spend some time with the young couples to find out what their skill sets are, what their interests are and what we can do to help out. My idea is to run this through a foundation here in DC. My job will be to find the donors. Your job will be to find the local resources that we can tap in to for training and job placement. But we are getting ahead of ourselves. First you need to set up some day cares."

"Okay. We'll be leaving shortly."

Wildfire

The intercom in Matt's office buzzed.

"Matt."

"Yeah."

There's a Carl Lowenstein on the line for you."

"Who?"

"Carl Lowenstein. He said he can only talk to you."

"Okay. Put him through."

"Colonel Mathews?"

"Yes."

"This is Carl Lowenstein. I have been instructed by our mutual friend to contact you."

"What mutual friend would that be?"

"The one who refers to go by color."

"Okay. Do you have a secure phone number?"

"Yes."

"Give me that number and I'll call you back." Lowenstein rattled off a series of numbers and Matt wrote them down. He disconnected the call and walked down the hall to Wog's office.

"Wog, I need a secure line to this number. Can you set it up in my office?" Matt handed the piece of paper to Wog. The first two numbers and the last two numbers had been circled. The significance was not lost on Wog. He reversed the sequence of numbers on the paper and said,

"It'll just take me a few minutes to set up the equipment." When everything was set up, Matt placed the call.

"Mr. Lowenstein?"

"Yes."

"Sorry for the delay. It took a few minutes to set up the secure link. What can I do for you?"

"I was told you could get some specialized equipment that I need."

"Okay."

"Do you have a drone that can fly over a computer and extract all the information from that computer without ever being attached to the computer?"

"Whoa. When you said specialized equipment, I thought you meant directional microphones, video surveillance, that sort of thing."

"That equipment is commercially available for the right price. What I am talking about is not."

"No kidding. What you are talking about is breaking and entering and theft. Such equipment, if it did exist, would be highly classified." There was a moment of silence on the line.

"Were you instructed to help me out or not?"

"I was."

"Do you need approval from a superior to provide this particular piece of equipment?"

"No. My superior does not want me asking permission. He wants me making the decisions."

"Do you need some time to consider your decision?"

"No. What the hell? This job just keeps getting better and better."

"Had a rough week?"

"It's been an interesting couple of weeks. We've been busy."

"Well, I won't take up any more of your time than necessary."

"No, no. It's fine. We're kind of calmed down now. Let me explain the situation to you. The equipment is proprietary to my unit. We designed it, we built it, and as far as I know, we are the only ones who have it. If it is even discovered that such a thing exists, there will be hell to pay. So you can see why I am reluctant to let it out of my possession. The key is the algorithm that we designed. I put together the basic program, but my guys refined it. I've got some guys working for me that are way smarter than me. We basically took a sniffer program and welded it to a WIFI interface and powered it with a brute force cyber key and attached a random cipher key. In other words, once we break in, it only takes a matter of minutes to down load the data. We may be able to break in quickly or it may take up to fifteen minutes. It just depends on how securely the computer is protected. Also, the data may be encrypted which means the data will be brought back and run through a Cray system. There's no telling how long that will take."

"You have a Cray?"

"Access to a Cray, but only for national security emergencies. I don't think you're going to run in to that kind of problem."

"No. I wouldn't think so. My applications are personal home computers. I'm in LA. Is that a problem?"

"No. We can get it out to you. The drone has to be stationary during the incursion so a nighttime attack is the best to keep the drone from being detected. With a remote data extraction, there are a lot of variables, including weather, power lines, metal in the building, dead zones, other WIFI interference, you name it. There are dozens of things that can go wrong. Once the door is open and the link is established, we can get what we need pretty quickly."

"What about putting data into a computer?"

"Well, that's a whole other thing. It's one thing to take a peek at information. It's a whole other thing to plant evidence of a crime that wasn't committed. We don't do that. The military has no application for such action. We want to know what the enemy is going to do before he does it so we can counter it. We don't have a need to put false information into the enemy's computer."

"What about sending the troops to a wrong location or at the wrong time or false coordinates for a missile strike. Wouldn't that have military applications?"

"Yes, but you'd only get to do it one time. The enemy would catch on and it probably wouldn't work anyway. There are too many checks and balances in a military command structure to plant false attack orders. It just wouldn't work on any type of large scale command structure."

"So you have thought about it?"

"We're getting into classified areas here. I'm not comfortable talking about what the military may or may not have thought about."

"Okay. Fair enough. Let's get back to my problem. Is it possible to download images to a computer remotely using your technology?"

"Possible yes. Likely no. Theoretically, once a door is open, you can walk in or you can walk out. That's where the analogy ends. What we are doing by extracting data is like going to a stream and scooping up a bucket of pebbles and bringing them home so we can sort through the bucket for the one we want. Down loading the data into a computer would be akin to going back to that stream and putting that one pebble in the right place without disturbing the other pebbles and not letting the water move it. The drone would have to be completely still during the entire process. Inserting a document, or a file or an image would be a pain staking process, and it would take time. Even if you could do it, which is highly unlikely, it would never stand up in court. A forensic computer expert would find it in a heartbeat."

"I'm not planning on going to court."

"Oh. Well in that case, you can try it. If you get caught, you're on your own. They'll put you under the jail and throw away the key. When do you need it?

"Tomorrow."

"No can do. It will be at least a week before we can get it to you. My guys will have to build it from our existing components. The software is ours, but the hardware is cobbled together from several sources. We'll test it, get the bugs out and fly it out to you."

"Okay. I need it in a week then."

"My guys will bring it out, show your guys how to use it and then turn it over to you. My guys won't be involved in your operation in any way."

"Understood."

"How long do you think you'll need it?"

"Not long. A couple of months, maybe longer. We only have a couple of targets that we have not been able to penetrate. All the others are well in hand. I plan to wrap my operation up within the next few months."

"You'll have to turn it back over to us when you're done."

"Understood."

"There's one other thing. There will be a self-destruct feature included. I hope you don't have to use it, because if you do, we'll all be running for the hills."

"Roger that."

"Okay. I'll call you back in a few days on that same secure line and let you know the details."

"Let me give you another number. Call on that number first and say your food order is ready. I'll set up the secure link and you can call back in five minutes."

"Okay. Good."

Matt looked up to see Agnes standing in his doorway.

"Is this guy Lowenstein going to be a problem?"

"No. He just wants to borrow some equipment. I'm going to need military transport. Two of my guys and a large case will need to travel to LA, and the MP's can't look in the case."

"I can set that up. When do you need to go?"

"I'm not sure. It will be at least a couple of days from now. Let me talk to Wog and I'll get back to you. They'll need a van and hotel accommodations. We'll bill it to All Tech and keep it off the military books. Other than the flight out and back, they'll be off base."

"Okay. I'll see what's available." Matt walked down to Wog's office.

"Wog, I need you to get together with Max and set up a sniffer drone."

"We've got two that are operational now."

"This one can't have any serial numbers or anything else that trace back to the military or us."

"You want to tell me what's going on?"

"No. I don't know what's going on. All I know is I was told to provide this guy with equipment if he asked, and this is what he asked for. We'll build it out, test it and send our guys out to California to show them how to use it. Our guys will not be involved in their operation. Our guys will go back out and get it when they are done. One more thing, I want a self destruct mechanism so we can fry the components remotely if necessary."

"That's not going to do us much good if we turn it over to them. We won't know if it's been compromised."

"What go you suggest?"

"I don't know let me think about it."

"While you're thinking on it, get Max started on the build out. Remember no trace to us."

"Boss, you know this is classified technology. If we get caught, we all get court-martialed."

"Well, let's make sure we don't get caught."

Four days later, the testing was complete, none of the components could be traced back, and a self-destruct mechanism with a back door fail-safe was installed. A series of commands could be relayed to the base station which would turn the sniffer into an ordinary drone and even the most sophisticated technician wouldn't be able to figure out what the drone had once been. Agnes arranged transport for the two technicians and their cargo. They spent two days in LA. They returned on military transport.

Carl Lowenstein went to see his two technicians who were operating the drone.

"So how's it working out?"

"Just like advertised. Once we establish a link, the extraction of the data is pretty quick. Establishing the link is a little tricky. The drone has to hold perfectly still for a few minutes, but we've done a few practice runs and it worked just fine."

"So are you going in tonight?"

"Yeah. We're going to try it on the guy in the Hollywood Hills tonight and that other guy up north tomorrow. The weather looks right for both nights. These are the only two computers we haven't been able to get into here due to the security. After that, we are taking it on the road. There are several professors we haven't been able to get to, not because of security, but because there are always people in the house. There are only a half dozen, but with travel time, we're probably looking at several weeks."

"Okay. Don't rush, take your time, do it right. Hand off the data to the local team and get back here. I'm going to need your help coordinating the timing of this thing. It's crucial that we hit everybody at the same time for maximum effect."

"You know boss, this wasn't nearly as hard as we thought it was going to be. A lot of these guys are going to be arrested. We thought we would be entrapping these guys and using illegally obtained evidence, but that wasn't the case at all. Most of these guys had two prior instances of predisposition to be involved in this type of conduct, so we didn't have to entrap them. Jack Livingston set the whole thing up based on his time in the Bureau and these guys fell right into the mold. We've got 17 here in Hollywood and another 28 college professors. There are just a few we had to entrap. Most of these cases are legitimate sting operations."

"I know, but prosecution isn't our end game. We want everybody running for the hills including those people we didn't target. In order to do that we've got to have maximum exposure followed by innuendo, paranoia and guilt by association. We need to run a smear campaign against all the targets. We need to drop hints, gossip and use social media. I'll need you two to handle this campaign and it has to be coordinated for maximum effect. The arrests are just the opening salvo. What comes next is the important part. We don't care about convictions. We want to drag this thing out as long as possible. We want everybody looking over their shoulder. We want them to think their phones are tapped. We want them to think there are informers at work. The only way to stop this KGB program is to scare their assets to death."

"You know boss that list we got from the CIA is pretty accurate. I mean these guys are dirt bags. They were easy to catch. These guys were so sleazy that they didn't think twice about going after young kids."

"That's because they've been getting away with it for so long. They are arrogant. The whole gay rights, transgender thing has gone main stream. It's cool to celebrate an alternative life style and to look down on traditional marriage."

"So are we really accomplishing anything by taking out a few dirt bags with a kiddie porn sting?"

"Maybe not. It may be too late. We'll at least have the satisfaction of knowing we rolled up a KGB network that was started over 50 years ago. The CIA should have rolled this thing up 20 years ago, but they didn't, so here we are. I think the people who are actively promoting the gay, lesbian, transgender lifestyle on our college campuses and in Hollywood will keep quiet for a while. We won't stop it, but we may slow it down for a while."

"Maybe if there isn't a strong movement pushing this agenda, people will come to embrace family values."

"That's what we are hoping, but we at least get to spit in the KGB's eye. Is Jack running the show tonight?"

"Yeah, he's pretty much doing all the raids out here. He set up the script and the teams back east are handling their own raids. They're kind of doing double duty. They handle protection of the asset during the undercover, then switch to agents and handle the raid. The raid is the easy part. They just pretend to be cops serving a search warrant. The hard part is 'Stanley Goldfarb.' That guy should get an Oscar."

"Yeah, he's pretty good. I hope we are not over playing our hand on that one. We need to have about half the cases result in real arrests in order to make the scam work."

"Jack's got that under control. Everyone is coordinating their cases through him. He's sorting the cases and deciding which ones will be turned over to law enforcement and which ones will just be used as informants. It's going to be pretty close to half. Still, 'Stanley Goldfarb' has a lot of clients. We're helping him keep everything straight by creating files on all the clients and cross-referencing other participants. A lot of these guys know each other. There is more of a network than we realized. When the KGB set this thing up years ago, it was independent. Over the years, these guys just naturally gravitated towards each other. You know birds of a feather and all that. The Hollywood types all know each other and the college professors know a lot of their counterparts as well. There doesn't seem to be any connection between the professors and Hollywood. That part of the network seems to have maintained its independence. There may be some connections, but we haven't seen them yet."

"Okay. I'm headed east. I'm going to check in with the various teams and see what their status is. I know I could do this by phone, but I want see the operations in person get a feel for the lay of the land."

"You know boss, we're headed east too. We've got a half dozen computers to hit. That could change if the local teams get a chance to do a sneak and peek. We plan to end up in Virginia. We could drop this equipment off in DC. It would save those guys a trip out here."

"Good idea. Let me know when you're ready to make the drop and I'll set it up. Just be careful driving this stuff around. We don't want some local getting curious."

"No problem. This stuff is packed up as electronic components. We're electronic technicians delivering equipment to All Tech Security. Very expensive and very delicate. I doubt if some local is going to want to pop open the crates and even if he does, he wouldn't know what he is looking at."

"Okay. Keep me posted."

Later that day, Jack Livingston and his team of 'federal agents' conducted a search on the home of Max Goodwin, an executive with a well known Hollywood studio. Max was divorced and living alone. He had been consorting with Suzy Lynn an aspiring actress who was trying to get a part in one of Max's TV shows. In reality, Suzy Lynn was an undercover operative for Operation Wildfire and had been playing Max like a fiddle. She sent him pictures of herself and her friends. She had introduced him to some of her friends and she had been photographed in compromising positions with him. There was audio, video and enough images on Max's phone, laptop, and desk top that Max was in deep doo doo. The agents secured the residence and then brought Max to the living room and sat him on a couch. Suzy Lynn was in the kitchen wearing a bikini bathing suit and high heel shoes. She immediately started crying when the agents arrived. Jack sat across from Max and asked him,

"What is your relationship to this person?"

"Oh, that's Suzy Lynn. We've been dating for a few months. She's trying to get a part in one of my TV shows. We're just friends."

"Ms. Lynn, could you come in here please?" Suzy Lynn quickly kicked off her high heels and came in to the leaving room.

"Mr. Goodwin could you stand up please?" Max stood up next to Suzy.

"Ms Lynn, would it be okay if we took your picture?"

"Sure." An agent quickly snapped a photograph of the diminutive Suzy Lynn and the large Max Goodwin.

"Ms Lynn, how old are you?"

"Fourteen."

"What? She told me she was eighteen. I didn't know she was that young. I swear I thought she was eighteen. You've got to believe me, I had no idea."

"Ms Lynn, go get some clothes on, and an agent will take you to your parents." Suzy Lynn disappeared down a hallway and an 'agent' escorted her away from the residence. Another agent produced a portable printer and printed out a photograph of Suzy Lynn standing next to Max Goodwin.

"Mr. Goodwin, as you can see the quality of the photograph is not that great due to the portable printer, but we'll get a nice glossy 8 x 10 when we get back to the office. Take a look at that photograph and tell me, do you think there is any jury in the world that is going to believe that you thought that child was eighteen years old?" Max looked at the photograph and swallowed hard.

"She's a run a way from Ohio. We've been tracking her for several months. We got a lead from one of your neighbors. Apparently she likes to sun bath in the nude by your pool while you watch."

"Look that was her idea. I had nothing to do with that."

"Hey boss, look at these." An 'agent' brought in a monitor with images of various children in various stages of undress. Max said,

"She sent me those. She wanted me to meet her friends. I didn't ask for those." The agent said,

"Those were on the desk top." Another agent brought in a different monitor and said

"This was on the lap top." Jack looked at the image and said,

"Oh my." The image showed a naked Max with an erection standing next to a giggling Suzy Lynn.

"We were just joking around. Nothing happened." Jack started flipping through the images.

"Boss, they're still working on the cell phone. That's going to take some time. There are a lot of files."

"Okay. Keep me posted. So Mr. Goodwin, it appears from some of these date stamps that Suzy Lynn was not your first conquest. Some of these images go back years."

"She wasn't a conquest. We were just friends. We hadn't actually done anything yet."

"Okay. Who is this young boy?"

"I don't know. I don't remember his name. Tommy something I think. He was hitch hiking. I gave him a ride. He said he was hungry so I brought him here, gave him a sandwich and he left. I never saw him again."

"But you took a picture of him before he left?"

"Yeah, probably not a good idea in hindsight."

"Tell me, your TV shows all have a gay component, a gay character, a gay love scene with men kissing men in almost every episode. Is that your doing or does that come from the writers?"

"How is that relevant?"

"It may not be, but we try to be thorough when examining sexual motivations when investigating sex crimes. We could go talk to the writers if you prefer. I just thought I'd give you an opportunity to clear that up, without us having to go to the studio. It's you choice."

"So if I say it's the writers, you're going to go to the studio and see if you can catch me in a lie?"

"Would it be a lie?"

"It's not the writers. It's me. I'm pushing that agenda."

"Mind if I ask why?"

"It's time for Americans to embrace the vast diversity of sexual orientation and break down the barriers of what was once taboo in this country." There was silence in the room as both men realized what had just been said and it's possible implications. Jack took a moment to write down the quote. That wasn't really necessary because the entire conversation was being recorded, but he played the game. Just then one of the agents came into the room.

"Hey boss, Stanley Goldfarb has shown up again."

"Oh crap. This is getting ridiculous. Look, Mr. Goodwin, you don't have to talk to this guy. It's totally up to you. We can send him away. It's you call."

"Who is he?"

"He's a pain in the ass is who he is. He's a lawyer who show's up sometimes. He tries to get people off."

"I'll talk to him."

"Damn it. Okay. Show him in."

"Hello Jack. Good to see you."

"Counselor."

"Mind if we have a few minutes alone?"

"Yes, I mind, but it doesn't seem as if I have a choice."

"That's a good fellow."

"We're going to continue to do our thing. Let me know when you're done." The agents left the room.

"Mr. Goodwin, My name is Stanley Goldfarb. I'm with the ACDU, the American Criminal Defense Union. We're a non-profit organization that is funded by a foundation to provide services to people such as you. There is no cost to you, however if you decide to retain my services, I work strictly for you. Nobody else. Before you decide, let me explain what we do. You can hire your own attorney, and you may want to do that. Your lawyer works for you, but he also works for himself. It is in his best interest to have billable hours. So he files a Motion to Suppress, A Motion to Dismiss, a Motion for a Continuance, Motion for Discovery, A Bill of Particulars. The list goes on an on. He interviews witnesses. He does research and he does trial preparation. All of this is in your best interest as well, but at the end of the day you go to trial or you make a deal. Maybe you go to jail, maybe you don't. We don't do any of that. We nip it in the bud. There is no trial, there is no arrest, there is no indictment. There is no record of this at all. It is as if this never happened. We make it all go away."

"How do you do that?"

"We have a special arrangement with the prosecutor."

"What about those guys?" Pointing towards the agents in the other room.

"They have to do what the prosecutor says. As long as you stay on the good side of the prosecutor, this whole thing goes away."

"How do I do that?"

"You cooperate."

"What's that mean exactly? What am I, some kind of snitch? I have to wear a wire?"

"No. Nothing like that. You don't have to wear a wire. You just answer a few questions, make a few introductions, maybe send a few e-mails. That's it. Every thing goes through me. I am your back channel to the prosecutor's office. You don't deal with law enforcement any more. You just deal with me. I'm the guy who keeps you from being prosecuted. It's up to you. If you don't want the arrangement, I walk out of here and you never see me again. You hire your own attorney and fight this out in the normal criminal justice process." Stanley stood up as if he was ready to walk out the door.

"Wait, wait. I didn't say I didn't want it. I just want to make sure I understand it."

"Well let me make one thing perfectly clear. The operative word here is cooperate. If the prosecutor thinks you are not cooperating or not telling the truth, the deal is off the table and you are back to square one. We can make it all go away, but you have to do your part. So what's it going to be?"

"I want to cooperate and make this whole thing go away."

"Okay. Let me go talk to the agents and see how long it's going to take them to finish up and then you and I can sit down and talk."

And so it went. This scene was played out over and over again in residences throughout Hollywood and on college campuses. The college professors didn't have as much to lose as the Hollywood executives, but all loss was relative. When tenure, reputation and academic standing are all you have, losing it coupled with the possibility of jail time is a serious consideration. For all their bluster and righteous political beliefs, when it came right down to it , everyone acted in their own best interest. This whole network of ideological strategy, so carefully crafted and set in motion years ago, folded like a cheap tent and went away. The one thing the KGB never counted on was they were using people as agents who were never trained as agents. They were willing to put forth a philosophy designed to destroy American culture, but they weren't willing to go to jail for it.

The Meeting

The meeting began when the last member to arrive took his seat. As it was with every meeting, there was no small talk, no banter, no pleasantries. These were serious people with a serious mission. Mr. Blue looked at Ms. Brown and simply said

"Report." Ms. Brown stood as was her custom when speaking to the group.

"As you all know, indictments have been returned and the trial is due to start shortly. After several months of pretrial motions and negotiations, it looks like there will be a trial. What you may not know is this strategy worked flawlessly. The deep state has all but been destroyed. After the indictment, there was much gnashing of teeth and blustering and name calling by the media and many in the political arena. When the dust settled, calmer minds prevailed, and many people realized that they did not want to tie their fate to a sinking ship. These people were suddenly on their own with only their lawyers screaming for their advocacy. I must say that the use of the grand jury was brilliant. They slowly built their case and tested out theories and witnesses. They tied people down to their stories. They didn't let them wiggle off the hook or make speeches. They brought journalists in and showed videos of what they said on the air over a two year period. They had the journalists confirm that the videos were an accurate representation of what they said. They then read excerpts from the Miller report, the IG report and congressional testimony that showed the journalists were either lying, incompetent or both. They did the same with a few politicians and some government employees. When you have testified under oath before the grand jury and shown to be a liar, you are somewhat reluctant to run your mouth on TV for fear that you are going to be called to testify again. Members of the deep state were sent a message, loud and clear. You commit perjury, you get indicted. You use your power to influence an election, you get indicted. These people have all been subpoenaed for trial. Records have been subpoenaed, e-mails have been obtained. People who haven't been subpoenaed or interviewed, are looking over their shoulder. The deep state was arrogant because they had the media on their side, and they told themselves they were acting for the greater good. When the curtain was pulled back and the lies, the deceptions and the corruption was exposed, nobody wants to admit they were a part of it. The trial will be interesting, but no matter what happens, the deep state is gone." Ms. Brown looked around the room at all the heads nodding in approval and sat down.

"Mr. Black, I believe you have the floor."

"Unfortunately the Southern Baptist operation has not been as successful as the Plumber's Union. We didn't expect it to be. This is a long term plan. It will take a generation to see any results and maybe two generations. We are moving forward. There are day care centers running out of church basements all over the country. We are setting up more every day. The operatives who are setting up these programs are becoming vey good at coordinating services through foundations, charitable organizations and corporate sponsors. We've had a few set backs. A few of the ministers want to go their own way and provide day care for everyone, not just married couples. That's a complete failure from out point of view. And we just have to back away from those situations. There aren't that many of those, but there are a few. Our people have made it clear from the beginning that they can't be involved in those situations. We are trying to change attitudes, and it is going to take some time. In that regard, we cannot continue to run this thing through the federal government under the radar forever. Sooner or later somebody is going to get wise and shut us down. We aren't doing anything illegal. We can completely justify our actions under the banner of 'head start' 'affirmative action' 'equal opportunity' or any number of federal programs, but the courts will put an end to it if we are challenged. The Under Secretary is aware of this, and he is working diligently to create a foundation where all these employees can go. All of these employees know that this thing is temporary, and at the drop of a hat they will report to a different location and no longer be federal employees. The plan was and remains to use the resources of the federal government as long as possible. We are getting to a point where the program is up and running, and it might make sense to disband before we get caught. That decision is being left to the Under Secretary. He has a better handle on this than I do. I think his decision will be guided by the results of the next election. If the administration changes hands, then the cabinet secretary position changes as well as the under secretary position. If that happens, it will trigger the transition to a foundation. If not, he may try to hold on a little longer. It's just a matter of funding at this point. The organization and structure exist at this point. It can continue to function regardless of what you call it. The key to this program was getting the right people involved. He has done that. These people are dedicated, hard working and true believers in the mission. Some of these folks will go on to do other things, maybe even great things. Most of them will see this thing through to the end, believing that they did something truly great. Only time will tell. Most of us will be long gone before the results of this initiative will be realized. The basic concept is working. Day cares are operating all over the country and new one are opening every day. The ones that are open are being monitored and supported by the operatives in the field. The program is not growing as fast as we had hoped, but it is growing. Day care is not the end result. It is a means to an end. Two parent family households is the ultimate goal. Change comes slowly, but it has begun." Mr. Blue looked around the room and asked,

"Any questions?" There were none.

"As you know, I provided security for both the Plumber's Union and the Southern Baptist operations. That security has been withdrawn and the security function has been turned over to a private security company, All-Tech Security. Some of the more sophisticated equipment has been removed, but the M Street Building is still locked down pretty tight. Once the indictment was returned, the secrecy element went away and there was no longer a need for the tight security. Some of the officers and the non-coms are still in the area and are on stand by, but the vast majority of the work force has been returned to the 'normal' duties. This unit performed flawlessly and I intend to reconstitute it as a special forces unit. I will have to jump through some hoops, but that is neither here nor there. The reason I bring it up is because we had some complications that I think the group needs to consider." Blue Man had everyone's undivided attention. He rarely spoke this much.

"There are currently seven individuals being held at Gitmo. These seven individuals attacked the Plumber's Union. They kidnapped a young girl, they shot one of my agents and they tried to fire bomb the building. Like I said, my people performed flawlessly. The girl was rescued unharmed within 24 hours, my agent wasn't seriously injured and the attempted fire bombing was thwarted. All of the suspects were captured unharmed. Due to the sensitive nature of the security operation and its methods of operation, the suspects could not be turned over to law enforcement. The decision was made not to terminate them so they were put on ice at Gitmo for the last nine months. My inclination is to let them go. With the trial starting, they can't do any damage and they are essentially broken." Mr. Green spoke up,

"How do you know they won't talk?"

"We don't, but I have a woman who works for me who was involved in the operation. She wanted to kill them, still does. She went down to Gitmo and had a talk with each of them individually. She told them if they ever appeared on our radar again or if they talked about this, she would kill them. I think they believed her. I would."

"Who is this woman?"

"You can't have her."

"Okay. Just curious."

"So before I order them released I want to make sure there are no objections."

"Like you say they are no longer a threat. I don't see any need for termination."

"Any body else?" There were negative head shakes all around.

"Okay. Good. Mr. Green, you want to talk about Wildfire?"

"Wildfire was a complete success in terms of its operational parameters. Of the seventeen Hollywood executives, nine were arrested. The others are scared to death. Of the twenty-eight college professors, fourteen were arrested. The rest are panicked beyond belief. Immediately following the arrests, a smear campaign was begun with social media, anonymous phone calls to university presidents and network executives and unsolicited photographs being sent to and from the targets. Those who weren't arrested, provided a wealth of information on like minded individuals and even some on their proteges. There have been firings, resignations and a whole host of loss of prestige and influence in the academic community. The sting operation has been dismantled, but the harassment component is in full force. Those writers, actors and industry associates who were influenced to push the envelope of sexual orientation are now rethinking their position. There has been a great deal of discredit brought to bear on these folks and no one is taking their phone calls. All of the individuals who sent and received images through he mail and on line at the request of Stanley Goldfarb now find that his number has been disconnected and he doesn't exist. They thought they were part of some undercover operation. They now find that their actions are not protected. That doesn't mean that the gay, lesbian and transgender issue is going to go away. It's not. It just means it is not going to be shoved down our throats on college campuses and on television every night. Without the constant bombardment of the politically correct point of view, there will be room for a rational discussion of the issue. There is room for more than one point of view. Both sides need to come to grip with the notion that you can agree to disagree. There will be a pause and that will allow an examination of the issue without tearing apart the moral fabric of our society. That's all, we were trying to do and we have done it." There was a slight pause as heads nodded all around the table and the group basked in the glory of a successful operation. Finally Mr. Blue spoke,

"Ms. Red, you have a proposal you want to put forth?"

"I do. Thank you. As you all know, the Justice Democrats is a communist front organization from India. They had no success in influencing political policy in India so they came to this country where there is a little more freedom to deviate from the norm. They are based in Chicago and their goal is to fundamentally change American society and destroy capitalism from within. They ran four congressional candidates in the last election and all four won. These four candidates have pushed their party further to the left than it has ever been. They plan to run twenty candidates in the next election and a hundred in the election after that. They appeal to the millennials because they offer free stuff and couch their arguments in climate change. Millennials have been told their whole lives that we're all going to die in twenty years because of our carbon footprint, and most of them believe it. You can sell them anything as long as you wrap it up in climate change. They are self-righteous, sanctimonious little shits who live in their mom's basement and play video games. They only work when they have to and have no problem with destroying society because it doesn't treat them fairly. The Justice Democrats appeal to them but they also appeal to other left wing groups as well. They are motivated and well organized. They latch onto the issue du jour to capture the emotion of the day to support their candidates. Their mission is to fundamentally change society from a capitalist viewpoint to a socialist utopia."

"You say they plan to run twenty candidates this time around. What are their chances of winning twenty seats?"

"Who knows. Maybe they only win ten. Look what they did with four. Their ambition is off the charts in terms of what they are trying to accomplish. They want to destroy capitalism. Their green new deal would have been laughed at twenty years ago, even ten years ago. Today serious politicians are considering aspects of it. Not because they believe any of this crap, but because they are catering to the far left wing of their party. We can't stop the left from moving to the left, but what we can do is stop this organization from trying to destroy us."

"How do plan to do that?"

"We are taking a page out of Mr. Green's book. We are going to sting them. Same concept, different product. We are going to use drugs as our sting. We are going to sell them drugs and then buy the drugs back. That way no drugs get loose on the street. They are going to make a lot of money just being the middle man. We start off small with just some marijuana, which is damn near legal anyway. We will gradually increase the amounts and the amounts of money they can make. Eventually we will shift to different drugs which are more lucrative. Once they get addicted to the money coming in for their political campaigns, we will give them huge amounts of drugs and turn the cases over to the DEA and local law enforcement. Before we do that, we will track all the money, identify all the bank accounts and be ready to seize all their assets. We're going to use Mr. Green's guy, Carl Lowenstein, and his guys to do the initial undercover. There's an outfit called FINCEN that does forensic accounting of money laundering operations. Each of the federal law enforcement agencies donates manpower on a rotating basis. It's kind of like INTERPOL in that you pay your dues for a couple of years at FINCEN, you go back to your agency and you get promoted. Well, like all things, some guys get really good at it and don't go back. We've hired some retired FINCEN agents to do our forensic accounting. This is totally legit. They will be a private consulting firm comprised of all retired law enforcement agents consulting with the U.S. Attorney's office or local prosecutors. They will be on the 6(e) list, the whole bit. They do all the tracking and asset identification. The law enforcement agency, DEA or local, will get all the credit, but our guys will do all the work. The bank accounts will be seized, and the funds will be part of the criminal indictment. We are not going to use civil asset forfeiture. We are going to use criminal. Either you plead guilty and forfeit the money obtained from the sale of the drugs or you go to trial and we show how the money moved traveled through the organization. Either way, the organization is destroyed. We are not going after boats or luxury condos or anything else. We are simply going to seize money obtained from selling drugs.

The money will be a part of the criminal indictment or the plea bargain, either way we will get the big part of the money back. The smaller amounts that will be used to track the financial operations of the organization will be lost. We won't be able to recover those funds. That's a cost of doing business. Those funds will allow us to establish money laundering by political candidates, which will be helpful in the long run."

"Where are the drugs coming from?"

"Let's just say there are some individuals who are facing some severe mandatory minimum prison sentences who are highly motivated to provide some product in exchange for witness protection consideration."

"Where is the money coming from?"

"I'd rather not get into the specifics of that. It is complicated."

"So you're going to use cash that was seized in drug deals to buy more drugs? Is that even legal?"

"Ms. Brown?"

"It is not unprecedented. Forfeiture funds are used all the time to combat the war on drugs. That was one of the stated purposes for creating the forfeiture program in the first place. Using funds that are being held as evidence is a little tricky, because they may be needed as evidence. Once the cash looses its evidentiary value, that is, the trial is over, the appeal process is complete, there is a plea bargain, whatever. Then the cash is just part of a big pile of forfeited funds and can be used according to the guidelines of the program. The truth of the matter is, there aren't big piles of cash sitting around in evidence rooms all over the country. Large sums are deposited in non- interest bearing escrow accounts for security reasons and to prevent problems. The Supremes haven't weighed in on this issue, and with the nature of the court, it is a 5-4 split, you pick them. Bottom line, I think we're safe to use some of these piles of cash that we can get our hands on before they are deposited. We just need to be careful and only use cash that is no longer needed as evidence. We need to make every effort that we can to recover it and we need to follow the guidelines. The money that we plan to lose so we can track it through the system probably should come from a different source."

"So let me get this straight. We're going to run an undercover operation to talk some political operatives into becoming drug dealers so they can raise funds for political candidates. We're going to provide the drugs. We're going to provide the money. We're going to set the whole thing up and then arrest the political operatives. Does anybody see an entrapment issue here?" Ms. Brown turned to Ms. Red.

"You want to take this one?"

"Your reasoning would be spot on if we were a law enforcement agency. What we are doing is the very definition of entrapment, i.e. the idea for the crime originating in the minds of law enforcement. We are not a law enforcement agency. Our involvement is not a matter of public record and never will be. The law enforcement agency, DEA, locals, whatever will have no knowledge of the undercover operation, of where the drugs came from or where the money came from. A confidential informant is going to show up with information about a large drug deal on a certain date at a certain place. The CI will have had his bona fides established through some previous smaller drug deals. The CI will be available to testify if necessary, hopefully not. If he is required to testify, he will have a cover story that will stand up to scrutiny. We will have to be careful with the money laundering aspect of the investigation because it could expose our involvement. The CI will just be some guy who knows about some previous drug deals. The forensic accountants will have to put the whole thing together and trace back the network. We won't be able to help them, but we might be able to give them a hint or two without exposing our involvement. There will be some gnashing of teeth and ruffled feathers. The FEC will claim it's their jurisdiction to examine financial dealings of a political party and the FBI will claim it has jurisdiction over national security issues. The DEA or IRS or whoever will just be following the trail of drug money. If that trail exposes ties to the communist party or other foreign interests, then so be it. Once a few of these people are arrested, the rest will head for the hills. The Justice Democrats will no longer be a player in out political process. The key of course will be the initial contact. Mr. Lowenstein will have to put an operative in the organization and wait for an opportunity. He can't push. He's going to have to make it seem like the other guy's idea." Mr. Green spoke up for the first time.

"I like your idea. I think it is operationally sound. Operation Wildfire worked beyond our wildest dreams, and this is base on the same concept. The difference there was that our targets were inclined in the direction that we pushed them. Here we are assuming that a political party is interested in getting some easy money. I think that is a valid assumption. All political parties are driven by money. My question is this. If the millennials are the problem and we take out the Justice Democrats, won't the millennials just gravitate to the Beanie Bros or Antibra or some other left wing nut job organization that hates America?"

"Yes. They probably will. We will fight today's battles today and tomorrow's battles tomorrow. It's never going to end. Our group needs to be vigilant. Your question, however, raises a larger concern. How do we, as a group, combat the hatred for America that is being nurtured in today's youth? This is no accident. Young people in the age group of 18 to 28, by in large, hate this country. They think everything about it is immoral, and they want to tear it down. They want to build a utopia in their own image. This is a question that this group will have to grapple with at some point. How do you undo fifty years of liberal ideology put forth on our college campuses, our high schools, social media and even main stream media? It's not just young folks either. There are people who are old enough to know better, who want free stuff. Capitalism is considered evil by a large percentage of our population. All of us in this room need to think about this to see if we can't come up with a solution." The room went silent for several minutes while each member contemplated the future and what part they could play in it. Finally, Blue man spoke.

"If there are no objections to the plan, we will proceed." There were none.

"Okay. Please consider the problem just presented and be prepared to discuss options at out next meeting. With that we are adjourned."

End Game

The courtroom was packed. The judge had decided that there would be no video cameras. Jury selection had taken the better part of a week. Kathy Solove and Debbie Brinkman sat at counsel table with Bob Williams and Dale Brickler sitting behind them in the first row of the gallery. By agreement with the judge, Bob and Dale would rotate to counsel table as needed for certain witnesses or for cross. This strategy was not so much to give them some thing to do, but rather to provide a much needed break to Kathy and Debbie in a high pressure trial. The defendants and their lawyers sat on the other side of the courtroom. They had been smug and indignant at the arraignment. Now after months of pretrial motions and discovery, the façade of indignation had faded away. Many in the news media who had been summoned before the grand jury and shown to be less than objective, were now silent expecting to be called as witnesses at trial. The media had not turned on these defendants, but the word had spread that even a member of the media can be called before the grand jury and put under oath. Grady sat in the back of the courtroom. To all but the most knowledgeable observer, he was seemingly not involved. The truth of the matter was, Kathy had become the general and Grady, the administrator. The four AUSA's had settled into a rhythm of trial preparation. The agents had less and less to do. All the agents were in the courtroom and were involved in document and video retrieval and help with the witnesses, but eight agents were a bit of overkill for trial. During the indictment process, the agents had been unbelievably busy and worked incredible hours. Now there was a lull, and it was up to the attorneys. Grady found himself thinking, if this thing goes south, he would go home to Cincinnati in disgrace. If the trial was successful, he would go home to Cincinnati as a virtual unknown. He had held a press conference on the steps of the courthouse when the indictment was returned, but he didn't say anything other than what was in the indictment. He didn't take any questions and the media quickly forgot his name. He assumed he would say something at the end, but he didn't know what that would be.

"All rise." The judge entered the courtroom through a side door leading to chambers. The judge walked up the steps to the bench and looked out at the courtroom. The clerk continued,

"This honorable U. S. District Court for the District of Columbia, the honorable Hastings Meadows presiding, is now in session. All persons having business with this honorable Court shall draw nigh and be heard. God save this honorable Court and the United States of America." The judge took his seat and said,

"Please be seated. The clerk will call the case for the record."

"Case Number 19 CR 17474, the United States of America versus:

>James Homey
>
>Dennis McCoy
>
>Robert Lowenstein
>
>Paul Ruck and

Linda Pugh…..

And so it began.

Epilogue

The preceding book is a work of fiction. The themes are real. The characters and the plot lines are not. The author is not aware of any secret cabal that protects capitalism and the republic. Nor is the author aware of any secret group of super soldiers who can do anything. There is no sting operation to thwart the moral depravity of Hollywood or our college campuses. There is no government group that is trying to reestablish a two parent family in the black community. There is unfortunately a hatred of our country by the younger generation. Previous generations were taught that our country is the greatest country that ever existed. They believed it, and they still do. Less than 300 years ago, the founding fathers created a country out of whole cloth. This was a phenomenal accomplishment. There were only thirteen states at the time. The country has continued to grow and evolve. This experiment in self-government has proven to be the envy of the entire world. The accomplishments of the nation are too numerous to mention here. The founding fathers created a document that established a country. The preamble to the document states that "We the people of the United States, in order to form a more perfect union, establish justice, insure domestic tranquility, provide for the common defense, promote the general welfare, and secure the blessings of liberty to ourselves and our posterity, do ordain and establish this Constitution of the United States of America." THIS DOCUMENT CREATED A COUNTRY. Unfortunately, the youth of today is not taught the greatness of this history. They neither appreciate the significance of this great event nor do they care about the sacrifice of others who have continued this great experiment.

Late in the book, the question is posed that this thing is broken and how do we fix it? There is no easy answer. At least there is none apparent to the author. It turns out asking questions is easy. Answering them, not so much. There are many moral dilemmas presented throughout the book, but none more poignant that this, how do we fix that which is broken? The End Game reveals five individuals from the Justice Department, the JD-5, going to trial. This fictional accounting for the wrong doing chronicled in the book may satisfy some and leave others wanting to know the end result. As they say, truth is stranger than fiction. If you want to know what really happened, I recommend <u>Witch Hunt</u> by Gregg Jarrett, a well researched and well documented expose that tells the story of what really happened.

A special thanks to my wife for putting up with me during this process and for helping with some of the typing, also to our friend, Susan, for reviewing the manuscript for my many typos.

Cast of Characters

Donald Trump	as himself
Robert Barnes	Attorney General
Jim Homey	Director of the FBI
Tim Dapper	Director of National Intelligence
Rex Brenamore	Director of CIA
Hildy Claxton	presidential candidate
Summer Dewdrop	adult film star
Michael Abadabado	adult film star lawyer
Donovan Stuhl	dossier author
Denny McCoy	Acting Director of FBI
Paulie Ruck	FBI agent
Linda Pugh	FBI lawyer
Ben Stinson	Owner of Fission CVS
Ronald Miller	Special Counsel
Rob Lowenstein	Acting Attorney General
Carson Pugh	Trump campaign worker
Allen Stiff	Congressman

Jack McCormack	Senator
Jim Goetta	FBI agent
Rey Rowdy	Former Congressman
Grady Franklin	Special Deputy Attorney General
Bill (Matt) Mathews	Colonel U. S. Army
Agnes Frobush	Colonel U. S. Army
Joseph Sizemore	General U. S. Army
Andy Anderson	General U. S. Army
Carl Lowenstein	former NSA operative
Kathy Solove	AUSA
Debbie Brinkman	AUSA
BobWilliams	AUSA
Dale Brickler	AUSA
Susan McCoy	Matt's girlfriend
Lieutenant Malloy	U.S. Army M Street Bldg.
Captain Oster	U.S. Army Ft. Belvoir
Chet (Wog) Woginiewski	Warrant Officer U.S. Army

Ralph Simmons	Corporal U.S. Army sniper
Larry Maxwell	Sgt. U. S. Army drones
Charles Johnson	Sgt. U. S. Army cleaning crew
David McGee	Sgt. U. S. Army interrogator
Jack Livingston	former FBI agent
Max Goodwin	Hollywood Exec.
Suzy Lynn	undercover operative
Stanley Goldfarb	undercover lawyer
Roy Johnston	Secretary DGRED
Samuel Parson	Undersecretary DGRED
John Sizemore	Deputy Chief Criminal D C District
Stanley Berger	FBI Chief Counsel
Jim Martin	reporter
Judith Sams	employee DGREDG

The Author

W. Gary Claytor is a retired Postal Inspector who lives in Cincinnati Oh with his wife. They have two children and four grandchildren. The Trump Legacy is the second installment in the Grady Franklin series. The first book A Day in the Life tried to give the reader an idea of what it was like to be a Postal Inspector prior to the turn of the century. Those who read that book seemed to like it. Unfortunately, not that many people read it. It is hoped The Trump Legacy will reach a wide audience, if for no other reason than the name in the title.

Synopsis

The Trump Legacy offers the reader a fictional look at what might have been, had things been just a little bit different. Several scenarios are presented that question the prevailing wisdom. Hopefully the book will leave the reader asking why not. The story has a decidedly conservative point of view and would be of little interest to those who already have their minds made up. For those who wish to examine these issues from a different point of view, the story offers an opportunity to do so.

Made in the USA
Monee, IL
31 December 2020